THE MURDER OF AMOS DUNN

A small business owner, Amos Dunn, has been found murdered in the lowcountry town of Morgan, South Carolina. The initial reaction of the local police is that the robbery of Dunn's convenience store got out of hand resulting in the owner's death. The robbery and murder receive token coverage in the local and regional press, which is not uncommon. But nothing is what it seems.

Tillie James, the housekeeper for Professor Sidney Lake, a retired professor of English Literature at Morgan College, doesn't believe it and convinces Sidney Lake that something is very wrong. Enlisting the aid of a new black police officer and a recently arrived county assistant coroner, they band together to seek the truth. And so begins a wild ride though the politics and changing culture of a small, quiet lowcountry town that endangers all of their lives as they seek the truth.

The story of Amos Dunn's murder and its aftermath will forever change the way the town of Morgan views itself as it is thrown into a spotlight it has tried to avoid. This is a town where big city problems aren't supposed to exist. A quiet family place where the local churches are still the center of life and Wednesday night suppers and meetings in church education buildings are a mainstay of its social fabric.

Tim Holland's weaving of the story through common everyday events in Morgan brings the town and its people to life. Everyone from Professor Lake and Tillie James to tourist, pastors, policemen and especially Mrs. Micawber, Sidney Lake's Labrador retriever find themselves entangled in a web they thought could only be woven by the decadence of a large city. This is one you won't want to put down.

KUDOS for *The Murder of Amos Dunn*

You may want to pick up this really good mystery set in the lowcountry. I really enjoyed it!

-**Ellen C Priest** – Editor/publisher, Sommerville South Carolina *Journal Scene*

I really like the way the first chapter sets up the mystery. Very effective. The reader knows how the victim died, but not who did it or why, and is able to watch the characters make inaccurate assumptions. The story moves along seamlessly. I found it hard to put it down.

- **E. Compton Lee** - Author of *Native*

The way the professor and his housekeeper play off one another is very effective. The dialogue is real and the way each chapter ends makes you keep looking for the next one.

-**Peter Stipe** – Author of *Remember Me*

Tim…is a writer. With two novels to his credit and two on the way, he is passionate about words. *The Rising Tide* is an interesting murder mystery thriller set is a fictional town in the lowlands (sic) of South Carolina. It follows Sidney Lake, an English literature professor, and his friends as they investigate a murder in their small town. The two forthcoming novels, (*The Murder of Amos Dunn* and *Deception*) will be the next installment in the Sidney Lake series.

-**Ben Mackin** – Collins Group LLC *Next Door Neighbor*

The Murder of

Amos Dunn

Tim Holland

A Black Opal Books Publication

GENRE: Mystery

This is a work of fiction. Names, places, characters and incidents are either the product of the author's imagination or are used fictitiously, and any resemblance to any actual persons, living or dead, businesses, organizations, events or locales is entirely coincidental. All trademarks, service marks, registered trademarks, and registered service marks are the property of their respective owners and are used herein for identification purposes only. The publisher does not have any control over or assume any responsibility for author or third-party websites or their contents.

DEDICATION

For Crystal Holland and Michael Betcher

Chapter 1

The Murder of Amos Dunn

T hat makes me mad," Tillie said as she came close to Mickey with her broom. Sidney Lake watched as she cleaned the kitchen floor and tried to keep Mickey out of the way. As Tillie made her way around the room, Mickey would move in front of her by about ten feet and then lie down, only to get up again as the broom approached. It was a biweekly routine that never changed. Every Monday and Thursday Tillie would sweep and Sidney would get Mickey to move. A treat would usually solve the problem, which really wasn't a problem, as the three of them were well aware of the bribery routine being played out. Mickey loved people and if Tillie and Sidney were in the same room, she assumed it was a family conference so she had to be there. If they were in separate rooms, she would position herself to keep an eye and an ear monitoring them.

"Make you mad? What has you upset today?" Sidney Lake said.

Tillie mumbling along about something as she worked seemed to be a part of her daily routine. Most of the time it involved a comment one of the other Gullah housekeepers said about their employers, but problems with children, husbands and grandchildren were also high on the list.

"Somebody killed Mr. Dunn."

"Excuse me. Amos Dunn?"

"Yeah, they's lots a people around that could use a bop on the head, but Mister Dunn ain't one of um."

"What in the world happened?" Both Sidney and Mickey stared at Tillie.

"Professor Lake, don't you ever read the newspaper?"

"Of course I do, but Mickey and I went for an early walk this morning. She brought in the paper and left it in the office and then we went out for breakfast at the City Hall Café."

Tillie kept working as she spoke, pushing the broom a little stronger for emphasis from time to time, "Some low-life broke into his place last night and hit him on the head. Police say it's a straight forward robbery. Which don't make no sense since he don't keep anything there of value and everybody knows it. He don't even live above the place anymore."

"I know. He told me he bought a place two blocks away last year and rented out the apartment above the store."

"That's right." Tillie stopped working and leaned on the broom. "Has a standard routine. He closes up around seven. Goes for a walk around downtown, then heads home for dinner. You can pretty much set your clock by him."

"He was found in the store?"

"Musta gone back there for somthin' since the police think he was killed around eight or so. Routine walk is only a half hour long. Usually doesn't pass the store on his way home. Either got a late start or maybe remembered something in the store he forgot and went back."

"Was all this in the paper?"

"No. Paper never gives any specifics 'bout nothin'. Jimmy Smalls does the cleanup at City Hall and the police department every night. Nobody pays attention to him. It's like he's invisible so the police just talk like he ain't there. Rita, his wife toll me."

"Hmmmm." Sidney looked off into space.

"You got that look again Professor Lake."

"What? Oh, I was just thinking there might be another possibility."

"You thinkin' what I'm thinkin'?"

"Somebody he knew asked him to open the store as a favor. Probably forgot to buy something earlier."

"Yeah, you thinkin' what I'm thinkin' all right."

"No one who's local who went to the store would ever try to rob it. It doesn't make sense. Cedar Street is probably the safest place downtown, even more than Market Street."

"Yeah, you thinkin' it's somebody he knows, but not from downtown."

Sidney stopped but didn't answer. He quietly looked at Tillie. Mickey caught the pause and sat up. Then Sidney said, "Why are we always doing this?"

"What?"

"Assume a sinister event instead of a simple straight forward one. The logic would be a simple robbery gone wrong. Open and shut."

"Maybe we got that fairytale disease?"

"Fairytale disease?"

"Yeah. Like that lady who every time she heard the story of Humpty Dumpty fallin' off that wall thought 'did he fall or was he pushed.' I think that's what we got. Never can take somethin' for what it seems to be—the logical simple answer. The easy 'open an' shut' answer."

Sidney had a smile on his face and Mickey's tail thumped the floor when he said, "I think you're right. Yes, I think you're right."

"Problem is we both know that 'open an' shut' is

probably the right answer in the white neighborhood, but in the black one it's just the easy one an the 'shut' part ain't always really shut."

e/ɔe/ɔ

Pete Hornig celebrated his tenth anniversary as Morgan's police chief just a month earlier and had been silently reflecting on how much had changed during that time when Corporal Sam Cashman came into his office. Sam covered the downtown area and had two officers assigned to him. The Amos Dunn robbery and murder, so far, was his responsibility. Hornig had not yet made the decision about which of his three detectives would be assigned to the case. He wanted to see all the medical and forensic reports first. If it confirmed that Amos Dunn was killed in a random act of violence during a robbery, he would give it a different priority than a premeditated killing. So, for the time being he would just keep Sam noseying around and digging up whatever he could. Besides, he valued Sam's thoughts, especially as Sam was from the Gullah community. Hornig knew Amos Dunn from the Morgan Rotary Club and couldn't imagine someone wanting to kill him. Besides, Amos' Cedar Street Market sat at the edge of the black community downtown and the chief figured Sam Cashman would have an easier time getting people in the area to talk than any of his white detectives.

"So, Sam, any thoughts?"

"Mind if I sit?"

"No, go ahead. I don't have anything scheduled. Something bothering you?"

Sam sat down and took a deep breath "Yes and no. Amos' murder. The logical conclusion is a petty robbery gone bad. The cash register was empty, a wine bottle broken on the floor, some other stuff on the floor as well and the back door open. Looks like he was hit from behind. All kind of fits…and yet it doesn't. Anything from the coroner yet?"

Hornig made his way around to his chair behind the desk but didn't sit. "No, but Cooper promised some preliminary stuff by noon. So, are we looking at a break-in gone bad?"

"Preliminarily, I'd have to say yes."

"Well let's keep it that way for now. I've got Ed working on the vandalism problem up on Layfette Boulevard and Kent's only here temporarily. Patton's not due back from vacation for another week so you're the acting detective on this one. I just don't have anyone to put on it and I'm not going to ask for county help unless this proves to be more than a simple robbery."

"Understand."

Chapter 2

The more Sidney thought about the murder of Amos Dunn, the more it bothered him. Certain that Tillie's instincts were correct, he decided to have a look for himself. He knew the best way to do it would be to take Mickey for a walk along Cedar Street to Amos' market, but to do it the long way around. He wanted to walk as much as possible on Cedar and reacquaint himself with the neighborhood. Besides, with Mickey along he'd get a chance to stop and chat with people along the way.

One advantage of walking with Mickey is that no one would question your moving slowly. Although, given Sidney's size and weight—five foot eight and 230 pounds—speed was not an option anyway. The junction of Market Street and Howard reflected a typical southern town center. To the left the main business section started, while to the right were some of the old, lumbering homes of centuries and economies gone by. Once a fishing village with canneries and warehouses, they were all gone now, torn down and replaced with restaurants, banks and shops. But off to the right, the old houses were still there and went right down to the water. Large lawns and giant live oak

THE MURDER OF AMOS DUNN

trees were common, but many of the houses now contained charitable and government organizations: visiting nurses, Meals on Wheels, the local hospice group, the county Department of Social Services, the Board of Education.

As they made their way closer to Cedar Street, the Morgan River came into view. Many of the old houses had been preserved and renovated by the town's newly wealthy, who saw dollar signs in the river view rather than the mosquitos that caused them to be abandoned for lack of air-conditioning.

Turning onto Cedar Street, he and Mickey slowly walked on the right side of the street. The grand houses still used as residences extended for only one full block and then the neighborhood began to change. The houses with large lots had been torn down and replaced by groupings of one-story cottages of about 1,000 square feet, tightly squeezed together. The deeper you walked into the neighborhood the less affluent it looked, but it had a neat, well-kept appearance. Up ahead on the opposite side of the street was the Cedar Street Market, Amos Dunn's store, which now had yellow police tape on it that blocked the entrance. Standing just up ahead of Sidney a man looked across the street at the store. He was an average height man with a slim build wearing a white shirt, tie and sports jacket.

Jim Cunningham, the editor of *The Morgan City Times* spotted Sidney and Mickey coming and gave them a wave. "You and Mickey out for your morning walk?"

"Second one actually. We had breakfast at the City Hall Café this morning. Not much of a walk to get there so we're making up for it."

. They shook hands and Jim greeted Mickey with a pat on the head and a rub behind the ear. "Getting your boss out for some exercise, hah?"

Mickey responded with an enthusiastic wag of her tail,

which slapped against Sidney's pants leg. Two men wearing sport coats and ties at the beginning of August anywhere in South Carolina would stand out, but in Morgan it proved to be a car stopping event, as a green pick-up pulled up to the curb next to them and Ted McGraw, the owner of The City Hall Café called out to them. "Don't you guys know it ain't healthy to stand out in this sun with those jackets on?"

Jim responded with a smile and a laugh, "Hah, at least I'm smart enough to stay away from your place at breakfast time. Talk about unhealthy."

"Abuse, abuse. That's all I get around here. Ha, ha. Have a good day gentlemen. I'm off to pick up some more *organic* ingredients for that shrimp, grits, biscuits and gravy Sidney there had for breakfast." He waved, rolled up his window and took off down the street.

"Yeah, I suppose the only people around here dressed like us are either police, lawyers or bankers," Cunningham said.

"Speaking of police, anything new about what happened to Amos?"

"Have a meeting with Hornig at eleven when the coroner is supposed to give him a preliminary report. Find out more then."

Another pick-up passed with a honk and a wave.

"Any unofficial theories you'd like to share?" Sidney asked.

"Everyone seems to think it's just a robbery gone badly. Pretty straight forward. Probably surprised Amos inside. Can't imagine anyone could believe there might be something pre-meditated going on."

"Well, not everyone."

"Really?" Cunningham looked surprised.

"Tillie can't imagine anyone trying to rob the store in the first place. Said everybody knows Amos never kept anything in the store after closing. Says it isn't logical."

"Someone with a drug habit isn't always logical."

"True, but then you never know these days." Another car passed and gave a honk. Sidney continued, "Jim, why don't we walk across the street where we won't stand out so much. Have you been inside?" Referring to Amos Dunn's store on the corner in front of them.

"No, just got a peek along with my reporter and his camera." All three of them stepped out into the street. "He took some pictures of the outside. Sam Cashman wouldn't let us in. Told us to come back after I had my meeting with Hornig." After crossing the street, they stepped around to the side of the building to get out of the view of passing traffic. The building was elevated to stay above the estimated storm flood level. The front entrance had four steps up to a porch area where Amos usually positioned brooms, mops, pails and other cleaning utensils. There was also a newspaper rack and a table and chairs for four to accommodate local domino and checkers players. Yellow police tape cordoned off the area. The building originally housed two apartments, one up and one down, with the lower one being converted to the store in the 1930s.

Sidney walked over to the side of the building and stood on tiptoe to peek through the window, but was still having trouble.

Cunningham came up alongside him and also peeked in. "Thought so. Checkout and register right up front by the door. Lots of visibility from the street. It's been a while since I've been inside. Yeah, Amos was found down from the front door. In the entry aisle about two rows back."

"Not by the cash register?" Sidney stepped back from the window and tried to remember what it looked like inside. The checkout counter, a backwards lazy 'L' shaped affair, stood just to the right of the entrance. The long side of the 'L' touched the wall next to the doorway and the short side provided an entryway into the rectangle space between the end of the short side and a side window. To the front a double sized window fit between the door and the side wall giving a clear view of the porch's table and chairs. The cash register sat on the short side and a large paper roll-fed calculator sat on the left of the long side, indicating the checkout person was left-handed. The empty cash register drawer was lying upside down in the middle of the long side of the counter.

Cunningham said, "Unless they moved something before I got here, that's the way it looked last night."

"And the cash drawer upside down and empty that way?"

"It was. Which seems to make a case for the robbery, but I'll know more later. All looks pretty straight forward though."

"No sign of a struggle?"

"Well, there's the broken wine bottle and some stuff from the shelves scattered on the floor. What's left of the bottle the police took, but the other stuff is still there. One of the officers that responded to the call told my reporter that it looked like he was hit with the bottle from behind and fell against the shelf knocking that stuff on the floor as he fell."

"Everything does seem to lead to robbery as an explanation." Sidney stepped back from the window to allow Jim to get a better look. "Understand the killer went out through the back door that was found open. Wonder if that's how he came in?"

Cunningham thought for a moment before answering, "Again, seems logical. May have just followed Amos in. If that's the way he came in? Don't know yet."

"Hmmmm…wonder why Amos wanted to go back to the store in the first place?"

"Cause somebody asked him to." Tillie came up behind

them.

"Tillie, what are you doing here?" Sidney said. Even Mickey was surprised by her but recovered quickly with an immediate move in her direction, energetic tail wagging.

"Saw you and Mickey going down the street an' figured you were coming here. Morning Mister Cunningham, you lookin things over too?"

"Yes, but that's my job. Sidney's just being curious."

"That's my job," Sidney said.

Jim returned to the conversation addressing his question to Tillie, "So you think that's why he opened up the store?"

"Only logical answer. Doesn't ever even come this way after he goes to the bank. Goes straight on down Market Street to *The Ridge,* then comes over the other way to get to his place on Queen Street. He mostly crosses Cedar two blocks up."

A police cruiser pulled up alongside the curb and interrupted Tillie. Sam Cashman exited the passenger side and Officer Hampton Butler came out of the driver's side.

"Hello Sam, your meeting over?" Jim asked.

"Hasn't started. Just saw three people standing in front of a crime scene and thought it might be a good idea if Hamp here extended that tape out to the curb. Looks like a larger perimeter is needed."

"Oh, sorry, you're right. Sidney here was just curious about where things happened. Peeked in the window."

Officer Butler opened up the trunk of the cruiser, took out a roll of 'crime scene tape' and started to wrap it around the streetlight pole that stood on the corner. Sam removed two orange traffic cones and two metal pipes that fit into the top of them and placed one on Cedar Street and the other along High Street.

"Say Sam, as long as you're here, Tillie just said

something that's interesting," Jim said while Tillie just stood silent and crossed her arms. "She said Amos goes to the bank every night after he closes up. Is that true?"

"It is. We just came from there and Randolph Byron confirmed the night depository bag was placed in the drop box as usual the night of the murder." Sam held up his hand. "No more for now. Chief Hornig will give you a full update when you see him later."

Sidney said, "Is that why you're putting extra tape around the store? Doesn't really have anything to do with us does it?"

"No more for now. You just read it in *The Times,* as I'm sure Mr. Cunningham would like you to. Now you'll all notice you're standing inside a police line." Sam pointed to the other officer having stretched the tape from the lamppost to the iron bar sticking out of the traffic cone on High Street and then attached it to the side of the building.

They all began to move. "How are you, Miss Tillie?"

"Oh just fine, Sam. Give my regards to Miss Deede."

Sam said with a big smile. "I will."

They all moved out into the street while the two officers completed putting the tape in place along the Cedar Street side of the building and then got into the cruiser and drove off.

Sidney spoke first, "So there was no money in the store."

"Everybody knows that." Tillie said. "That's why he always turns the cash draw upside down in clear view to show there ain't no money in it. Also makes sure there's a light on it. Tellin' anybody lookin' through the window that if they break in they's gonna get nothin' but wine and corn flakes. Mr. Sam knows that." Then, with a smile on her face she added, "That's why he checked with the bank. Good man, Mister Dunn. Hope they throw the book at whoever did this to um."

"People who do this sort of thing aren't too smart to begin with," Cunningham said. "Sam's also a good man. I think he'll figure it out."

Tillie agreed. "Amos had lots of friends and they're all ready to help."

"Well, I have to get over to Hornig's office and see if he's ready to give me an official version of what happened. Have a reporter who'll meet me so he can take some pictures. Get the whole story out for tomorrow morning. We'll put a preview online tonight if you want to know what the official story is. Sidney, Tillie, if you come up with anything interesting, let me know." Cunningham gave Mickey a pat on the head and left.

"Well, Tillie, what do you think? Did Amos jump or was he pushed?"

"Pushed. By somebody he knew. Amos knew who bopped him on the head. He invited him in the store."

"Why him instead of her"

"When's the last time you heard of a lady doin' somethin' stupid like stickin' up a place like this, or even a liquor store. Ladies do things you can understand, like knockin' off a no-good cheating boyfriend or a good for nothin' lazy husband who sold her a bill of goods. Ladies don't stick up stores."

"You make an interesting point. But what do you think happened here?"

Mickey, realizing the meeting conversation didn't end with Cunningham leaving, stretched out her lead and moved into the shade of a tree by the curb. Feeling a tug, Sidney moved a few steps over, as he talked, and Tillie moved with him and said, "Got to believe he knew who did it or he wouldn't have opened up. Also would have gone in by the back door. Wouldn't want to open the front door as that might signal he was still open an someone else would come in. Heck, he already closed up for the night.

Been to the bank and everything."

"Okay, seems reasonable, but why would he open up for someone?"

"Knew um."

"Somebody in the neighborhood?"

Tillie thought for a moment. "Not sure. Probably not likely. Don't think he would open up just so somebody could buy something. Not good business. And Amos was good business."

"You're probably right. What bothers me is that he came all the way to the front of the store after coming in the back and the person followed him. Then he gets hit over the head with a wine bottle when he's heading to the back door. Although, we don't really know if that's what killed him. The coroner will tell us that later today, but let's say he did. Why wait until you got to the front of the store where you might be seen? The lights were on. Why not do it in the back by the door? You can't see that area from out here."

"How 'bout if they had an argument and the bad guy was a hothead and got real angry and bopped him when Amos turned his back on um?"

Now it was Sidney's turn to quietly think. "Actually, he could have shoved him into that shelf first and then hit him in a rage after."

"Maybe. Amos was a nice man and all, but when it came to somethin' he didn't agree with, especially a business thing, he didn't take no prisoners. If he was convinced he was right, he could be just plain ornery. He's a good church goin' man an all, but when money got involved, he's gonna have trouble with that 'eye of the needle' thing."

Sidney smiled. Tillie always managed to get to the heart of the matter. She might not get to all the ins and outs and nuances of what occurred, but she had uncanny perception skills about people. If she didn't trust or like a person, she might not provide a 'court of law' reason, but her instincts were rarely wrong. It was Sidney's job to put the meat on the bone and come up with the logical, provable explanation. Between the two of them they usually got it right.

Chapter 3

The official version

By the time Jim Cunningham arrived at Chief Hornig's office, it had just turned twelve-thirty. His reporter had arrived at the original appointment time of eleven and then called the editor about the meeting being delayed at the coroner's request. Cunningham used the extra time to go over to Coastal Rivers Community Bank to speak with Randy Byron and confirm Amos Dunn's reliability in always dropping off the night depository bag.

After having listened to Sidney and Tillie, Cunningham began to wonder if this could turn out to be more than a simple robbery and whether everyone should just slow down a bit. He knew Hornig had staffing problems. The battles with the mayor and the city administrator about the police department's budget were no secret. Morgan, with its influx of retirees from all those cold places up north, was getting the traffic and tourist problems, while the county was getting all the property tax revenue—the newcomers were moving to those new real estate developments outside the city with their golf courses and deep water access. He knew Hornig was stressed and complained about having to make unpopular decisions about where scarce resources would be allocated.

Hornig's office was a bit tight, with the extra chairs that had to be brought in. There were the usual two that sat in front of the Chief's desk, but now there were four more spread around the room. The door to the office stood open so Cunningham went in. He and a reporter were invited to these sessions with the coroner as a time saver to keep the press from pestering everyone separately. As an accommodation, Cunningham agreed to offer Hornig a preview of what would be reported—if the chief wanted to see it.

When Cunningham came into the office, he found his reporter sitting just to the left of the entry. They greeted one another and chatted for a moment. Hornig sat at his desk fumbling with some papers. He gave Cunningham a quick acknowledgement, which the editor returned. The other people in the room were Sam Cashman, Hampton Butler and a woman he didn't recognize. Detective Kent came in behind Cunningham, closed the door and took a seat behind the unknown woman.

Hornig officially introduced the mystery woman as Mary Coffey, the county's new assistant coroner. Sam Cashman sat in the chair next to her in front of the desk. Cunningham raised his hand to speak, but Hornig preempted him. "Don't worry Jim, I'm sure Mary will stay around for a while afterward so you can get some background on her."

The editor dropped his hand.

Hornig looked around the room and made sure all the right people were present, "Okay, let's get underway. What do you have for us doc?"

"All seems pretty straight forward," Mary Coffey began. "Time of death between seven-thirty and eight-thirty pm—severe blow to the head." She stopped and then said, "I'm giving you the non-technical version. The coroner will be back from Columbia on Friday and he'll issue the formal report with all the usual bells and whistles. But for your benefit, these are the basic facts as I see them. Everybody okay with that?" No one said anything.

Hornig finally waved his hand at her to go on. "It's fine, maybe we'll actually understand it this time." A few chuckles from everyone.

Mary continued, "Okay, as I said, a severe blow to the head. Definitely the wine bottle." Everyone in the room started making notes. "Hit from behind. Really hard. The full technical report will define all of that. He went down and out immediately. Didn't seem to have any reaction. The hit was slightly to the left side of the top of the head. Main force came from the end of the bottle where the glass is the thickest, not the middle where the break is the easiest. The bottle was full and unopened when it hit him. Don't think he knew what happened. Wine splattered over everything. Also had a gash over his right eyebrow. Hit the corner of the shelf to his right as he went down. Nothing else to comment on. Oh, yes, he had a brain tumor. Nothing to do with this though. I haven't received any additional material from the scene that needs to be analyzed. If you've found anything that you believe needs to be looked at, please get it to me as soon as possible. Any questions?"

Sam Cashman said, "Haven't finished with the crime scene yet. It was pretty busy last night. We secured the store and will be back in there this afternoon. Based on what you said, would you say we're looking for someone taller than Amos and possibly left-handed? And is there any evidence that there were more than two people in the store at the time?"

"Unless you can come up with something else, it looks like they were alone. And the left-handed hit, yeah, that seems like a reasonable assumption. That's why he fell into the shelf on his right. The force pushed him that way."

Detective Kent asked, "Do you believe the bottle came

from the store? What I'm getting at is the killer didn't bring it with him. Could have been just a drunk passing by and saw an opportunity. He just used what was available. Say the killer became angry at something and acted instinctively."

"Could make a case for that. The wine was a brand the store carried. There were a couple of bottles missing. Wine section would have been to the killers left. Dunn seemed to have been hit only once, possibly by someone in a rage or out of control. If we find anything else, we'll get it to you right away."

"Body was not moved in any way?" Sam asked.

"He was not moved from the position he fell into, but it does look like he was moved slightly. By that I mean shifted slightly. Like someone trying to lift him up a bit. It was very slight. If you stop by the office later, I have everything that was in his pockets. We can go over it if you like."

The room went quiet for a moment. Then Jim Cunningham asked, "Could it be consistent with someone checking to see if he was alive?"

"Possibly. It would have been pretty cursory though. The arms do not appear to have been moved from the position they took from the fall. Probably didn't try to check a pulse," she said turning slightly in her seat to look at the questioner.

"So what makes you think there was movement?" Cunningham followed up.

"It looks like the torso was moved slightly."

"In what way?"

"As though it was lifted just a tiny bit. Dunn was dead when he hit the floor, so he didn't move himself."

"What about other signs of a disturbance? Nothing pushed over? Nothing out of place?"

"No. Just the material from the shelf where he hit his

head and the ones he bumped into on the way down. And, of course the empty cash drawer sitting upside down on the check-out counter."

The Times reporter asked, "Who discovered the body?"

Sam shifted in his chair and said, "People upstairs, the Ambers, Tonya and Ronald…let me correct that. They didn't actually discover the body but did make the nine-one-one call. They had been out to dinner. The Morgan River Grill. Saw the lights on in the market when they came back about nine p.m. The entrance to their apartment is up the rear stairs, which goes over the back entrance to the market." Sam had his notebook out and double checked the information as he spoke. "Spotted the rear door being open and Ronald called in to Amos Dunn, the owner, who he assumed was inside. Did not get an answer. Called again. His wife, Tonya, commented that he never leaves that door open. Even during business hours, unless he's getting a delivery. She actually made the nine-one-one call. Said they never went inside. Stepped over to the curb on High Street to wait. Cruiser showed up in about five minutes. Officer Shawn Green discovered the body at nine-ten p.m.

"Another point of information, the Ambers said they were sitting in a booth in the front of the restaurant, facing Market Street, and they saw Amos Dunn walk past carrying a large paper sack. When he went to the bank after he closed up, he always put the night depository bag in a paper sack so people wouldn't spot the money bag. They estimated the time as after seven-thirty, as that's when they got to the restaurant. Their drinks had just been delivered so we know Amos was alive between seven-thirty and eight."

Mary Coffey quickly made a note and said, "Good, I'll refine my 'Time of Death' window."

The reporter followed up. "Did they see him on his way

back?"

Sam said, "No. Didn't expect to. Amos always went for a walk over toward *The Ridge* after the bank deposit. Made a wide circle back to his residence on Queen Street. That's at least a twenty-minute walk. Also checked the art gallery next door to the market. No one there. They closed up a little after five. Also talked to some of the neighbors. No one saw or heard anything."

"Thanks," the reporter said as he wrote in his notebook.

Jim Cunningham addressed Hornig, "So you're still going with the robbery angle?"

"No reason not to at this point," Hornig said.

"But there was nothing to steal. Amos already deposited whatever he had in the bank."

"Doesn't change anything. Guy who killed him didn't know that. Assumed the money was still there."

Sam Cashman got a word in. "I think it's too soon to make any definite statement. We've got some work to do yet. The instinct is to say robbery, as that's what you would expect when dealing with a convenience store, but...it just doesn't look right."

"In what way?" Cunningham asked.

The chief interrupted, "Hold on, Jim, I don't want any of our internal discussions in the paper. You know that. No speculation."

"Not a problem. We'll discuss that separately. I know you want to keep your investigation under control. Don't worry."

"Okay. Just as long as we're on the same page on this." Then addressing Sam, Hornig said, "Tell me what doesn't look right."

"It's still too neat and clean. If the guy was there for a robbery and finds out there's no money, the usual reaction is to not believe it. Mess up the place. Push Amos around a bit. If I'm reading you right, Doctor Coffey, there's no sign of a struggle. I know I didn't see one. Also, the place didn't seem to be searched. The cash drawer was still in the exact place where Amos usually puts it when he closes up: upside down, on the counter, under the night light. He always kept it visibly empty to anyone looking in. The killer didn't seem to touch or check it. The storage area under the counter wasn't touched and there's no indication the storeroom was entered by someone looking for a safe or some other hiding place."

"I agree," Mary said. Hornig gave her a serious look as though he wanted her to stay out of it. She saw the look and ignored it. "This may be one of the cleanest—except for the wine—crime scenes of a convenience store I've come across."

"You've seen a lot of them," Jim Cunningham said looking at the thirty-something, auburn haired woman sitting in the chair in front of him. He had not seen her before, although he knew the coroner had recently taken on an assistant. He made a note to make sure his reporter got a full resume and personal background for a separate story.

"Enough. Came down from the coroner's office in Dekalb County, Georgia."

"You can get your background stuff later, Jim. Kent what do you think?" Hornig said, calling on the senior detective sitting behind Mary.

"Maybe yes, maybe no. Sam's right about the general look of things, but we may just have a scared rabbit on our hands. Especially if Amos told him to go to hell and get out. He probably turned his back on the guy and started for the back door. The guy panicked, grabbed the first thing that was handy, hit him with it and took off. Open and shut. Probably lives in town. Made a mistake. Did it on a dare. Who knows? Wouldn't read too much into it."

"Sam, what do you think?"

"Kent's got more experience than me and he might be

right, but I wouldn't count on it this time."

"Hamp?" addressing the officer that was at Dunn's earlier with Sam.

"Lean towards Kent's view a bit. But I have to admit Sam's got a point. Think we need to go slow on this one."

Cunningham couldn't resist, "Sidney was saying the same thing earlier today."

The chief looked at the editor. "Sidney?...Lake? Let's not go there. I don't want him and his housekeeper getting their fingers into this. They're not part of the police force. Let's not blow this out of proportion. No amateurs! I repeat. No...amateurs. Understand?"

Sam immediately answered. "Agreed. I'll go where the evidence leads, but...I'm not going to close any avenues that can be helpful."

"I don't expect you to, but I do expect you to stay in control. And I don't want to find Sidney Lake in here telling me how to do my job." Then looking at Cunningham, "An' I don't want you encouraging him. We have a good relationship, Jim, let us do our job. We'll keep you and your people informed, as we always do. We have a deal here?"

All agreed.

"Good." He said as a dismissal and then stood up, "Mary, you and Sam stay behind for a couple of minutes." Addressing Detective Kent he said, "Close that door as you go out."

"Doctor Coffey," said Cunningham, "If you have a few minutes after you're finished here, could we have a chat? Just need some background for the story."

"Sure, no problem."

Once the door was closed Chief Hornig started in, "Sam, you know how I feel about amateurs. I want Sidney Lake kept under control. It's not that I don't think he's a smart guy. I know he is, but so are we." Switching to Mary

Coffey, "Doc, in case you haven't figured it out, we have a couple of amateur sleuths in town. So far they really haven't caused any major problems. In fact, I have to admit they pointed us in the right direction a couple of times—not that we wouldn't have gotten there by ourselves anyway—but their nosing around can be risky. Some people got hurt last year. They're not trained professionals and I don't want to spend scarce resources watching out for them when I could be doing something more productive. I'm referring to Sidney Lake, a retired English professor from the college and Tillie James, his housekeeper. She's from the Gullah community. So is Sam here. If you want to know what Gullah is all about ask him. What I can tell you is that they're a close-knit group and information travels around faster than anything on the internet, and Tillie never misses any of it. Trouble is a lot of it's misleading."

"I'm familiar with the Gullah. Been to Penn Center over on St. Helena Island and I've even watched *Gullah, Gullah Island* on *Nickelodeon* with my nieces. I found it really interesting."

"That's good. I think that'll help a lot, but be careful. Those two will sneak up on you and before you know it, you let something out you shouldn't."

Sam, at this point, had a smile on his face.

"That goes for you too," Hornig said. "Don't think you're immune to those two...nobody is."

Mary raised a finger as she spoke. "Can I make a suggestion? Back in Dekalb County we had a situation with two little old ladies in one of those fifty-five and over places, the Miss Marple syndrome, I would imagine something like you've been experiencing with your Sidney and Tillie. The old ladies were actually helpful a couple of times and then thought they knew it all and started to get in the way. We solved the problem by giving them more access rather than less. Threw technically worded reports

at them but didn't give them access to the 'English lan-
guage' versions. Buried them in paperwork. Most people
don't realize just how much paperwork is involved in a
normal, routine event like a traffic accident, but when
there's a death involved...." She rolled her eyes.

"I don't know about that. These two aren't a couple of
old ladies. Knowing Lake, he would probably do an analysis of the reports and extensive research on everything in
them. Then he'd submit a document back to us that's twice
as long as what we gave him."

"Well, I don't know them, but since Sam does, why not
just let him control it and decide how involved they should
be? Keep them out of your hair. Sometimes it's better to
embrace the problem than let it fester.

Hornig put his head in his hands, then ran the fingers of
his right hand through his hair. "Okay, I'm going to give
you two this problem. You're going to be working on this
together anyway. You figure out how to deal with them,
but I'll tell you both right now," mainly addressing Sam
Cashman, "I don't want to see either one of them in this
building."

Chapter 4

Finding a discrepancy

*T*he *Morgan City Times* came out with a more detailed story on Friday but shed no extra light on Amos Dunn's murder. It read as a straightforward tragic, senseless robbery that '…the police believe got out of hand.' *The Post and Courier* in Charleston gave it some coverage with a regional news mention on an inside page and *The Island Packet* on Hilton Head did the same. One of the television stations in Charleston also gave it a five second mention.

By Monday morning, when Tillie came to Sidney's on Howard Street, it seemed to be following a familiar pattern of how violence in a local neighborhood is supposed to be covered: a quick blast of news, interview with neighbors, one or two pictures, police comments of no leads, ask for help from the community and move on. A sad, tragic event that would eventually be solved when someone was picked up for another incident and then be tied back into the Amos Dunn murder.

Once in a while the person of interest would be caught quickly when the victim was well liked in the community. Anonymous tips were not unusual, and the police were very quick to promote them where possible, although no help was coming their way this time. However, they knew it sometimes took a little longer for the information to drift out, but Chief Hornig and his people were certain they would eventually get to the bottom of it. The trick would be to keep it off the front pages so they would have control over their own resources. They would certainly pursue it and try to get everything cleaned up as soon as possible before the next crisis hit Hornig's understaffed department. Hornig also wanted to keep the option open to shelve the file temporarily if he had to.

Sidney thought long and hard about it over the weekend, but, based on what he'd learned so far, couldn't see any other avenue to follow other than the way Chief Hornig was handling it.

When Tillie arrived at eight-thirty, she found Sidney at his desk with his literary research spread all around him.

"Mornin', Professor," she called out as she came through the unlocked front door. She didn't even attempt to use her own key, as Sidney always left the door open for her on her cleaning day. Tillie also made her greeting before actually seeing him. She knew he would be at his desk in the front office, where he camped out every morning to work on his latest literary project. It's not that he was a slave to a specific routine, but just that he had an extremely methodical nature.

The library in the back of the house—originally a large bedroom that was created for a previous owner and stood just off the kitchen—figured in his routine for later in the day. The big, comfortable chair with the matching footstool—just right for reading and napping—proved to be an excellent afternoon hide-away.

Her morning greeting was anticipated as Mickey heard the door close on Tillie's car and went from Sidney's side to the front door.

"Kinda miserable out there today. Hot and humid. Hi

Mickey. We gonna get an afternoon thunder-bumper for sure."

Sidney looked up as she came into the room, "My thoughts as well. The Mortons seemed to have picked a good couple of weeks for their vacation up north. Although I could use his police contacts around here with regard to Amos Dunn's murder. I'm really curious to know how the police chief is going to handle this one."

"Yeah, that Mister Morton sure knows everyone in the county."

"Retired policeman do like to keep their hands in."

"Retired college professors seem to have the same problem," she said with a sneaky, little smile, not missed by Sidney who responded with his usual look of peering over the top of his reading glasses.

Tillie continued, "Bet Mr. Morton doesn't know anything 'bout that new lady body snatcher person from the county."

"Body snatcher? What body snatcher?"

"The lady who works for Doctor Cooper."

"The new assistant coroner?"

"That's her."

"But why body snatcher?"

"Cause that's what they do. Come look things over after someone like Mister Dunn gets killed and then they snatch up the body and take it away. Saw her and Mister Sam goin' into Amos' store just now when I drove past." As Tillie spoke, she and Mickey walked into Lake's office and stood next to the sofa positioned in front of the fireplace.

"Mary Coffey?"

"Mary Coffey, yeah, that's her. Came down from Georgia to work for Doctor Cooper. She's a doctor, too. Mother lives in that condominium off Mill Creek Road. Husband died about six months ago. Her mother's that is. Miss

Coffey came down to live with her mother and help her out. Christina said her mother's havin' some troubles. Miss Coffey ain't married...at least not now she ain't. Worked in a clinic and did body snatchin' outside Atlanta."

Sidney sat back in his chair and shook his head from side to side. "None of this was in the newspaper article on Amos Dunn. And who is Christina?"

"Does the cleaning for Mrs. Hoteep, that's her mother's name. Man who died was the second husband. Don't really know much about the first. Think he was a lawyer or somethin'."

"Since you seem to know just about everything, you wouldn't happen to know who killed Amos Dunn would you?"

"Not yet. Nobody seems to know. No one's heard a thing. Got to believe it was someone from the outside. Who knows? Maybe it's really what they say it is: random act of violence?"

Tillie moved away from the sofa and started toward the hall and the closet behind the stairs where she kept the cleaning equipment.

"Do you really believe that?"

"Not for a minute."

Just then a knock came at the front door and Hattie Ryan came in. "Good morning everyone."

"Morning Miss Hattie."

"Hattie," Sidney greeted. "You just gave me an idea."

Hattie stopped in her tracks. "Well, good morning to you, too."

"Oh, sorry. Of course. Good morning." He quickly got up from his chair. Not a particularly elegant maneuver for a man of his bulk, but when he had something on his mind, something that consumed his thought process, he seemed to ignore obstacles that would limit him, as a bird dog would charge ahead through almost anything to retrieve the object he had been trained to find and bring back to his master. "I could use you."

Hattie got a smile on her face. "Interesting choice of words. Sidney, you know you're impossible. Okay, now what are you up to?"

Tillie chuckled to herself as she opened the closet door.

"Amos Dunn's murder," Sidney said. "I need to do some snooping and you can be my cover. Tillie and I were just talking and the new assistant coroner and Sam Cashman are over at Dunn's right now. I need to find out what they're doing and if I go by myself, without Mickey, they'll think I came there on purpose to spy on them."

"You really think you're going to fool Sam Cashman?"

Sidney didn't respond, he just lifted his shoulders and one eyebrow in a motion that said, *why not.*

"Okay," Hattie said, "I came over to see if you were going to the library this morning and it's sort of on the way. I have some research I want to do on Wordsworth's involvement in stopping the rail line from going into the Lake District and you said something last week about needing to confirm Patrick Brontë's church connection in County Down. I thought we could go together and maybe do lunch."

"Ah, excellent idea. That also gives me an excuse for not having Mickey with me when walking around. Sorry, Mickey."

Not knowing why Sidney expressed being sorry to her didn't stop Mickey from wagging her tail at the mention of her name, clearly understanding that Sidney's penance would result in her receiving a treat, for which she was always thankful.

"Don't worry, Mickey, you can help me this morning," Tillie said from the hallway.

"So, Sidney, tell me what's this all about?" Hattie

spoke as the professor ushered her toward the front door.

"You got your phone with you?" Tillie made the comment more as an instruction to make sure he took it with him rather than checking that he already had it.

"Ah, good catch." He stopped and checked the pocket of the ever-present sports jacket he wore. Sidney was not a mobile phone fan, often mentioning how intrusive it could be, but he did find it useful to have on occasion.

Tillie treated him like an older, forgetful brother she needed to watch over. "Don't worry. I got it right here for you." She went over and picked it up from his desk. "Make sure you let me know if you decide not to come back here before you go to lunch so I can feed Mickey before I leave."

The walk to the Cedar Street Market didn't trace Sidney's path of Thursday afternoon, but a more direct one, which took no more than five minutes. A police cruiser could not be seen as Sidney and Hattie approached the building and the police caution tape had been removed from the perimeter of the building, but still remained across the front door. As they made their way along High Street toward the building's back entrance, Sam spotted them as they passed the store window.

"I think we're about to get some company," Sam said.

Mary looked up from the area around the cash register, where she stood and got a brief glimpse of Sidney going by. "The professor and his housekeeper?"

"No, his lady friend...or colleague. Well, maybe a bit of both. She's another professor from the college. I spotted Tillie earlier so I think she reported back to him that we were here. We'll see. Her name is Hattie Ryan. She still teaches at the college. He retired last year."

"Okay, should be interesting." She then returned to her inspection of the counter.

In less than thirty seconds she heard a male voice call

out. "Hello? Is that you Sam?"

"Yes it is."

"Professor Lake. Can we come in?"

"Sure, it's okay now. We're just tying up a few loose ends. All the tape will be gone when we leave." Sam moved to his left slightly, as the back door was offset so it could be seen from the cash register position, but not from the aisle leading directly from the front door, where Sam now stood. Mary, on the other hand, had a clear view of both of them as they came in the rear entrance.

"Couldn't resist getting a look inside. Haven't been here in a while. Tillie comes in all the time and described it pretty well though. Sam, you know Doctor Hattie Ryan don't you?" he said as they came up the center aisle.

"Oh, yes, we've met a number of times." They shook hands.

"And you, I presume, are Doctor Coffey," the professor said as he moved toward the check-out counter.

"Yes, sir. And I understand you to be Professor Lake. I've heard of you." She reached across the counter to shake his hand while Hattie engaged in conversation with Sam.

"I don't think I've ever been in here," Hattie said. "I've walked by on occasion. I live over in the Palmetto Place condominiums. We have a convenience store right on the corner. Great for local emergencies."

"Yes," Sam answered, "that's true here as well. The big shopping for everyone in the neighborhood is the Piggly Wiggly on Market and Front Streets. I guess that's why the market is considered a convenience store."

Sam was trying to listen to both conversations, the one with Hattie as well as what Sidney was saying.

Sidney carefully noted the check-out position and everything around it as he spoke to Mary Coffey. "Amos did well here because a good many people in the area don't have cars, or, if they do, they only have one. Lot of walking goes on in a local neighborhood like this one. The Cedar Street Market is an easy walk for everyone, and Amos kept his prices down."

"Amos was a good man, well liked." Sam said.

Hattie took in the large but shelf-crowded room as she said, "That's what Tillie said. It's why she doesn't believe someone local was involved. Sidney said she's convinced it was an outsider. She also said she saw something when she peeked in the window the other day that also didn't look right. Said she couldn't put her finger on it."

Sam considered what Hattie said before replying. "Well...she comes in a lot more than I do. Amos Dunn was part of her source network," He now smiled. "She'd come and just chat to pass the time of day and find out what was going on in the neighborhood. I know all this from Deede, my wife. She's also one of Tillie's sources...though she won't admit it. I swear there are no secrets in this town that Tillie doesn't know."

"I get that impression, but she also has the reputation of not spreading anything around unnecessarily. She can keep a confidence. I suppose that's why people trust her." Hattie's attention shifted as she noticed Sidney becoming animated while speaking with Dr. Coffey at the counter.

"But it's wrong!" Sidney said, raising his voice, which caused Sam and Hattie to turn toward them—Sidney in front of the counter and Mary Coffee in the position Amos would have been in if he was checking out a customer. "Somebody moved it. They had to. Tillie's right. It's all set up wrong by someone who really didn't know Amos Dunn. It's all been moved around and not been put back right."

"Something the matter? Sam asked.

"Has anyone else been in here but us?" Mary Coffey looked around the cash register and then under the counter.

"Not unless there's another key I don't know about.

Aside from Amos Dunn and Grace Carter, she opens up sometimes, no one else admitted to having a key. Even his nephew, William, who arrived in town late Tuesday, couldn't get in. I brought him over on Friday morning and was with him the whole time. I had three extra keys made, one of which you have, the one I have and the other is locked up in the station."

Mary stood behind the counter with her hands on her hips. "I have to check all the pictures that were taken and the notes I made from my original visit here immediately after the body was discovered, as well as the other pictures that were taken the following morning."

"What's the problem?" Sam said.

"I may not have spent the time I should have on this. We had three nursing home deaths since Wednesday, where there was no medical professional in attendance at the time, and with Cooper still out of town—he's the one who usually concentrates on those—I lost my focus here. Everyone kept looking at this as a simple B and E gone wrong and I took it for granted as well."

Sidney couldn't resist. "You see, it's all set up wrong. Everything is arranged for a right-handed person, Amos was left-handed. If you're using a scanner it doesn't matter, but everything here is manual."

"He's right," Mary said. "We verified that in the lab when we did the work-up on Amos."

The professor shifted to analysis mode. "I'm sure that's what Tillie saw when she looked in the window. She saw how the counter was arranged. You see here," he pointed to the calculator which sat just to the left of the old, bulky, 1940's era cash register. "It should be a body width to the left. I commented about the position to Amos one time when I came in. The credit card machine is supposed to be where the calculator is. Amos' routine consisted of the customer putting the hand-held basket of groceries on the end of the counter here." Sidney placed his hand where the basket would sit on the end of the long side of the L-shaped, linoleum covered counter. Everyone looked at the spot, envisioning the filled, brown, plastic grocery container. "As he emptied the basket with his right hand, he would enter the price into the calculator with his left hand. There was also a pad on the left side of the cash register— which is missing. Has anyone seen that pad?" Then to Mary and Sam, "Something else to check. That pad was used to keep track of cash sales. The card reader on the right kept track of the debit and credit sales. Once he got the money part of the transaction out of the way, all the signed receipts and any checks went into the plastic tray under the counter below the credit card machine. Next, he would bag everything. Plastic and paper bags were under the counter just below where the calculator is supposed to be." As Sidney spoke, he moved around behind the counter and Mary stepped back so he could stand exactly where Amos would have been. "I'm sure you'll find a folder someplace with a bunch of cash position work-sheets. He may not keep completed ones in the store though. They're probably in his house on Queen Street. There definitely should be some blanks around here someplace. If they aren't under the counter, I'll bet they're in the storeroom."

Mary had a look of dismay on her face as Sidney gave her a lesson in careful observation. She had heard he was observant, but this level of detail surprised her. He was nothing like the 'little old ladies' she ran into in Georgia. "I think I know what you mean. You're right, there's a shoe box in the storeroom with some printed forms in it." Mary pointed to the underside of the counter. "Everything else you said holds up, too. It's all under there in the places you mentioned."

"But no sign of the other pad," Sam said. "The one with all the numbers indicating the cash sales."

"Not that I recall seeing when we looked last week."

Sidney made another suggestion: "You may want to take another look at the house on Queen Street. That pad with the numbers on it was used to reconcile the cash register. He may have taken it home with him every night. I don't think Amos stayed around the store after he locked up the front door. I'm sure he just did a simple close down routine. He added up all the cash, set aside what he would need to open up with the following morning, put the remainder in the night deposit bag and made his way to the bank. After depositing it, he went for his walk. I suppose it's possible he had his cash number pad, the cash position sheet for the day and cash for tomorrow, all in that shopping bag he carried. The one he took with him to the bank that contained the night deposit bag. Of course, that would mean he carried the money with him on his walk, if he didn't leave the whole shopping bag at the bank, which I don't think the bank would allow."

"Some serious food for thought there, Professor Lake." Sam admitted. "I think I'll just have another talk with his assistant, Grace Carter. If what you say is even half true, then she would be expected to follow the same procedure when she opened up...or closed the store for Amos. Also, we know he had three part-time workers that he scheduled so no employee was ever in the place alone. We've only talked with one of them so far. A Jan Liston. She lives about two blocks from here. The other two live out on the islands and we haven't caught up with them yet."

Mary reclaimed her space from Sidney. Looking at him as she spoke, "Are you sure of all this? You remember all of this just from coming in a few times?"

"More than just a few times. Also, keep in mind that four blocks from here is Church Street. You have Episcopal, Baptist, Presbyterian, AME and Methodist churches along there and they all have pantries to keep full. They do most of their shopping at the supermarkets, but the Cedar Street Market is where we all do our emergency runs. Been in here more times than I'd like to tell when we ran out of something ten minutes before a Wednesday night supper at church. Besides, this place fascinated me. Manual things do. In the age of computers in the twenty-first century, you'd be amazed how efficient and cost-effective manual can be. Sometimes electronic things can be a nightmare."

Sam stepped back from the counter and looked around the room, "Why would someone want to steal a pad with numbers on it? Mary, you have to come up with those pictures."

"Actually, I'm going to take some more. I have a camera with my case in the car. There are a couple of other angles I'd like to get a picture from, as well as reshooting some I already have. The original pictures are in my office, but what if the missing pad is in the original picture? That would mean someone took it after the body was discovered and my team arrived. However, if there's no pad, then someone may have taken it at the time of the murder."

Hattie decided to add another possible option: "Is everyone sure the Ambers never came into the store, despite what they said? Did they really just call in and then go outside and dial nine-one-one? I realized when coming in a few moments ago, that you can see the counter, cash register and the whole check-out area from the back door. Although, that's an awful squeaky door. I don't imagine anyone could sneak in or out without Amos knowing it, regardless of where he was in the store. But then, of course, he would have already been dead unless, God forbid, they killed him."

"We've looked into that. Being the first people on the scene they were natural suspects. We checked out their story and also their relationship with Amos Dunn. Tenant-landlord disputes are not that unusual. But no, no holes anywhere. Got along real well. No bad history. No disputes. I believe they told us everything accurately. Besides, if either one of them were involved there'd have been wine over one or both of them when we showed up."

Sam continued to play the congenial cop. Despite what Chief Hornig said, Sam encouraged Hattie and Sidney to expound upon their theories, as he wasn't getting too much help elsewhere. He was also pleased with Mary Coffey's theories and approach to the murder. She proved to be very thorough, not that the coroner, Doctor Cooper, wasn't, but she acted like she cared about what had happened to Amos Dunn and she really wanted to find out the full story. Sam and Mary had a lengthy discussion the day after that first meeting with Hornig. He told her he'd appreciate her keeping to herself that he had no problem enlisting Sidney Lake's help where he thought the professor and Tillie—and anyone else—could help him solve the murder of Amos Dunn.

"Another possibility," Sidney said while moving away from the counter and over to the position where the body was found. "How do we know that the intruder wasn't still in the store when the Ambers called in to Amos? I'm sure it was in their minds that he could still be in there, which is why they didn't go in, even though they didn't see anyone. I know it would have been in mine. In fact, the murderer would have been standing right about here after hitting Amos." Sidney took a position behind where the body would have been and acted out his theory. "Let's say he hits Amos, who bounces against the shelves here," He pointed to the spot. "And then falls here." Another point. "Then he—I refer to 'he' instead of 'she' as Tillie has convinced me that this is a crime that only a man would commit—he then leans over the body looking for something." Turning to Mary, "Footsteps in wine?"

"Negative."

"Okay, that tells us he didn't panic. But it also raises the question of how he got away from the body without stepping in the wine spatter?"

Sam and Mary gave one another a look that indicated they were well aware of the puzzle that faced them when it came to the lack of footprints in the wine.

Sidney continued with his analysis, "He then carefully leans over the body and moves it slightly in his search for something when he hears voices."

"Why looking for something?" said Hattie.

"If he was checking to see if Amos was still alive, he would have gone for the head or wrist or someplace he could easily catch a pulse."

Mary nodded in agreement.

"But he didn't see what he was looking for. Now startled by the voices outside, he straightens up and carefully hides behind the shelf to the left of the body." Sidney turned and stood sideways against the end of the shelf and tried to pull in his midsection to be concealed from anyone looking in the High Street window.

"If he was about your size, he'd do better facing the end of the shelf, you're sticking out at both ends," Hattie said with a mischievous smile. She and Sam moved out of Sidney's way as he performed his demonstration.

"Ah, yes, well, thank you for that." And then ignoring the comment he continued. "When the Ambers come across High Street—I'm assuming they come up Cedar from Main on this side of the street—they take a quick look in the window. Some of the lights are on."

Sam nodded his head in agreement, since the route Sidney has chosen for the Ambers is the one with the most streetlights.

Sidney continued, "Once they pass the window, he quickly goes to the cash register position," Mary gave way as he came behind the counter. "He's looking for something small and sees the calculator on his left and picks it up to see if anything is under it. The same with the cash register drawer. Nothing. Then he tries the credit card reader." Then to Mary again, "No fingerprints, right?"

"Right. Assume he used a handkerchief, or something similar. Another reason for believing this may not have been an impulsive or random act."

"Okay. But he's still in a rush—hurriedly moving things around. Still he can't find what he's looking for. Gets down under the counter and starts looking around the shelves. He finds Amos' cash counting book. He tries to figure out what it is and hears the rear door squeak. It's Ronald Amber and he calls for Amos. Our murderer stuffs the book into his pocket, stays down and out of sight behind the counter. Mr. Amber calls again and then turns and speaks with his wife. Tonya Amber tells him to come away and close the door. Our murderer is frantic. He tries to get everything back into place, but sets it up for a right-handed person, the common denominator, then heads for the back door. The Ambers are still there and talking about what to do. He can't leave with them standing there as he would come out right in front of them. There are only two places to hide: the washroom and the storeroom. He chooses the storeroom because it has windows where he can watch the Ambers. He monitors their conversation and, when they go out to High Street to wait for the police, he slips out the back door. Hiding behind the garbage cans just off the porch, the murderer waits for the right moment and while the Ambers have the police occupied on the sidewalk, he makes his way, quietly, over the back fence into the Art Gallery's yard."

Quiet.

Sam finally spoke. "Interesting theory, but it doesn't change the robbery gone bad suggestion. In fact it could enhance it. If you're right about him keeping start-up money around, as a lot of the small businesses on the street do, where is it? Could have been just enough to satisfy the murderer. I'll admit you've raised some interesting points, but they won't mean much unless you can come up with a motive for Amos' death that doesn't involve robbery in some way."

"Just a thought," Mary said, as they all walked toward the back door. "What if there is a bag of cash and coins hidden in the store someplace and we just haven't found it? Might be a good question to ask Grace Carter who opens up sometimes. She would need the cash to prime the register drawer when she started for the day."

"Good point." Sam held the door for everyone as they exited the store. "If it's still in the store someplace it raises the question as to whether Amos would be willing to risk his life for a hundred dollars in small bills and coins by not handing it over. I'll give Grace Carter a call. It may answer some more questions but may still not alter the robbery motive."

"Probably," Sidney said, "but I don't think so. It's the moving of the body, the way he did it that still has to be answered. And then the question of what was being looked for, what prompted Amos to open up the store after he closed it for the night? Lot of loose ends here Sam, a lot of loose ends."

"That may be. Could be we'll never know. All I do know is Chief Hornig has given me until the end of the week to put it all to bed and move on. Have a feeling Doctor Cooper's going to have a few other chores for Mary to switch to as well."

As Hattie stepped through the doorway to the back porch, she moved to the side where the stairs to the second-floor apartment began. "You know when you were all talking before, I took a walk around the front of the store, looking at the shelves and the general layout. Are you sure

Amos and his killer didn't come in the front door? I mean, just because the front door was locked and the back door open doesn't really confirm anything. What if Amos met someone he knew on his walk after the bank visit, who asked, as a favor, to open the store for him, as he just forgot to pick up something earlier—as Sidney mentioned—it could be a local church member he wanted to help? So they went through the front door from Cedar Street. The killer could have locked it behind him and went out the back in a hurry, where it was dark. Could have moved Amos' body to get the keys from his pocket."

Mary hesitated in the doorway. "Keys were still in his pocket. Also these locks are really old style. You need a key to both open and close from either inside or out. They don't lock automatically. Don't have a button on the door-knob. Deadbolt on the front door doesn't use a key. Once you throw it, it can't be opened from the other side."

"Oh, well." Hattie seemed resigned to Sidney having the only viable alternatives as usual, but figured she'd continue to try and punch holes in the professor's theory, something she loved to do. She decided on one more try. "Another thing, what if Amos set everything up for Grace Carter to open up in the morning? She's right-handed isn't she?"

"No," Sam said. "I mean, yes. She is right-handed, but she wasn't scheduled to open up on Thursday. It's an interesting point though. How did Amos leave everything when he closed up for the night he was killed? And the issue of the book where he kept the cash receipt records, why isn't that around someplace?"

"What about his office at home on Queen Street?" Mary said.

"We've looked there and didn't see anything out of the ordinary...but we didn't have a list of what to look for." Sam looked at his watch. "I really have to close up now. I have a meeting with the Chief in twenty minutes."

"Do you mind if I stop by Amos Dunn's place and have a look around on my way back to the office? I still have some pictures I'd like to take here. I can lock up."

"It's okay, Mary, especially about here, but you better check with William Dunn, Amos' nephew. He stayed in a hotel the first couple of days but moved to Amos' yesterday. The funeral is tomorrow. There's a mobile phone number for him in the file."

Sidney listened to the back and forth between Mary and Sam and would have loved to go with Mary Coffey to look around Amos' office, but he knew that would be pushing it. So he looked at Hattie and said, "We better be off as well. The library and research beckons. Sam, I appreciate you're putting up with us and believe me we'll do everything we can to stay out of Chief Hornig's hair."

"I appreciate that Professor Lake, just keep in mind that the chief plans to shelve the investigation by end of the week, so if you come up with something new let me know. If the murder of Amos Dunn comes back to the front burner in the future, I have a feeling Detective Kent will take it over." Sam just shrugged his shoulders and both Sidney and Hattie received the message.

Chapter 5

A secret hiding place

ary gave Sam a wave as he pulled away from the curb, but instead of heading immediately back inside, she walked over to the window on High Street that looked out from the storeroom. It wasn't possible to see inside. She made her way to the back of the building—the area that was under the outside stairway to the Amber's apartment upstairs. When she tried to look through the back window to the storeroom her view was blocked by stacked cartons. *Interesting,* she thought and then went over to the rear of the black SUV with the coroner's sign and county logo on its side, which she had parked behind the store. Retrieving her case she returned to the market and the storeroom.

Wasting no time in getting to work, Mary took another complete set of pictures, but this time focused on the perspective of someone entering the room. In another set she went after specific areas, such as the location of the shoe box with the printed forms in it and the area around it. The box sat on the far end of a shelf at the back of the room near the window that opened to High Street, the same window she was unable to look through from the outside a few minutes earlier. Tucked into a space between the end of the shelving and the High Street wall sat a folding card table with a matching chair. As she focused her camera on the area, she realized this would be Amos' work area. He could set up the table and chair to the left of the High Street window, where he would not be seen, and with the rear window blocked by the stacked cartons, he created a protected location where he could work unobserved. She focused her camera on the area and took pictures from every possible angle. Finished, she opened the shoe box, took a form from the box and opened it. It was filled with 8 1/2 x 11 inkjet paper sheets folded in half. The heading on top of each form read CASH POSITION WORKSHEET. Sidney was right. The first line began with 'Starting Cash:' and the amount $150.00. *So, where did he keep the $150 overnight? Did he keep it out of the depository bag and take it home with him or hide it someplace in the store? Probably the store, but where? And it wouldn't be all bills. Fifty dollars of it would probably be coin to prime the cash register. He must also have a computer somewhere. How else would he be able to make up those worksheets? At home? Sam didn't mention it. Has it been examined?*

Mary looked around the room. Most everything was on the shelves, having been removed from their original cartons, except in front of the rear window. Everything in the storeroom was non-perishable. What frozen foods and dairy products the store carried were in the refrigerated bins in the front of the store along the High Street side.

Mary looked from shelf to shelf. Canned goods, cereals, pastas and similar products were stacked along the interior wall, while paper products were on the other side of the room. At eye height next to the cereals, she spotted a stack of large, paper, grocery bags with sturdy handles, the size that Amos used to conceal the night depository bag on his walk to the bank. She touched a few just to get a feel for their strength. Sitting next to them on the same shelf were the classic round containers of Quaker Oats. They were neatly stacked three high and three deep, but her eye caught the position of the last container on the top in the back row. Something about it didn't seem right. Having a career that demanded strict and close attention to every detail, she noticed that the position of the Quaker on the box looked to the left while all the others looked straight ahead. Instinctively, she reached back to turn the box so it conformed to the others, but it wouldn't be moved with a simple twist. She tried again. This time it did move, but did its best to resist her shove. She gave it a long look and then put her hand around it, instead of just trying to move it with her fingers, to see what caused the resistance. It was heavy, a lot heavier than oatmeal should be. She took it down from its place and almost dropped it because of its unexpected weight. In keeping it from falling, she squeezed it and the top popped up. It had been opened. A plastic bag filled with coin and currency looked back at her when she fully removed the cover. *Sneaky little devil weren't you, Amos Dunn?*

Mary immediately dialed Sam on her phone and left him a message to call her. Opening the case, she took out her Dunn file, found the phone number for Amos' nephew, William, and dialed him.

"Mister Dunn, this is Mary Coffey from the County Coroner's Office, I'd like to come over there to take some pictures of your uncle's office, if it's not too inconvenient?"

"Oh, yes, Miss Coffey, but I'm not there."

"Oh, I was advised that you had moved into three-ninety-one Queen Street."

"That was my plan, but I decided to wait until after the funeral and you people finished off your investigation. Have you?"

"No. We're still piecing some parts together, which is

why I wanted to get a look at your uncle's office."

"The police have been there already."

"I know, but I never had a chance to take any pictures. It didn't seem important at the time, as we were just focusing on the store, but we really need them for the full record. Has anyone been in there or moved anything around?"

"No. As I said, I decided not to move in until after the funeral. I'm still at the Holiday Inn. Nobody's been in the place since I was there with that policeman."

"Ah. Good. Well, if it's not too inconvenient I would really like to get in there this morning."

"That's all right. I can meet you there in about ten minutes."

⊘⊘⊘

Sidney and Hattie made the walk to the college library in a leisurely manner. They passed the time with some minor chatter about political intrigue in the English Literature Department, one of their favorite topics, and everyone else's on campus ever since Sidney retired at the end of June. Although expected, his decision to leave had not been taken seriously and no plan for his replacement had been put into place.

Once at the library, they followed their usual routine of choosing an unoccupied area and set up their chosen space with two chairs between them along one side of the ten-seat table—effectively securing it completely for themselves. While Sidney carried his material in a traditional, brown, expandable briefcase, Hattie's choice was a small backpack. There were few materials in either of the cases so weight was not a problem when lugging them from Sidney's to Dunn's market and then to the library.

As they both switched their priorities to the research before them, they didn't speak of the Dunn murder during the entire walk. However, once Sidney'd had a chance to look at the issue of *Brontë Studies* from January 2013, which held the articles in which he was interested, he said, "What could possibly be a motive?"

The question addressed itself to no one in particular and he spoke in a low tone, although loud enough for Hattie to hear it, which she did. But there was no way to determine if the question dealt with his research on literary forgery or murder in the first degree. Hattie, having known Sidney ever since she came to Morgan College in 2006, had a pretty good idea of how his mind worked and knew he had an idea about something and wanted to bounce it around a bit.

"You have some thoughts about something?" she asked keeping the subject matter up for grabs.

"Yes, I'm glad you asked." He put down his fountain pen and turned to Hattie. "It's got to have something to do with the walk."

"You mean after Amos made the deposit at the bank?"

"Yes. I'm sure he met someone toward the end of it. I wonder if anyone saw him. I meant to ask Sam that, whether they checked along the route to see if they found anyone who spotted him walking on Wednesday evening."

"Do we know the route he took? Is it always the same?"

"Unanswered questions, I believe."

"And what about the reason he took it? Does anyone know that? I mean, it's not as though he was overweight and needed exercise…like some people." Hattie said, raising her eyebrows and giving Sidney a sidelong glance.

Sidney ignored the reference to his 230 pounds. "Well…he did have that tumor. I wonder if he knew about it."

"Knew about it? I don't know about it. It wasn't in the paper. How do you know? Oh…of course, Tillie. Right?"

"Right." Sidney gave a nod of his head and smiled.

"But how?"

"She doesn't always tell me how and I didn't ask. But you do ask the right questions and I have to wonder if it doesn't play a role in his death? As far as she knows he wasn't aware of it. I think what we really need to know is more about that daily walk of his." He closed the notebook in which he had begun to write. "I have to talk with Tillie. She's still at the house," he said while checking his watch. "I think she has the information that may shed some light on a few things, although I'm pretty sure doesn't know she has it or she would have said something already."

Seeing Sidney continue to pack up his material Hattie asked, "What about your research?"

"It's not what I expected. The email I received said there were some letters from Charlotte Brontë to Monsieur Constantin Heger in Bruxelles that had come into question and I assumed the question had to do with their authenticity since some reference material referred to T. J. Wise."

"Ah, your infamous but very learned literary forger."

"Yes, well I've already found evidence of some Brontë forged and doctored material and believed this would feed my research. However, there is no dispute over the authenticity of the letters only their whereabouts for the past hundred and fifty years. So, I don't think they will help me, but you keep going with what you're doing. I don't mean to interrupt your research…although there is something you can do for me. Could you call on the Rector of Saint Luke's and talk with her about Amos Dunn? Just general conversation about him and see what her impressions are?"

* cɔcɔ *

When Mary pulled up to the curb in front of Amos Dunn's house on Queen Street, William Dunn was in the process of opening the front door. Seeing the coroner's car stop he didn't continue inside, but waited on the porch for Mary to join him. As she came up the steps he greeted her, "I was afraid you'd beat me here. A housekeeper at the hotel, who's a customer of the market and lives down the street from it, wanted to know when I was going to open up again. Seemed to be really concerned. In her seventies and working as a housekeeper at three places, two on a regular, part time basis and one as a fill in. Doesn't have a car, lives with her sister on Church Street." He shook his head. "Don't know how they do it."

"I know only too well." They shook hands. She put her case down and showed him her I.D. that hung on a lanyard around her neck. "Sorry to have to interrupt your morning. Got delayed myself with some phone calls. The police took the tape off everything earlier today so you could open up if you needed to. By the way we found the start-up cash hidden in the storeroom. Someone from Chief Hornig's office will probably give you a call about it."

"Yes, they told me the tape was down. Haven't heard anything else though. I've talked with Grace Carter about the procedure Amos followed. I can't stay past next week so I'll just have her run things for the time being. Have an appointment this afternoon. Well, come on in and I'll show you the office."

William turned, opened the door and held it as Mary, lugging her ever-present case moved past him. She stopped immediately. Mary's halting was so quick that William bumped into her.

"Oh, I'm sorry. Oh my God!" he exclaimed, as he looked past her into the living room.

❧❧❧

Sidney found Tillie wiping down the counter tops in the

kitchen. "You're back early," she said. Sidney, followed by Mickey, peeked into the room.

"Yes, a bit of a false alarm, as far as research goes, but I need your help with something that came up at Amos Dunn's market."

Tillie stopped her cleaning. "Whad you find out?"

"First of all it's becoming clearer that this was not just a routine, neighborhood break-in."

"No news in that. There ain't no routine, neighborhood break-ins over there. They're all good people. Local bad folks don't go there." Her stance stiffened as she spoke.

"Point taken. I know, but that doesn't stop the police from classifying it as one. Our job is to show them that they're on the wrong track. It seems clear that Amos Dunn knew his killer, who may have met up with him during his evening walk and opened the store as a favor for him."

Tillie thought a moment, "Make's sense. Amos was a no-nonsense kinda man, but he had a good heart. He'd probably do that, especially if the reason was a good one. Yeah, I can see him doin' that."

"Okay, so my question is, do you know the route he took on his walk and was it always the same?"

"Oh, sure. Seen him walkin' lots a times. Sometimes give Gloria a ride home. She works full time at Mr. Ross'. You know, the former State Treasurer. He's got that big, cream colored, stucco place on Ridge Place. She'd wait for me at the curb on Marianne Street. Every now and then we'd see Amos come walkin' by. Always say hello. Then he'd go up another block on Marianne and turn left. Then he'd make the next right and then another left. Couple of dead ends in there and it's the only way he can make his way over to Church Street and home. Don't know why he went that way, but he's been doin' it now for about three months."

"I have one of those downtown street maps in the

cupboard above the toaster. Take it out and let's have a look at it."

"Yeah, I know where it is." As Tillie opened the cabinet door, Mickey immediately came over to see what she was doing, sticking her nose in the air and sniffing in Tillie's direction. "No, it's not a treat an' you know it. It's not food an' you can't read so you might as well just sit and watch. We'll talk about treats later." She opened the small map and placed it on the island where Sidney moved one of its stools to sit down.

"Tillie, could you bring over one of the pencils by the phone? We'll see if we can trace just where he went every night."

She took a pencil and then walked around the island and sat on the stool next to Sidney.

Lake looked at the map. "How long do you think the walk is?"

"That I can't say. Never walked it."

"All right, so show me where you think he walked."

"I don't *think* I know where he walked, I know. Seen him do it. Not all at once but he does it—or did it—every day an' I'm down there every day. An' if I didn't see him, somebody I know did."

"Point taken. Okay, show me where he walked."

Tillie looked at the map. "Well the map don't show it, but this is where the store is." She pointed to a spot indicating the corner of Cedar and High Streets. Sidney made an 'X' there. Tillie then, with her finger, traced an imaginary line down Cedar Street to Market Street and Sidney followed with his pencil. "He always went right down this way and then turned toward downtown where the bank is. He put the money in the bank and then threw away the paper bag he carried so people wouldn't know he had a bank bag—that was just for strangers, everybody else knew what was in there. Next, he headed up Market Street all the way to Marianne Street, where he made a left. Kept walkin' along there till he got to George Street and made another left turn." Sidney kept moving with the pencil. "When he went down there he only went one block, as it ends up in a sort a dead end."

"What do you mean?"

"It kinda peters out. I mean it's a dirt road back there, but it don't really go nowhere but to some old houses and a fence that's behind the City Hall parking lot. They were left over when they built the new City Hall. Nobody wanted to buy them. Right up against that fence. So they's abandoned. The usual bad stuff goes on there, even if the police station is right there in the City Hall building."

"Ah, I know where you mean now. Understand there's a proposal to take the buildings down and turn it into a park."

"Yeah," she laughed, "Good luck with that one."

"Well, so where does he go from here?" He pointed to the corner of George and Marianne Streets.

Tillie resumed. "As I said, he goes down the one block on George and turns onto Pond Lane. Some nice houses in there. The road crosses King Street and goes over to the pond which backs up on the college, but comes to an end at the pond. He don't go that way. Goes down King till he gets to College Street and takes that all the way out to Church Street where he walks past all the churches till he gets to Morris. He makes a left there down to Queen Street and then heads on home. That's it."

Sidney looked at the convoluted path he had drawn. "Well, it comes out as a basic square with a few cut-outs here and there. Have to put a highlighter on it. Are you sure about this?" He, of course, knew the answer before he asked the question.

"'Course I am. Seen him do it…mostly. Got people workin' all around there. You know that. The fancy houses, the churches, we got 'im all covered."

"Yes, I know. Nothing escapes the housekeeper network. You and your friends must be a great source of information for the police."

"Hah, they don't talk to us less they think we done somethin an' we don't tell them anythin' less we have to. Then we don't tell 'im who said it."

Chapter 6

*M*ary made three quick phone calls: the first to 911, the second to Sam Cashman and the third to Coroner Cooper. She instructed William Dunn not to enter the house. When he protested, she stood in the doorway with her hands on her hips, stared him in the face and said: "Look, I know what dead people look like, and this one's been dead for a while."

☙❧

As Sidney walked in the direction of Main Street on the way to a lunch appointment with Hattie, a police cruiser cut across the intersection of Howard and High Streets in front of him—lights on but siren quiet. His research finished, he had left the library well before her but they decided to meet again for lunch at the Morgan River Grill on Main Street. The restaurant sat next door to Amos' bank. He was sure there had to be something more to Amos' death than the police believed. There had to be a motive and he knew it didn't have anything to do with robbing the market. Had Amos stumbled into something unintentionally? Sidney kept running ideas around in his head while watching the police cruiser disappear down the street. *The walk*, he thought. *It has to be the walk.*

During lunch, the idea consumed him. Hattie tried to change the subject a number of times. Wordsworth, The Lake District, T. J. Wise, the maligning of Anne Brontë— his most vehement topic—but nothing worked. He just kept coming back to the murder of Amos Dunn.

"You know, Hattie, I've got this bad feeling about what happened to Amos. I don't think it's over."

"Well, they haven't closed the case yet, have they?"

"No, Sam said he has until the end of the week, but that's not what I mean. Until we know why he was killed there's no way we can figure out the identity of the killer. There's something else at work here. I'm not even convinced Amos knew why he was attacked, hit from behind as he was. I'm sure he never saw his attacker as a threat. So there has to be something going on that Amos didn't know about…maybe…something the killer saw him do or say that led to an assumption that Amos had the potential to be a real problem. But how? He ran a small local market. Boring stuff all day long made bearable by friendly banter, gossipy news and tidbits of neighborhood information. There are no official reports of previous threats, although Tillie assumed he probably wouldn't report them if there were, believing the police would ignore them anyway." Sidney paused and rubbed his chin for a moment while considering Tillie's assumption. "As much as I respect Tillie's views, I don't buy this one. Amos was active in the downtown business association, as well as Morgan Rotary. The police chief, the mayor, the coroner, a couple of judges, the sheriff and a whole host of potential political adversaries are all at the weekly Rotary club luncheons, and readily available for Amos to pester, which I've seen him do. When that streetlight on his corner wasn't being fixed fast enough, Amos went after everyone, including the local power company's representative, who's also a member of Rotary. So, no, this time Tillie's wrong because Amos was empowered, he had connections to the right people, and they couldn't avoid him. I don't see him complaining about shoplifting. I think he could handle that. No, there's definitely something else here. If he was having trouble with someone he wouldn't be quiet about it. No, there's something else going on here."

"Is that another police car?" Hattie interrupted as the car caught her eye as it went on past the window of the restaurant. "That makes the third one. There must be a terrific accident someplace. I hope it's not at the college. The whole country's going crazy with everyone having a gun and shooting one another. Not to mention the fear mongering over terrorists. You don't know what to expect."

"Which way was it heading?" Sidney had his back to the window.

"Heading south toward Front Street."

"I'm sure we'll find out pretty soon, but back to Amos. It has to be something outside the store. Something in his personal life, maybe. Or, perhaps his business. Not the market but the real estate he owns and rents. Like the Amber's apartment upstairs. I still wouldn't rule out the Ambers, although that might be stretching it somewhat. He also owns the building next door, where that art gallery is, the one that specializes in local island arts and crafts. Are they in trouble? Pay their rent on time? How does he get along with the two people that run it? Then there's the building he owns on the corner of Queen and Morris Streets, just down from Bay View Presbyterian. He rents that out to a lawyer and an accountant. What's the relationship there? And the Episcopal Church where he belongs, you said you would check with the rector."

"Already called her. I'll be over there at two-thirty. You

realize that a lot of the questions you're asking are probably the same ones the police are asking."

"I do, but how actively are they pushing their inquiries
if they have already classified the murder as the result of a
break-in and robbery?"

"But you don't know that for sure."

"No, but it certainly looks like it. I'm going to stop into
the bank after lunch and see what I can find out. Randy
Byron's in Rotary and he won't mind my asking questions.
Also, Tillie, Mickey and I are going for a walk around
seven-thirty this evening to retrace Amos' path. Tillie as-
sures me he took the same route every evening. Is there
something special about it? I have to figure this out."

ϾﾀϾﾀ

Chief Hornig was not happy. Murder and mayhem in
the downtown area was not supposed to happen. Admittedly, the argument could be made that Queen and North
Cedar Streets were not part of the tourist area, but he knew
it was close enough to make the wealthier residential areas
and the local business community nervous. The power
base of Morgan resided in *The Ridge* neighborhood, which
began a mere five streets away. The downtown business
district started only two streets in the other direction. As
long as disruptions of the usual type occurred on Main
Street and the Morgan River front, where the bars, restaurants, park, gift shops and local mainstream art galleries
were located, it could be tolerated. The usual disruptions
were regarded as the drunk and disorderly type. Acceptable since the perpetrators were spending money. They
were having a good time, that's what they were supposed
to do, that's why they came to the area. They're not supposed to feel threatened.

The touchy problems occurred when someone decided

to exercise their perceived second amendment rights and openly carried a sidearm into one of the bars—or any other place surrounded by tourists. This was seen as a business problem, as it really made the tourists—especially all the big city ones with the money to spend—uncomfortable. So, the tourists would leave, quietly, but then loudly spread the word of the perceived threat.

The Morgan City Administrator had been pushing for a 'Wyatt Earp' ordinance to keep guns out of the tourist areas—and out of town, if possible, but the mayor had been wary of the reaction at the state legislature level. So now Hornig had two dead bodies on his hands inside of a week and no leads as to who did it, assuming they were connected—a realistic assumption given that Amos Dunn seemed to be the focus of both. It may have nothing to do with the second amendment, but the arguments would erupt anyway and the anger would be directed at him...by everybody.

Mary confirmed the death was caused by blunt force head trauma, just like the attack on Amos. However, that's where the similarities ended. No wine bottle, or any other blunt implement had been found, and no surprise attack from behind. This was a major struggle, given the disruption in the living room and the adjacent office. It was unclear where the fight began, but the body ended up on the floor of the living room angled toward the front door face down. The victim died from repeated blows made with a blunt object after being softened up with apparent punches to the head and, presumably, other parts of the body. She told chief Hornig and Sam that she couldn't say any more until they had a chance to go over everything. No one could immediately identify the body. Mary was certain the killer paid a penalty during the struggle as well and told Dr. Cooper, when he called her back, that she felt state help should be brought in right away. Too much evidence lying around. Too much blood and probably from both parties—if there were only two of them. Cooper said he wanted to see everything for himself before he made any decisions. However, he seemed to be in no hurry, as he went back to his meeting at Morgan Medic-aide, the emergency care clinic on Front Street he owned with another retired doctor. They were planning the expansion of the existing facility and the possibility of starting a second one.

❧❧❧

Sidney anxiously waited for Tillie to show up for their Amos walk. He paced back and forth in his front hallway, periodically looking out the front window. Mickey watched him quietly from her favorite napping place in Sidney's office. Her leash was in Sidney's hand so she had no need to lobby him to be involved in the upcoming walk.

News of the second killing was all over town, but the police and Mayor Wilcox were keeping quiet. TV news trucks were showing up from Charleston so the pressure was really on for some type of official response. The mayor, who had been the coroner prior to Doctor Cooper, usually liked the limelight, but not this kind.

"Sorry I'm a few minutes late. Traffic is backed up with everyone wantin' to see what's goin' on. You sure you still wanna go Amos walkin'?" Tillie said as she met Sidney on the front porch.

"All the more now."

"Kinda figured that's what you'd say. I was gonna suggest we just ride the route, but with this traffic, walkin's the only way now. They got part of Cedar Street blocked an' all sorts of stuff going up and down King Street between Amos' and City Hall. Mickey, you ready?"

Even though Sidney had walked from Main Street to

the Cedar Street Market the week before with Mickey, he wanted to do it again, but this time from the other direction, as he had a different purpose in mind. With Tillie and Mickey in tow, he took the shortest route to the market and went directly to its back door. The market was still closed and there didn't seem to be any activity upstairs. The Ambers were keeping a low profile of late. They had become tired of telling their body-finding story over and over to everyone they met.

"I have seven forty-five as the time. I think that's close enough for us. I know he officially closed at seven-thirty, but I'm sure there's a fudge factor involved. When I was at the bank earlier they said he dropped off the bag between seven forty-five and eight, usually not earlier but sometimes later. In fact, he was more likely to drop it off between eight and eight-fifteen. This time of year we have pretty good light until almost nine."

The three of them started walking at a good clip, assuming Amos would usually do the same, as he carried the cash and checks from the store. He used to also have food stamps included but now the program had gone electronic, with SNAP EBT cards, it made it easier and safer for him.

The bank confirmed that he had a sizable cash component to his deposits, which was not unusual. Many of his customers didn't have bank accounts. Before Social Security required payments be electronically direct deposited to a bank account, Amos had to keep extra cash on hand so he could accept Social Security checks in payment for groceries. At Amos' prodding, Coastal Rivers Community Bank came up with a special no-fee account, as long as the customer had a direct deposit arrangement and also opened a savings account and kept a minimum of twenty-five dollars in it. It served as another example of how Amos fit into the local community and didn't have any reservations about using his connections to get something done. It also added to Sidney's theory that Amos' murder didn't have anything to do with an attempted robbery.

The walk to the bank took just over eight minutes, even with Mickey's desire to stop from time to time. They stood out on Main Street, the big black woman along with the short, fat white man wearing a white shirt, tie and sport coat leading a big black dog. A number of tourists, as well as some locals, couldn't resist passing the time of day, especially to say hello to Mickey, who's tail never stopped wagging no matter who came by. Sidney estimated that Amos would have covered the distance to the bank in about the same time.

At the bank night deposit box, they agreed that this part of the trip held no real meaning, other than getting the daily receipts to a safe place. The real walk would now begin and Sidney posed his first questions to Tillie, Mickey and himself. "Why did he go for a walk after he completed his assignment of depositing the money? Why, after a long day's work, take a walk at all?"

Tillie's simple response typified her usual straight forward manner, as they began walking down Market Street heading toward *The Ridge* neighborhood and Marianne Street. "Why not? All cooped up behind a counter all day. Stackin' boxes and shelves, makin' small talk, noise all around with all that traffic outside. Good way to unwind. Take a nice walk where you can see the water, maybe stop if you want an' watch some sailboats goin' by. Then go walk past the big houses an' quiet streets with big tall trees all around. Sometimes, Professor, I think you try to over think things. Sometimes people just do things because they like to. Make um feel good. Nothing wrong with that. Smell the roses. It's good for you. You an' Mickey do it all the time. Long walks around town—well, long walks for you. Don't need no fancy reason. Do it because it's good to do."

"Yes, I know, and I agree for the most part, but are you telling me that you think I'm all wrong about what happened to Amos Dunn?"

Tillie looked at Sidney and they both stopped walking. "Well no. I think he found out somethin' he shouldn't a, an' got bopped on the head for it." Then came the big smile and the little laugh. "Gotta keep you honest though."

"Excuse me." A woman coming from the other direction stopped in front of them. "Could I say hello to your dog?" She had just crossed Magnolia Lane and carried some plastic bags from one of the gift shops.

"Oh, she would love that." Agreed Sidney, as he put Mickey into a 'sit' position.

"We have a chocolate Lab at home. Didn't bring her along, as it's too difficult to find decent places to stay."

"Oh, I know. I try to take Mickey here just about everywhere I go."

"So that's your name, Mickey. Are you a boy or a girl?" she said trying to get a look at Mickey's rear while she patted her head.

"Lady. Missus Micawber's her full name."

"So, you're a Dickens dog."

"Goes if you got a boss who teaches at the college," added Tillie. "That Best Western place up by the college takes dogs. Don't charge for 'um either. Nice place too. Bring your lady dog along next time."

"Oh, I'll have to make a note of that. Thank you so much. And thank you, Mickey, it's been nice to meet you," giving Mickey's ears a rub. "And thank you both for letting me say hello. This is such a wonderfully friendly place." Sidney and Tillie agreed. They exchanged a few more pleasantries and then went their separate ways, having satisfied the Chamber of Commerce's directive to be kind to tourists whenever possible to make sure they came back.

They continued their walk and stopped when they reached Marianne Street. "Well," he said, "that was an uneventful section. He turned left now, you said."

"That's right." Tillie waved her hand in the direction they would now take. "I usually drive up this way when I come to get Gloria. As I said, I'd sometimes see Amos right around here. Exchange a wave and go on."

"Did he just keep walking or sometimes stop and talk?"

"Both. Though not as much lately. Seemed to be movin' faster, like he was goin' somewhere an' not just out for a walk. Had somthin' on his mind an thinkin' about what he would do when he got there. Don't really know for sure since I never actually followed him. We just come across one another a couple times a week. Sometimes here an' sometimes later on."

"Interesting." Sidney looked up and down the street as they stood on the corner.

"I can't say if it is or it isn't. As maybe I just imagined it, but…I don't know. Some people when they got troubles they never shut up, an' others keep it all to themselves. Everybody's different."

"True," said Sidney, thoughtfully. "But…well, let's walk on a bit. Come on Mickey. Now, you said he stayed on the left side of the street?"

"Yes, sir. Never went no other way that I ever saw."

"I must admit he picked one of the most pleasant routes for his walk: quiet, wonderful old houses and gardens. Mickey and I come up here quite a bit ourselves, don't we Mickey? Only we cut up Ridge Place and usually walk on the other side of the street. That way we can be closer to the water. We have a few friends up that way and Mickey likes to pester the local water birds. We do it in the morning, mostly, when it's cooler and the tourist carriages haven't started yet."

They continued the walk at a comfortable, straight-line

pace, except for Mickey who tried to guide them across the street when they reached the area where Ridge Place came in, her usual turning spot. Sidney explained the reason they were not going the usual way. Mickey got the message and they continued on, meeting no one and keeping true to Amos' route. When they reached George Street, Tillie stopped at the corner.

"Amos always turned here. Can't really tell you why, he just did."

They both looked down the tree-lined street. While the houses on Marianne were fairly large and the street had a sidewalk bordered with three-foot-high fences, mostly white or iron and backed by hedges and bushes, George Street had a more modest look. The neighborhood was created in the 1950s from a small farm. There was no sidewalk and, except for the corner property, which faced Marianne, the houses were closer to the street and designed to accommodate cars rather than horses and buggies. Here, cars were not hidden in garages converted from stables in the rear, but sat alongside the house in their own driveway and, in some cases, they were parked at the curb. Many of the houses in *The Ridge* traced their lineage to the 1700s and originally stood on more than an acre. The George Street properties were more in the quarter to half acre range and predated the historic designation of the area. The Morgan City Historic District came to be in the mid-1970s and had been expanded a number of times since, mainly to curb the enthusiastic wallets of town-house builders, who were salivating at the prospect of acquiring multi-acre properties for development.

About halfway down the street Sidney could see the roof of the new City Hall building come into view.

"Ah, this is why he would turn right at the next corner. There's no outlet if you go straight."

"Never was. That dirt road ahead is how they got the

big trucks an stuff in when they built the building ten years ago. Town bought the property an made the road."

They had been walking down the left side of the street, but suddenly Mickey decided she wanted to cross to the other side and they followed. At this point they were about three quarters of the way down George Street. "That's Doctor Cooper's place over there." Tillie pointed to the house to the right of the one that Mickey favored. "Used to have his office in there too. Back before all the docs got together and made groups of themselves. Mother used to come into town to see his father, old Doctor Cooper, that's when there was mostly farms and Gullah on the Islands, Not many white folks lived there back in the thirties. Had some huntin' camps, but lived in town."

Sidney looked at the house and observed that it had a wing added toward the back with its own entrance. He pointed to it. "That must have been where the office and waiting room used to be."

"Yeah. Got it all made up as a library and stuff. Keeps lots of books an things in there."

Sidney kept looking at the house and Mickey decided to investigate the back of a car that was parked in the driveway of the house in front of them and pulled on her lead. "I think Mickey's trying to tell us to keep moving. She's probably right. I expect we're falling behind on Amos' pace. Mickey then stopped and sniffed at the right rear tire of the car. "Recognize a friend?" Mickey moved on but then stopped again at the license plate as though she was reading it. "Come on," encouraged Sidney.

"No, I think we're doin' okay," continued Tillie, "Amos used to stop once an a while too. Everybody knew Amos. Sometimes he'd stop an chat with someone an sometimes he'd just stop for no reason an stare at a house or a car an then move on. No, we're doin' okay."

The walk continued. The next turn would be a right on

Pond Lane. The neighborhood continued the same as on George Street. The same kind of houses and cars parked in driveways and on the street. Some professional people with families, but mostly local business owners. Morgan City people. Recent retirees from up north or inland places like Atlanta or Charlotte gravitated to the new developments. The residents who lived here had roots in Morgan. Deep roots.

"Your banker friend, Mr. Byron, lives over there on the left," Tillie said.

Mickey continued her practice of checking out every place another dog might have visited and managed to run out of marking material halfway down the street. However, that didn't stop her from making an effort whenever possible. Sidney let her go where she wanted as Tillie continued to recount how Amos liked to stop along the route and check out the houses and cars just as Mickey did, but not quite the same way.

"Yeah, I seen him just stop an stare sometimes. I'd always wave, but lately didn't get much of a reaction. Got a feelin he might a thought a buyin' somthin' along here. Saw him writin' somethin' down once. Had a little book he wrote in."

"Really? What kind of book?"

They stopped. "Oh, I only seen it once. One o' those little ones you see in the grocery stores, where they have the envelopes and stuff." She demonstrated its size by forming a rectangle with her thumbs and index fingers. "Had that wire around the top. That's Amos, always lookin' for another place to make some money."

"And that's the only time you saw him do it?"

"Think so. Coudda done it all the time, I just didn't see it."

"I wonder what was in that book."

"That accountant fella might know. The one that has

the office with the lawyer in the building Amos owns on Morris Street. We go by there later. How long we been walkin' now?"

"About twenty minutes since we left the market."

Chapter 7

The Amos Dunn Walk

Tillie kept giving directional instructions as they walked. "We make another turn to the left when we get on to King Street. Can't keep goin' straight as it goes to The Pond. They got themselves a gate. We can go in there if you want. I got the code."

Sidney pondered her suggestion, not the least bit surprised Tillie would have the access code.

"If you're sure Amos didn't go that way, we won't either?"

"Can't be sure, but it would take him outta the way. They's no way out but the way you go in."

"All right then, it's on to King Street."

They walked faster now as the right side of the street had no houses to see. A buffer of trees went from the curb to a fence that defined the perimeter of The Pond development. On the left there were no houses that fronted on the street, only back yards. Their next turn came when they reached College Street. They made a right and crossed to the left side of the road where there was a sidewalk.

Nothing much to see here either as the fenced Pond development just continued, while on their left the overflow parking lot for City Hall and the Court House took up a third of the area. The property of St. Peter's AME Church and graveyard had the rest. However, when they reached Church Street the possibilities for running into someone greatly increased.

The view down Church Street clearly demonstrated its most appropriate name. Over a four-block distance, Sidney and Tillie could see, in order: St Peter's AME Church, Coastal Rivers Baptist Church, Bay View Presbyterian and St. Luke's Episcopal. The grounds of each church occupied a full block with church buildings fronting the street and graveyards and parking lots in the rear. Amos Dunn knew—and called as friends—a wide variety of members in all of them. Most of his acquaintances were among the congregations of St. Peter's and St. Luke's, but from his involvement in Rotary and local business associations, Sidney knew Amos would have good contacts in all of them. If there was one stretch of the route that would be a prime candidate for an impromptu meeting, this one took first place. The questions begging an answer were: who and why?

Feeling comfortable that he was on the right track, Sidney said, "Tillie, I think we need to know what happened at each of these churches last Wednesday evening. We can cover them all if you check with the pastor of Saint Peter's. I know Hattie has already spoken with the rector of Saint Luke's and I can cover Cal Prentice at Bay View. Reverend Prentice is good friends with Jim Craft at Coastal Rivers Baptist and I'll have him check over there for me."

"Probably doin' the same thing this week as they did last week. Churches is like that."

"I know that, but it's not just the full congregation meetings like the Wednesday night suppers we have at Bay View, but the committee meetings. The finance committee, missions, stewardship, building and grounds, they all have meetings at least once a month, but on different days, and what I'm looking for is the one with activity in the eight-to-nine time frame. I can see a bunch of cars parked behind the Baptist church right now. In the evening this street can be a pretty active place during the week. Last Wednesday we had a representative of the Coast Guard Auxiliary giving a talk on general boating safety and a specific report on the environmental condition of the Morgan River. All this activity would be going on right in the middle of Amos' walk. Who saw him? Who talked with him? Who walked with him back to the market? Who agreed to meet him there later in the evening?"

"Yeah, I see what you mean. Saint Peter's has a dinner on Tuesdays. I don't know about Saint Luke's. Don't think they have one. That's where Amos belonged. Didn't join the AME Church. Said the family up in Philadelphia was all Episcopalians and he didn't see no reason to change just 'cause he now lived in the south, even if he was one of only four black people in Saint Luke's."

Tillie kept talking as they crossed the next street going along Church. Reaching the corner, they looked diagonally across the street to Bay View Presbyterian, Sidney's church. The cross street was Howard where Sidney lived, two and a half blocks away.

They kept walking and talking until they arrived at the next corner, Morris Street.

"Another turn here, Professor. He didn't go past St. Luke's. Went past his place at the corner of Morris and Queen, where the lawyer and accountant are. That Mister Beasley's a nice man. Helps a lot of folks in the neighborhood with taxes an stuff. Helps them fill out forms for Medicaid and SNAP an Social Security. Doesn't really charge'im for much…maybe just for mailing. Does all Amos' financial work."

"Do you use him?"

"No, have Mister George on the island. Mister Beasley

just helps out here in the neighborhood."

"Tillie, how in the world do you know all this?"

She just gave him a look.

"Okay," he continued, "I know, 'The Housekeepers Network.'"

Tillie smiled. "Not entirely, Mr. Beasley's secretary is my sister-in-law's gran'niece."

Sidney sighed.

"We keep in touch. It's the way it is. Families on the island watch over one another. Been doin it for a few hundred years. Only way we managed to survive. That's why we still speak Gullah. Keep the bosses in check, they think we're speakin' junk, but we ain't. We know what's goin' on…they don't. Things changin' though. Like Sam, he's movin' in both worlds and doin' it real well. Doesn't have to choose one or the other anymore. Don't have to go north to go to school. Can stay right here. So things are changin', but that white rabbit's a pretty slick customer an it's gonna take a while yet before we turtle's finally outsmart 'im. You keep watchin'. You know this already though, don't cha?"

Sidney's smiled. "Yes, I guess I do. I just wish the CIA had your kind of intelligence gathering. ISIS would be long gone." Sidney changed the subject as they got closer to the corner. "Well, this little walk has certainly given me some ideas. My problem is that it's raised a great many more questions than it provided answers."

When they finally reached the end of the block where Morris met Queen, Sidney stopped in front of Beasley's office and looked up at the converted two-family building. Beasley had the upstairs and Lawyer Marvin Colvin had the down. It stood out as the only commercial building on the street. All the buildings continuing down to within a block of Main Street were all residential and along the cross street, Queen, it was residential in both directions.

Sidney spoke out loud, but Tillie knew he really spoke to himself. "I wonder how Amos managed to have the only commercially designated properties in the neighborhood. The market, the art gallery and now this. Somehow I have a feeling Morgan Rotary has been really good for him."

He then spoke directly to Tillie. "Don't take this the wrong way, but do you think it might be possible he had something on someone in City Hall? You know, something he might trade for a zoning change."

"Not Mr. Amos. No, if he had something on someone, he'd either keep his mouth shut or open it wide. He was a good Christian man—a tough one—but it didn't pay to cross him if you had somthin' to hide and he knew it. He wouldn't ask you to do something you shouldn't so he could get an advantage. No, that wasn't his way."

"But still, I wonder if just knowing something he shouldn't could make someone angry enough to kill him?"

They were both silent for a moment and then Sidney said, "Well, let's keep moving. I can still see some police vehicles at Amos' place." He then checked his watch. "Come on Mickey, looks like we've been at it for almost an hour. Must be your fault. In any event, the real time is probably thirty-five to forty-five minutes without stops. I wonder if Miss Coffey has adjusted her time-of-death bracket?"

"What's that?"

"The coroner always gives a timeframe for a death. Could be fifteen minutes to an hour or more. They usually try to determine the last time someone saw them alive and work off that point as an estimate. From there they narrow it down on both ends. The police look for people who can't explain where they were during that time period."

"Oh, sure. The alibi. Why didn't you just say so?"

Sidney shook his head and smiled. How he did like Tillie. She was the bright spot that kept him grounded and on the right path. Many people were put off by her directness, but Sidney relished it. He was a pushover for her. She stood strong on the issues she believed in and you couldn't move her once she was convinced. Her instincts about people always turned out to be true and she could see through whatever smoke and mirrors were put in her way. There were some people she liked and some that she didn't, and she couldn't always tell you why she came to the conclusion she did, but you disagreed with her at your own peril. Sidney lived in a world of facts and history in which opinions were based on facts and defended. The written word and an historical context made up his logical world. Tillie came up with an opinion and a solution based upon 'gut' instincts and it became Sidney's job to prove her right in a logical and factual manner.

"Well," he said, "let's finish this off."

They began walking towards Amos' house and about halfway along the block a police car with its emergency lights on came down the street toward them. They watched it go by and then come to a stop at the corner they'd just left. Two uniformed officers got out, but left the lights flashing. Sidney, Tillie and Mickey reversed direction and headed for the car. By the time they arrived yellow police tape had already shut down the entrance to Mark Beasley's office and they were working on expanding the perimeter out past the sidewalk.

"What happened?" inquired Sidney.

Hampton Butler, the officer who'd found Amos' body the week before with Sam asked, "You're Professor Lake aren't you?"

"Yes, I am."

"They found a body in Amos Dunn's house earlier today and they just identified it as Mark Beasley."

еэеэ

Sam Cashman and Mary Coffey stood on the front porch of Amos Dunn's house. "Okay, Mary, what do we have?"

"Mark Beasley, white male, fiftyish, had no ID on him so we'll verify all of that later. Wearing running clothes. First estimate is he's been dead more than twenty-four hours. Figure it to be sometime yesterday morning. You can check his running schedule to see if he was coming or going and from where to where. Don't really know anything about him, but then you probably do. Cause of death was blunt force trauma to the back of the head, after he was softened up in the fight. Have a state rep here now collecting specimens for his lab in Columbia. Lot more capability there than here. Given the repeated blows to Beasley's head, have to say the killer was really angry and wanted to make sure Mister Beasley didn't survive the fight. Not sure what blunt instrument was used. No sharp edges on it. Who actually identified the body?"

"Neighbor across the street." Sam had his back to the street and pointed over his shoulder with his thumb. "We didn't let her see the body, but she said Beasley always wore red shorts and a blue or black T-shirt. Also wore red and white running shoes. I'm certain it's him. I've met him a number of times. Apparently this was his regular route for his morning run. Checking on all of this now. Had Hamp shut down access to his office as well as his home. Need to get next of kin information. Chief Hornig is not a happy camper."

"Wonder what Beasley was doing in Amos' place, especially at six or seven in the morning?"

"That's going to be an interesting question to answer. May never get to know, unless the murderer tells us."

"Well," Mary pushed herself away from the porch railing, "I'm going back inside for a while. I'll confirm everything later. Doctor Cooper is looking at the body back in the center now. Noticed there were file cabinet and desk drawers open, but seemingly not disturbed. I'm thinking Beasley interrupted an intruder and paid a price for it." She walked to the front door. "I wonder what Amos had that would cause two murders?"

C33C33

The following morning *The Morgan City Times* story of the second murder made the front page. It contained the usual carefully crafted wording agreed to by Chief Hornig and Jim Cunningham. They were not attempting to hide anything, but merely following their agreed to plan of not releasing information that could be of assistance to the murderer. The story touched on a potential link between the two murders without expanding on it. There seemed to be more interviews of friends and neighbors of the deceased for background and character purposes rather than presenting theories about who killed him and why. The local television stations in Charleston and Savannah gave the story about thirty seconds of airtime while the newspapers were more generous. *The Post and Courier* had the now double murders in Morgan on the front page—but below the fold—and were more inquisitive in their reporting than the other papers. Everyone at the Morgan City Hall could feel the pressure.

At police headquarters Chief Hornig gave Sam Cashman a wave to join him in his office. Sam expected it. The murder of the proprietor of a local convenience store had blossomed into something no one had anticipated: a high-profile crime that led to a second murder and contained political minefields for anyone with plans to move up in the political system. He assumed that Chief Hornig's decision to put a uniformed police officer in charge of the case would come under fire quickly. Detective Kent or Patton would probably take over. Sam's morale bottomed as he entered the chief's office.

"Close that behind you, Sam." Hornig stood behind his desk.

"Sure, Chief." He did and then took the right chair of the two in front of the desk and sat down simultaneously with Chief Hornig.

"Sam, I have to tell you honestly that I had some misgivings about your taking the lead on the Dunn killing. I really wanted Kent. But I talked him out of retirement to come back to the department while Ed is away. I needed him to help out with my short staffing problem and he really doesn't want to make a long-time commitment. Besides, he assured me you could handle it and it would be a really good test. Well, it was, and I think Kent was right."

Sam had a shocked look on his face.

Chief Hornig continued. "So, I'm not going to change anything. This is your case. I've had really good reports from Mary Coffey and Cooper. I've also watched you handle the interview pressure with *The Times* and Jim Cunningham thinks you've got a future with the department. Your own reports are spot on. I think you're the right person to keep running with this, but you have to be honest with me. Do you want this?

"There's going to be a lot of heat coming down from a lot of places, both internally and externally. I've decided I want you for my next detective in the Morgan Police Department. It means you'll be jumping over some people above you who may not be very happy, but that's my problem not yours. Same with the mayor and coroner. They're political animals and come at things a little differently. I run a police department. I'm not elected, I'm appointed. Ed is due back from vacation next week and he's already told me he's putting in his retirement papers, so I've got a permanent detective slot coming open. I want you to fill it. As I said before, my question to you is do you want it?"

Sam didn't say anything. His mind was racing through every conversation he'd ever had with Deede about why he wanted to be a policeman, what they saw as their future, the impact on their families, friends and co-workers.

Chief Hornig then said, "If you need to talk this over with Deede just say so, but I want an answer before the day is out."

"No, no, Chief. Deede and I have talked about this a lot. I want this. I planned to talk to you about the courses S.L.E.D is sponsoring this fall to see I could get into some. No, chief, we don't have to think about it. We want...I want it."

"Good man," he stood up and reached across the desk with his outstretched hand. "Detective, hope you have a suit at home you can wear for tomorrow. That uniform's going in the closet." He then came around the desk and put his arm around Sam's shoulder and gave it a squeeze. Sam was clearly taken aback. His relationship with Hornig had always been a somewhat formal one, even though the Chief clearly exhibited a protectiveness about all his officers, there always seemed to be a sense of distance about it with him. Perhaps he was just being defensive. Being black and a local Gullah, it came with the territory. So much of the time he felt tolerated rather than accepted, although there was something about the policeman's bond that complicated his feelings.

"Okay, Sam, better call Deede. And don't forget to tell her the bad news as well as the good." Sam looked at him questioningly. "You're now working twenty-four seven and you just lost your overtime," said the Chief with a big grin.

The rest of the morning proved to be a bit of a blur for Sam. Chief Hornig wasted no time in telling the rest of the department his decision to elevate Sam Cashman to detective and that he would, officially, be running the Amos Dunn murder investigation. Sam was particularly pleased when Detective Kent came to him and told him he could count on him in any way he needed to, as he understood what he was going through, being thrown into the middle of a murder case. Sam always saw the detective as a bit stand-offish with him and put it down to Kent being an old-timer not understanding Gullah and its community. He also realized that Kent's initial reaction of pleasure could have a double edge to it in that Kent wouldn't have to deal with the islanders as much anymore, it would all be dropped in Sam's lap. It also occurred to Sam that Hornig could be setting him up as a scapegoat if things got worse, but he really didn't want to believe that. Hornig retired from the Marine Corp as a major before getting into police work. He wasn't from the lowcountry and had a reputation for fairness, even if he did keep one eye on politics and the other on opportunities to advance his own career in a larger jurisdiction in or out of the state. *Lots of things to think about*, thought Sam, *lots of things, but if I don't figure out who killed Amos Dunn and Mark Beasley none of them will matter much.*

Chapter 8

Making soup

Sidney Lake took the frozen chicken bones from his freezer and put them on the kitchen counter in front of him. It was time to make soup. Tomorrow it would be a whole week since Amos Dunn's body had been found. Now, a second murder had been discovered, definitely connected to the first, and it appeared the police had no idea what was going on. Sidney knew his problem. With the first two murder investigations he became involved with over the past three years, Ray Morton, his retired Morgan policeman neighbor and good friend, helped him along by providing non-public information obtained from former colleagues. This time Ray couldn't help. He left town two weeks ago for vacation and wouldn't be back for another week. In the past, Ray had been able to confide to Sidney all the police theories about the cases. He needed help with this one, which is why he needed to make soup. There was something about putting together soup from scratch that made his mind work. Everything always seemed to become clearer when he cut up fresh ingredients and filled the room with their simmering aroma.

Mickey got up from her usual place near the kitchen

island, where she waited for something to come flying off the counter, and slowly made her way to the hallway that led to the front door. Someone must be on the porch. Someone she knew. "Who's at the door, Mickey?"

"Jus' me Professor," called out Tillie as she burst through the doorway. "We got to talk." She came bustling into the kitchen, an action that made her chronic limp clearly visible. Mickey trotted along behind her, delighted to see her on a day she wasn't expected. "Mister Sam's just been put in charge of the Amos murder and Deede's in a panic."

Sidney looked at her questioningly. "But I thought he was already in charge?"

"No, that was just a temporary thing. The police boss didn't have anyone else at the time an they thought it was just a robbery. Now he's gone and made Mister Sam a detective and told him to solve the murders."

"Well that sounds like a great opportunity. Sam's a good, solid, bright young man. Good for him."

"No, you don't understand, he ain't got a clue. Nothin'. That Coffey lady, she don't got no idea either. They's both in the dark an nobody ain't got no light to offer anywhere. Deede called me an said they's both in a panic. Mister Sam agreed to take the job, but if he don't come up with somthin' right away he ain't gonna have *no* job. So I told her you would help an that you had some ideas about what happened that made real sense."

Sidney was taken aback. "Tillie, that's not entirely true. I don't think I'm any further along than the police are. They're the professionals and have more information at their disposal."

"You know that ain't true. You're makin' soup ain't you? You got an idea about somethin' don't you?"

Sidney gazed at the ceiling of the kitchen and a small smile crossed his face. "How did you get to know me so well? Doesn't anything miss your observant eye?"

"Hah, only got the one good eye, but it sure sees people good. Got to. Got to know what kinda people I'm workin' for. I've had some pretty bad ones over the years. Deede said she talked with Mister Sam and he's gonna stop by this afternoon. Said he'd give you a call."

Sidney gave Tillie his usual look over his glasses. It was not a chastisement as it might have been for someone else. Sam's appointment represented the break he needed, the link to the police department that he didn't have and wanted.

Oh, how the world had changed since he'd found the solution to the Reed murder last year. He found himself looking for events to investigate, especially since he retired. His strength was research, drilled into him as a student and a teacher. Sidney became known for taking positions against established literary theories that he believed were incorrect and misleading. Challenging accepted interpretation of a novel—especially if it was long-held and rarely disputed—would get his juices flowing. He loved digging into literary history, reviewing 150-year-old publishing agreements and confidential letters held in private libraries, discovering where original opinions came from and the justification for them, learning of hidden agendas by critics based on their personal animosities spurred him on. It became an easy transition from literary history and criticism to delving into motivations for theft and murder. The predictable nature of human reasoning and justification for actions that seemed alien to a suspect—he always seemed to be such a nice, pleasant young man, I can't believe he shot all those people—translated to every situation he touched or read about.

"Well Tillie, I think I do have some serious soup making ahead of me, but don't think I'm going to let you off the hook. I've got something I need you to do and it involves you getting me some information from Amos' grandnephew, William. I have a germ of an idea that relates to that walk we took yesterday, so here's what I need you to do before Sam Cashman shows up at my front door."

ℰↄℰↄ

Tuesday continued its active pace after Tillie left Sidney to track down William Dunn, who continued to stay at the Holiday Inn. Amos' place remained an active crime scene and William wasn't too eager to move into the middle of it. Finding his whereabouts took very little effort for Tillie and involved one phone call to the head housekeeper at the hotel, who confirmed William was still checked in. In fact, while the room was being cleaned, she reported that he moved to a comfortable chair in the lobby near the fireplace and the newspapers. The Holiday Inn, being located on College Street at the intersection of Church Street, right along the route of Amos Dunn's walk, represented a three-minute drive for Tillie from Howard Street.

Right after Tillie took off, Sidney called Hattie to let her know about Sam's promotion. He invited her to come over later in the day so she could tell Sam directly what she learned from her talk with the rector of St. Luke's.

The soup making continued. In addition to the ingredients being laid out on the counter and the island, Sidney also had a yellow pad and a fountain pen ready to make notes about what he would say to Sam. A fountain pen could always be found near him. It was considered another quirk of the professor's, since he intensely disliked ballpoint pens and blamed them for the inability of students to write legibly. His quirks prompted a wide range of comments at Rotary meetings. These were not necessarily negative comments, but served to promote his visibility among his Wednesday luncheon companions and gave him a certain reputation.

ↄﾉↄℯﾉↄ

Sidney's meeting the previous evening with the pastor of Bay View Presbyterian Church, the Reverend Doctor J. Calvin Prentice, didn't provide a great deal of information about the night Amos Dunn was murdered, as there were no meetings scheduled for the education building that evening. However, Amos Dunn and his nightly walk often served as a topic of conversation on other evenings when active meetings *were* scheduled. Cal, on the other hand, had contacted his good friend and pastor of Coastal Rivers Baptist Church, who confirmed that a major administrative meeting occurred at that church on the evening Amos was murdered.

"Well Mickey, do you think someone spotted him? Maybe, hah?" The interrogation of Mickey did not require answers. Mickey's job was that of listener, of sounding board, a way for Sidney to express his thoughts out loud, which validated them. Speaking out loud to one's self or having a conversation with an imaginary person leaves one open to criticism as having, possibly, 'lost it' and in need of medical help. Metropolitan areas large and small all have their residential component of the homeless having endless conversations with those others cannot see. However, speaking to a living organism such as a pet dog, cat, bird, hamster and so on is extremely acceptable behavior and Sidney was an active participant.

"Well I think it's pretty certain more than one person saw him that night since Hattie received confirmation from the rector of Saint Luke's that she saw him speaking with someone across the street from her. Now, did that person set up a meeting with Amos or did he meet someone else who walked along with him to the market? Mickey, it's entirely possible there were other people who saw Amos that night." Mickey had resumed her position by the island and upon the mention of her name her right ear twitched, but her head didn't move. In fact, you would think she had gone to sleep except for the ear. She listened carefully, not because she understood what Sidney had to say, but because she understood him. He was making soup, which meant he had something on his mind and needed to talk and think out loud. Mickey understood her job well: be at Sidney's side and provide support, no matter what that would entail. "We need to talk to the person the rector saw him in conversation with so we can understand what happened. And then there's the book he wrote in. What was he writing down? Does anyone know about the book and what's in it? Mickey, I think we're beginning to get a sense of something here. I'm beginning to see a glimmer of something at the end of the Amos Dunn tunnel, but we're still a long way from identifying what that something is."

εʃεʃ

The banking floor at Coastal Rivers Community Bank always quieted down after two o'clock in the afternoon and that signaled the moment for P J Cross to start cleaning up. He knew the manager, Randy Byron, didn't want him visible with his broom or emptying trash cans when there were too many customers around, so he bided his time just out of sight next to the two conference rooms and the manager's office.

"I don't give a damn what you think, Byron, you made a commitment to that loan." A male voice boomed from behind the closed door of the manager's office.

P J jumped back when the volume of the noise startled

him. Loud voices in the bank were unusual, but he recovered quickly and leaned closer to listen.

"It's not what I think that matters. It's what the loan agreement covenants require and your associates violated them even before the first drawdown."

"That's bullshit and you know it. We've got the cashflow. We've demonstrated it over and over. Collections were slow in the last quarter. We can't control that. We're dealing with a major bureaucracy. They're erratic."

"We understand that, but to violate the covenants before the loan is even drawn isn't going to fly."

"We made commitments based on the money being there."

"Look, I'm not saying you won't get the money, but you've got to show the bank a positive cashflow number before anything can be disbursed. And tell your people they have to keep me informed."

The man took a long pause before responding. "The company's board asked me to lean on you and that's what I'm doing. They're not gonna be happy. We've got a lot of personal money in this place and even representation on *your* board. So, you're sayin' no?"

"I have no choice. Get that cashflow into positive territory. My hands are tied."

"Shit!" and then the voice lowered, as though talking to himself, "Fixin' the Amos Dunn problem was easy compared to you guys."

The door ripped open and P J quickly turned his back and started sweeping. The man flew past him in the hallway and headed to the banking floor and the exit. P J moved farther away from the door and closer to the entrance of the neighboring conference room and turned his back to the manager's office. The second man, Randy Byron, vice president and manager of the branch,, slowly exited his office, looked after the first man and then turned and walked back inside and closed the door. He never saw P J, who by that time had entered the conference room to empty the wastepaper baskets and tidy up the room from an earlier meeting.

As soon as P J finished with the conference room, he went farther down the hallway, opened the door at the end, walked through and then into the coffee/break room where he found Nala Foster, of the Coastal Rivers Coffee Service, replenishing the coffee and hot water thermoses as well as other break room supplies. They immediately fell into Gullah.

"P J, what you t'ink? Dey done an' tuk eberyting," she said lifting the empty coffee containers and looking at sugar and powdered creamers.

"Dis mornin' dey all ober de place. Done some howlin out dere too."

P J then went on to tell her everything he heard including the Amos Dunn comment. Just as he finished Randy Byron came in looking for a cup of coffee.

"I don't know how you do it," he said." I've lived in South Carolina all my life and I still don't understand a word you people say when you start talking Gullah. 'Course I don't understand half of what my teenagers say in English anymore either," he gave a little laugh, "and texting, my goodness, it all looks like hieroglyphics."

"Don't feel bad, Mister Byron, nobody understands their teenagers," Nala said as she continued replacing supplies and P J began to empty the trash.

Chapter 9

The Storm

The round table in Sidney Lake's office had pads and pencils in front of each of the four chairs. Tillie had placed two pitchers of iced tea on the table, but no one filled any of the glasses. Three of the participants in the meeting stood in the middle of the room waiting for Sam Cashman. They all looked toward the window facing Sidney's front porch. Sidney's mantel clock had just chimed five-thirty, but it seemed more like eight. The sky had darkened steadily over the past hour, as the 'pop-up' thunderstorm continued to develop. Such storms were common and expected in the low-country, although many of the new residents of the area were surprised at their violent nature and the local flooding they caused.

"Looks like it's startin' to rain," Tillie said.

Suddenly a gust of wind slammed into the front of the house, rattled the shutters and moved one of the oversized cane lounge chairs so it slid a few inches toward the window. Tillie, in anticipation of the storm, had removed all the cushions from the chairs and sofa and stored them in the bench seat next to the railing.

"Whoa! Look at that come down now," Sidney

exclaimed, as the sky opened and dropped its usual blanket of lowcountry rain. The wind pushing and driving it every which way it could. It came with such a pounding force that the other side of the street was barely visible. A palm frond went flying past the porch and down the street followed by a plastic garbage can cover.

"My, it looks dangerous out there now. I'm glad I got here ahead of it." Hattie said as she stepped to the side a bit to get a better view of the flying cover before it disappeared down the street. No one moved toward the window. Having experienced hundreds of these August storms, they knew how dangerous they could be. A good many carried 'microburst' winds that could reach fifty or sixty miles an hour. Simple objects like hanging plants and coasters on tables became flying missiles capable of breaking windows and damaging cars.

Tillie, watching the storm develop, spoke quietly, almost to herself, "Gotta feelin' Mr. Sam might be a bit late with this one."

Just then a dark blue sedan pulled up behind Hattie's car at the curb. It had a portable blue light on the dashboard.

Hattie said, "This looks like him now."

"Lemme get that door so he don't get too wet." Tillie rushed into the hallway.

Sam made it up the steps of the porch in two quick leaps after negotiating around a large puddle that had just formed on the concrete path to the house. In his left hand he carried an eight and a half by eleven notebook pressed to his chest to keep it dry.

Tillie got the door open just as Sam reached it. "You made that pretty good."

"Wow, that came on quick," Sam said while shaking some of the rain off on the welcome mat by stamping his feet. "How're you Tillie?"

"Jus' fine, come on in here."

Tillie closed the door behind Sam as he rushed by her and greeted Hattie and Sidney.

"We were afraid you might be delayed by the storm, get caught doin' traffic control stuff along Market and Front Streets when they flood," Hattie said.

"I would have if I still had a uniform on. I'd be the one out there directing traffic someplace. Walking around in a suit has its advantages. Of course, there are some disadvantages as well and I'm sure I'll find out what they are soon enough."

Sidney shook Sam's hand. "I hope you won't get into trouble speaking with us like this. I wouldn't want to be responsible for your starting off in a new position by being at odds with Chief Hornig."

"Well, that's going to be *my* problem. It's my decision. Besides, the chief specifically told me to get this Amos Dunn problem solved. He didn't tell me how to do it. I will admit though, he did say he didn't want to see you hanging around the department in City Hall. So, we'll just make sure you don't go there," Sam said with a smile. "If you have any information about Amos' murder or what happened to Mark Beasley, I want to know about it. That's why I'm here."

"Well good, we all want the same thing. Why don't we sit down?"

Sidney ushered everyone over to the prepared table just as a quick flash of light lit up the room followed almost immediately by a booming blast of thunder. They all jumped.

"Wow," Hattie said. "That was close." The lights flickered.

Sam took a step back toward the door and said, "Hope you have some flashlights around, that sounded like a transformer hit." The lights flickered again…and again then stayed on. Everyone remained silent and looked up at the recessed light that peered down from the ceiling just over the center of the table.

Sidney kept looking at the light and then said, "Looks like we're okay. For the moment anyway."

The rain and wind continued as they took their seats. Sidney sat with his back to the inside corner of the room, framed by the bookcases. Suddenly the sky brightened and the sun came out for a brief moment before disappearing again as the rain and the wind continued to pound away.

Sam decided it was time to get to the reason he agreed to come to the meeting. "So, you've got some ideas for me. I must admit I could use a few. Let's talk about Amos first. There are a lot of people who still believe that Amos Dunn's murder was a bad complication to a robbery, even though there's no evidence of one. That in itself doesn't mean it wasn't the intent."

Sidney replied, "I agree, but I think it's hard to hold to that conclusion under the circumstances."

"Okay, convince me a bit."

"For one, the market had been closed. All the cash, except what was in the oatmeal box…"

Sam interrupted with a surprised look, "Eh, how did you know about that?"

"Tillie heard it from Jan Liston."

"The part timer at the store?"

Tillie spoke up, "An' I confirmed it with William Dunn."

Sam now focused on Tillie. "When did you speak with him?"

"Earlier today."

Sam sat silent for a moment. He had some misgivings about attending this meeting but Deede told him he'd better. He didn't know if it would really contribute to anything but he was determined to leave no stone unturned just in case. Now he became intrigued. "Okay, simple enough. I want to know everything you heard from William."

"You will," Tillie said.

"Okay, go ahead Sidney."

Sidney shifted in his chair before he replied. He heard something in Sam's voice that made him pause. He realized he would have to be careful with how he presented his ideas and decided it would be better to lead Sam to where he wanted him to go rather than just tell him.

"As I started to say, Amos had closed everything up, went to the bank, deposited his receipts for the day into the night depository and then went on his nightly walk. This has all been confirmed, as you know. However, that walk he took on Wednesday night was different. His standard walk wasn't designed to take him back to the market but to his home on Queen Street, two blocks away. For some reason he deviated from his usual pattern and went back to the market. Why did he do that? Did he remember something he forgot to do when he closed up, or was he asked to go back?"

Sam listened carefully and said, "Asked to go back? What do you mean?"

"I believe he met someone along Church Street who asked him to go back to the market and they went there together."

"Eh…" Sam started to interrupt but Sidney raised his hand and stopped him

"Let me continue for just a moment. Church Street can be a busy place on a weeknight as you know, and Amos met people along that part of his walk all the time. I had a talk with Cal Prentice of Bay View Presbyterian, and he confirmed he often saw Amos chatting with people from the various churches along the street. In fact, Cal often passed the time of day with Amos as he walked by. Now he didn't see Amos on that Wednesday evening, but Reverend Craft, of the Baptist Church did. They chatted briefly and Amos ended the conversation when he saw someone wave at him from down the street. Amos seemed to know who it was although Reverend Craft didn't really see the person. At this point, I'll let Hattie make some comments about her conversation with the rector of St. Luke's."

Sam said, "Just a second." He opened his notebook and quietly made some notes. "Sorry Hattie. Go ahead, what did the rector say?"

Hattie gave a quick look to Sidney and then back to Sam and then said, "Amos Dunn is a member of St. Luke's, as am I, and is very active in its affairs as Rector Walker can confirm."

"I'm familiar with Rector Walker and with Amos' involvement with the church," Sam said.

"Good. Amos during his walk does not pass in front of St. Luke's, which is at the corner of Church and Morris Streets, but turns down the corner onto Morris. There was a meeting of the finance committee at the Episcopal Church that night and Shirley Walker, the rector, went out to her car to retrieve some notes she'd left there. She spotted Amos talking on the corner with a medium height, rather stocky white man. She said she didn't see his face but there was something familiar about him. The meeting seemed cordial and then the two men went off together down Morris Street."

"Mark Beasley the accountant and J. Marvin Colvin the attorney both have their offices in Amos' building just down the street on Morris. Could it have been one of them?" Sam asked.

"I asked the same question and she said no. She knows them both and she's quite sure it wasn't either of them."

Sam sat quietly and thought for a minute, no one spoke.

Finally, Sam summed up what he heard, "Okay, so we know he met someone during his walk that night, but it wasn't a planned meeting."

"Not for Amos," Sidney said.

Sam immediately challenged Sidney's conclusion. "You can't say that for sure. All you can say is that he met someone he knew and they walked down Morris Street together. I'll have a talk with the Rector and see if she can add anything to what she's already told you, Hattie. Also, we can't say that the person Amos met accompanied him to the market. Unless we can find someone else who saw him that night. I'll have Hamp check with the neighbors along Morris Street. At the moment I still have him interviewing Amos' neighbors along Queen Street." Sidney decided to accept Sam's interpretation for the time being to get more information out in the open so he simply said, "There is another curious activity that Tillie observed Amos doing while he made his evening walk. Tillie, tell Sam about the book."

Tillie thought for a moment, not expecting the conversation to move her way and then said, "Oh, yeah, the book. I remembered this when the professor and I made our walk. He used to stop and write things down. He'd stop in front of a house, look at it and then make notes. Couldn't see what he was writin', but it was real quick. Didn't write a lot. Just looked at the house an' maybe somthin' around it, make a note, close up the little book and move on. I axed Mr. William about the book an' he didn't seem to know anything about it. Of course, he being new around town didn't really know Amos that well. Knew him as a great uncle, an' member of the family, but not as a member of the town. Didn't know his habits and friends and neighbors. They talked about the market and money stuff. I know Professor Lake thinks Amos was speculatin' about buyin' some more property, but Mr. William didn't think so. Said he was happy with what he had. Said he did worry about his health a lot."

Sidney reached for some sweet iced tea as he spoke. "Can't disagree with Tillie on what she said. Anyone else want some iced tea as long as I have it?"

"I'll take some. That's the unsweet one isn't it?" said Hattie.

"No, Tillie always puts a piece of lemon in the unsweet one."

"I'll take the other one then."

"Sam, anything for you?"

"No thanks. I'm fine."

Sidney poured the tea and then said, "Sam, I have to believe that whatever Amos was writing in that little book has something to do with his death. You haven't found anything at the market or in his home that looks like the little book?"

"I'm quite sure there wasn't anything at the market, at least that we found. I'll raise the question with Mary Coffey and Hamp. We didn't have anything specific to look for, just listed what seemed relevant."

Tillie thought for a second and asked, "What about his pockets? That's where I seen him take it from and put it back. His front right-hand pocket."

"Don't recall seeing it listed in his personal effects," Sam said.

"What about his home and office?" Sidney looked at Sam as he spoke, with an expression that made it clear he knew he was on to something.

Sam thought for a moment before answering. "The house is still an active crime scene. We can go back over it again and just focus on the book. Tillie could you describe it again?"

"Sure. One of those little notebooks you see in the grocery store where they got the kids school stuff. Fits in your pocket like Amos put it. Black and white with the holes in the top with a wire windin' round the top to hold it together. You know the type."

Sam made notes as Tillie spoke then said, "Yeah, I got the idea. Know exactly what you're talkin' about."

Hattie then added, "Just a thought. Tillie, you said William Dunn mentioned Amos' health being a concern and just thinking about my conversation with the Rector, she also mentioned that as a concern with Amos. Said he mentioned it a couple of times recently and, not just to her, but to a couple of the members of the vestry as well. Amos was not someone who talked about himself very much. Personal things he kept closed up, so there must have been something that really bothered him. Sam, have you heard anything about this?"

"Well, all I do know is that Mary Coffey found that he had a tumor right around the spot where he was hit. She felt it could have been a contributing factor in his death, but said she would contact Amos' personal doctor to find out more. I haven't heard back from her yet, so I can't be sure Amos even knew he had it."

"What about Beasley? Where does he fit into all of this?" Sidney said.

"Another unanswered question for us. All we do know is that Beasley fought back. Why he was in Amos' house we aren't sure. He did have a key that was found in the pocket of his running shorts. In fact he had two keys on him. One was to Beasley's office, it was in a small leather key case, and the other was a single key to Amos' front door with no identifying tag. We've determined the running route he usually followed. It went from his office up to the Morgan College campus, around that and then came back to the office along Queen Street, right past Amos' place."

Sidney thought for a moment and then said, "Could it

be that he usually made a visit to Amos' on his way back from running? Amos would normally be up by then. A cup of coffee together before Beasley went back to his office?"

"Remember, Amos died last week. Even if that might have been part of his routine, he wouldn't have stopped in to see Amos yesterday," Sam cautioned.

Sidney realized his mistake and said, "Ah, yes, of course. Unless he needed something from Amos' office."

Tillie then said, "Maybe he saw somethin' an' went to see what it was. Saw somebody in the house. Police markers gone and no police car anyplace."

Sam said, "Just being in the wrong place at the wrong time. Hmm—no direct connection to Amos' death in the sense of being a party to it. He just saw someone and something he shouldn't have and paid the price."

Sidney hesitated before making his next comment. He didn't want to alienate Sam. He liked the young man and saw him as having a possible transitional effect on the Morgan police department, but the real world of the south still existed in 2014. Admittedly it had evolved from the 1950s and 1960s, but so many of the people who grew up in that era were still around and would be for quite some time. It became evident with the election of Barack Obama, where a certain percentage of the population of South Carolina—albeit a steadily declining one—couldn't bring themselves to vote for a black man. They just couldn't do it no matter how much they may have liked him or agreed with his view of the world.

"Sam, just how much support do you think you're going to get from your fellow officers in this investigation? Don't get me wrong, I'm not accusing them of doing anything to inhibit your progress. I just don't know how they feel. Ray Morton, as you know, is a good friend and he spent the last twenty years in police work in the county and city and he feels the department and the sheriff's office has come a long way, but there always seems to be just that little hold back. If you know what I mean?"

Sam carefully considered Sidney's question and then answered with, "No, I understand. I'm a realist. I think I have a pretty good idea about who I can trust and who I might question. Old habits die hard and change comes slow. But I can't think of anyone in the department who would object to solving a crime just because the person was black. That's one attitude that I'm confident is gone. There are a few people that might be tempted to take something less seriously if it occurred in the black community, as they would in the white. In most cases, they wouldn't be doing it consciously, in fact wouldn't be fully aware that they were doing it. Chief Hornig knows that can happen and makes a point of watching for it. I trust his judgement on it. He walks a good and careful line with the folks at City Hall. I won't mention anyone specifically, but I'm pretty sure the chief's analysis of the situation led to my doin' what I'm doin'."

Sidney didn't respond, but he agreed with everything Sam said.

No one spoke. For a long moment, everyone just sat quietly as the rain eased and the sun came out again.

Tillie said, "Looks like it's gonna stop for good this time. "Kinda like openin' one door and shuttin' another…." She stopped in mid-sentence. "I almost forgot. P J. At the bank."

Sidney said, "Excuse me?"

"P J. He cleans up at the bank. He tole somethin' to Miss Nala. Nala Foster, she has that coffee service around town. She said that P J heard someone say to Mr. Byron at the bank, 'It's a lot tougher than takin' care of the Amos Dunn problem.'"

"When did this happen?" Sam said.

"After the lunch crowd was gone at the bank an' he was

cleanin' up next to Mr. Byron's office. He heard some shoutin' and listened in. That's when he heard it."

Sam continued to question. "Did he know who said it?"

"Nala said no."

"Did he see who said it?"

"Don't know. Nala didn't say."

After Sam left, Sidney, Hattie and Tillie moved to the other side of the room near the front window, where more comfortable chairs were positioned around a coffee table. They sat talking for just short of a half hour. The storm had completely disappeared and a mist of steam began to rise off the sidewalks and streets, now being heated by the late afternoon sunshine. The rain had created a drop in the temperature but the humidity and heat were not driven far away. It looked like it would be a hot lowcountry evening. Not a single leaf stirred. Welcome to August. This was sleep on the screened porch weather. Open the windows wide weather. Crank up the air conditioner weather.

Sidney spoke first. "That storm didn't provide much of a break from the heat."

"Never do this time a year. Nothin' helps with this heat. Air conditioner better keep goin."

Hattie took a sip of her iced tea. "So what happens now?"

"Next move is with Sam," Sidney said. "He promised to talk with Mary Coffey and see if she has any more on Mark Beasley's death. Don't mention this to anyone, but he said on the way out that they found some strange material in the wound to his head that they think came from whatever it was the killer used to beat him to death. If it turns out to be something unique, that would be a big leap forward. Also, since he's going to have Mary find out if Amos' personal doctor knew about that tumor, I think that's also going to play into where we go from here. Tillie, you know there's something you said that piqued my interest. You said he kept the little notebook in his side pocket and not his back pocket. That seemed unusual to me."

"Well, I only seen him take it out and put it back a couple of times, but was always in the right side pocket. Can't say he always kept it there, but when I seen him with it that's where I seen him get it from an' put it back."

"Hmmm. I have to give this some more thought. The good news is that Sam wants to sit down and talk again."

No one said anything for a moment. Tillie broke the silence. "I don't know about you folks, but I got a family to feed." She took her phone from her pocket and looked at it. "Oh my, we're comin' up on seven. I got to leave. I think this is gonna be pizza night."

Everyone stood. Hattie looked at Sidney for a moment and then said, "Sidney, I have to admit I think you're really on to something. You know…"

Tillie interrupted as she headed to the front door, "Professor Lake, if you need anythin' just call an' if I think of anythin' I'll tell you right away."

"Thanks Tillie."

Hattie said, "Bye Tillie," and then continued the sentence she'd started. "As I began to say, I do think you're on to something. You know I don't always agree with your second guessing what you read in the paper or what you may have heard, but every now and then you latch onto something."

"Well, thank you for that. I think it may have been a compliment."

Hattie smiled. "Seriously, Sidney, there's something very wrong here. Something bigger. Something that we're not used to around here. Morgan is a small town—although with a more than forty percent growth rate in the last ten years and a population of almost 20,000—it's nowhere as small as most of the old residents think. The mayor just made a deal with that developer, Randall I think his name is, to annex Oak Island into the town. That's a big development he's planning to put out there. That'll make the second large land acquisition this year alone. I think the town's facing some major issues that just having a larger tax base isn't going to solve. They're facing problems they're not used to handling. This Amos Dunn thing isn't a family dispute or petty theft or an accidental event someone's trying to cover up, which is what the town usually has to deal with. This is murder. The real thing."

"You're absolutely right and I think both Chief Hornig and Sam know that. Sam doesn't want to go back to Hornig and say he's stumped and he can't ask for help from the other detectives, or at least he doesn't want to. If they offered it I think he'd jump at the chance to get it. If Ray Morton was around I think Sam would feel more comfortable, but he's not. Hornig, I think, would like to keep the state out if possible, but I also believe Hornig realizes that Sam needs to show some progress over the next couple of days. It would not surprise me to learn that he's been in touch with the state authorities just in case he does need backup. When the county coroner, Doctor Cooper, went to the state laboratory for help—pushed mainly by Mary Coffey—the door was opened."

"Sidney, what I'm trying to say is that I want to help. I know I play your foil much of the time. What can I do?"

Sidney smiled, "I've been thinking about that. You're in pretty close with the rector at Saint Luke's and if Amos had a confidante I think that's where we'll find him or her. I know you sing in the choir and work as liaison to the homeless shelter the church supports, are you aware what committees Amos was on? What meetings he would usually attend?"

"Good idea, Sidney. I know he was active in the annual white elephant sale for the benefit of the food bank. He also helped with the food truck the church usually set up during the annual *Art in the Park* event. He always bought all the hot dogs, chips and soft drinks at wholesale prices and also worked cooking on the two grills that were set up behind the truck. I know he was involved with a number of other events as well. Let me check with Shirley Walker. She's been rector for about five years now and keeps pretty close tabs on her flock. Shirley will know who's close to Amos. Is there anything specific you're looking for? You and Mickey have been talking again haven't you? What are you looking for?"

⟐⟐⟐

As Sam Cashman drove away from Sidney's place, his mind wasn't on the road ahead. He agreed with Deede that talking with Sidney might be a good idea. He had to admit there were some pretty good suggestions made during the past hour. The bits and pieces of information Sidney and his friends actually uncovered were proving to be extremely valuable. So, with his mind not focused on the road ahead, he missed the turn he would normally make on his way home. Now he suddenly realized he had gone straight down to Market Street. "Oh, shit," Sam muttered. With a shake of his head he turned right and headed down the town's main street.

It's not that Morgan was a bustling city, it's just that the roads hadn't kept up with its growth. It had stop signs everywhere to keep the traffic under control. The tourists—who spent their time admiring the old houses while jaywalking across streets—seemed to be in constant danger of getting run over by drivers trying to read non-existent street signs. There were a few crosswalks, but they were down in the heavy shopping area. Sam resigned himself to a slow drive home.

He managed to travel no more than four blocks when he saw the traffic ahead backed up to a full stop. Some of the cars were doing U-turns in an effort to find a better route. He had a pretty good idea of what the problem would be.

Sam turned on his emergency lights and moved out into the oncoming traffic lane. A block ahead he could see a police cruiser blocking the roadway and another one pulled in place just off the side of the road. A uniformed officer made his way to the middle of the intersection as Sam pulled up to the head of the traffic line.

The intersection had earned the well-deserved but polite nickname of 'accident junction.' Three roads came together at this point and traffic control consisted of a yellow warning light strung overhead in the middle of the intersection and stop signs at each corner. As traffic continued to increase, accidents became a frequent problem. A proper traffic light was in its own traffic queue with the department of transportation and at a dead stop waiting for funding.

Sam rolled down his window and got a good look at the problem. The yellow warning light was missing and two damaged cars were in the center of the intersection.

The uniformed officer leaned over and said, "Hi Sam, bet you're glad you don't have to untangle this stuff anymore."

"What happened?"

"Mother Nature stole the light an' a couple of ladies decided to play chicken. That storm had a few good gusts in it."

"Anybody hurt?"

"Doesn't seem so. Few bumps and bruises. EMS on its way." Then responding to a siren and flashing lights, "That's them now." He moved away and began directing traffic so the EMS truck could get to where the two women were standing.

Sam recognized one of the women and decided to pull over just to make sure she was all right. He left his lights on after he parked and then called Deede.

"Hi Hun, gonna be a bit late. Accident over at 'accident junction' an' it looks like Marla's daughter Sarah was drivin' one of the cars."

A note of concern was in Deede's voice as she said, "Are you sure? Is she okay?"

"Looks okay from here. I'm gonna go over and find out. Will call you back."

Sam walked across the intersection just as the EMS truck pulled up to the curb so it wouldn't block traffic. When Sam and one of the EMS people reached the two women involved in the accident and, although neither appeared to be hurt, they both looked shaken. Sam said hello to Sarah, and she introduced Sam to the other woman involved in the crash, Kristin McGuire, a nurse practitioner at Dr. Cooper's emergency medical clinic.

Sam said, "I know you both think you're okay, but make sure you tell Wally here every ache and pain you have."

"Don't worry, I know the drill. We get a lot of people over at Cooper's that end up with pain two weeks after something like this and don't realize where it came from. They don't make the connection. Making the connection is important—" Kristin hesitated and then thoughtfully added, "—for insurance purposes."

"Looks like we have the whole town represented," Detective Kent said from behind Sam.

Sam turned on hearing the voice. "Kent. Didn't see you there."

"Same as you. Got stuck in traffic. Came over to see what all was going on. Looks like just a fender bender. Anybody hurt?"

"Doesn't seem so. Lemme just double check with Sarah here, her mother lives just down the street from us. She also works at Coopers, X-ray technician." Sam shook his head. "Amazing stuff. Two people work at the same place. One comin' and one goin'. You heading in or out?"

"In. Paperwork to file. Sure forget the details real fast." Kent then waved his hand at the chaotic scene all around. "I retired last year to get away from all this. Too old for this stuff."

"That's right, the chief dragged you back after Detective Millar got herself transferred to Orangeburg. And now Ed's put in for retirement."

"Yeah, I gotta get out of this job. Place is getting too big." Then, almost to himself, "Came back for the money, but it ain't worth it."

Sam joked with a bit of a laugh, "Just don't leave yet. That'll just leave Patton and me and I can use all the help I can get."

"Don't worry. I'll get you up to speed. The faster I can tell the chief you're full-time ready, the faster I can get out of here."

"I appreciate that—I think. Anyway, I have to talk with Sarah."

"Yeah, go ahead. I want to have a chat with Kristin here." The two parted.

The paramedic had Sarah siting on a portable chair while he checked her blood pressure. Sam moved over to where they were and said, "Sarah, how you doin'?"

"Oh, I'm all right, Mr. Sam. Just stupid. Lookin' left when I should be lookin' right and went right into Kristin."

"Did you call your mother?"

"She called me. Miss Deede called her. News sure gets around this town fast. Just got off the phone with her."

"Good, as long as you're okay." Sam said and gave her a pat on the shoulder. At the same time he could see Kent in a serious discussion with Kristin. It seemed like he was chastising her over something, and Kristen didn't seem to be taking it well. Sam then said, "How well do you know Kristin?"

"Pretty well. We work the same shifts a lot. Do a lot of x-ray's at Cooper's. She sends everyone over my way. Insurance covers it so we do a lot." Sarah chuckled and continued with, "X-rayed a woman with a hang-nail this morning. They can do that as long as they suspect there might be a break in her hand. Can't take any chances, you know."

Sam noted the chuckle and seeing Kristen's reaction to Kent's chastisement asked Sarah, "How does she know Detective Kent?"

"Oh, he's in and out of Cooper's all the time. Knows everybody. Kinda watches over everything. Somebody said Doctor Cooper has him on the payroll on the side. Probably shouldn't say that since I don't really know. I guess my head's a little rattled."

"You're just upset. Easy to say things you normally wouldn't. Your checks and balances system is probably off." Sam then laughed and said, "Keep that in mind when you talk to your mother later."

Sarah smiled back. "Thanks Mr. Sam."

"Good. Well, before I leave I'll give Deede a call and tell her you're okay and then she can call your mother. That way she'll have independent verification."

"She's on her way over to get me." Sarah pointed to her car, "That's not goin' anywhere."

Chapter 10

Sidney and Mickey investigate

With dinner finished and the dishes done, Sidney looked at Mickey and said, "I think we need to take another look at Amos' market. Why don't we head over that way to-night?" Mickey hearing the word 'walk' knew the routine so she, with tail wagging gently, left the kitchen and headed for the front door where her lead hung on a nearby hook. Sidney carefully folded the dish towel he used to dry the dishes and placed it on a drying bar inside the cabinet door under the sink.

As they started out the door, Sidney stopped and reached back to get his flashlight. While he probably would be able to negotiate his way around the downtown streets if he were by himself, as there were streetlights in most of the tourist areas, eight o'clock in the evening in the lowcountry provided a diminishing amount of natural light. Besides, with Mickey along he would have some clean-up work to perform. The flashlight was kept in the drawer of the small table by the front door. "Hold on. I think we're going to need this." Mickey continued to pull. "Just a minute. I know you have to go, but even if you are a wonder dog you still don't pick up after yourself." The pulling stopped. "Okay, let me just close the door and we'll be off."

The walk to the Cedar Street market was an easy one and Mickey made the most of it. She seemed to be on sniffing patrol. Nothing escaped her. Every streetlamp and every corner received her blessing. By the time they were standing across the street from Amos' market, dusk had turned to darkness and the stars began to shine in the moonless sky. He checked his watch. Eight-twenty. The lights in the market were still on and he could see into the front of the store and the check-out counter. The 'closed' sign had been put on the front door and Sidney observed Grace Carter come up to the cash register, remove the drawer and place it upside down in the same position it was on the night Amos Dunn was killed. She then came back to the front door and checked it to make sure it was locked. She turned off the lights in the front of the store from a switch by the door. Then moving to the other side of the doorway, she flipped another switch and a single light came on, a low wattage one, that dimly illuminated the overturned cash register drawer, but also provided enough light to be able to move around safely. There was still a light on in the area of the back door.

"Mickey, if there was anyone on the street that night, they could see everything that happened. But was anyone here? And if they were, why have they remained silent? Even someone driving by could have seen something. Yet, no one has said anything. Could the killer just have been lucky? Took just the right moment to hit Amos? I suppose it's possible. Well, let's go across the street, I want to take a look at something."

By the time they reached the other curb, the main light by the back door had been turned off. It looked as though there was a low wattage light back there as well. Sidney guided Mickey over to the steps in front of the closed art gallery next door and stood there while Mickey sniffed around.

Within a few minutes, Grace Carter, having closed the market, came up to the corner of Cedar and High Streets, crossed High Street and headed down toward Market Street away from Sidney. She carried a brown paper sack with the night depository bag inside, just as Amos always did. She never looked back. Walking with a purposeful gait, she headed toward the bank and never saw him.

"Yes, Mickey, if you're not looking for something and you're focused elsewhere you don't pay attention to what's around you. I think the only chance of finding out what happened may be with Hattie and her talk with the rector of St. Luke's. Let's take a look at this walkway over here."

The walkway Sidney referred to went between the market and the art gallery. It led past a doorway entrance to the second floor of the art gallery building and then all the way back to a rear boundary fence.

The art gallery building had originally been designed the same way as the market with an apartment on the second floor and a private entrance for the tenants, but here there was no longer an apartment above the gallery, it had been converted to exhibit space. Sidney wondered if the entrance to the upper level still worked and if it was ever used. Could it have been a place for someone to hide? One of the theories that had been suggested envisioned the killer making his escape by going over the back fence into the parking lot behind the gallery to make a getaway but what if he came this way? Sidney looked to the end of the walkway. It was a dead end and backed up to the same fence that separated the two parking lots, the one for the market and the other the gallery. What if the killer came this way and just went into the gallery from here? Sidney looked at the door. He switched on his flashlight. There seemed to be a new, shiny, brass lock on it. "Have to ask Sam about this won't we." He said to Mickey who continued to sniff around the door.

A noise caught Sidney's attention. A car pulled into the back of the market. Its lights were off. Mickey kept sniffing and ignored it. Sidney switched off his flashlight and quietly started to walk toward the back fence followed by a reluctant Mickey. The boards were fit tight together and he couldn't see the car. Looking over the fence was not an option as it was clearly more than six feet in height. Pulling himself up to look over it never even came to mind. He heard a door open and close. Someone entered the market. Whoever went in had a key.

Sidney whispered, "Someone's inside, Mickey. And it's not the Ambers. They're still away, as far as I know. Quiet now." He was convinced that the person inside the market was not authorized to be there. But who was it?

He moved quietly back down the walkway watching the four windows that were along the side of the building. The window closest to him was the one at the very back and looked out from the washroom. He expected it to throw some light on the walkway once the light inside the back door was turned on, but it never went on and the light from the rear night light was blocked by the washroom door. Curious, he moved further down along the wall next to the market where he could not be seen from inside. Sidney could feel his heart beating as he felt the tension of hiding in an alley. A few beads of sweat appeared on his brow. The second window was in the main part of the store and, from inside, you had to be in the aisle right next to the window in order to see out. Since the lights had not been turned on, that window was dark, blocked by the shelves that made up the aisle. He and Mickey continued moving but stopped when they got to midway between the last two windows. They stayed pressed up against the side of the

building. The window closest to the street was right opposite the checkout lane and the cash register. The light that
shone on the empty cash drawer also filtered out into the
space between the two buildings and projected a rectangle
image of the market window against the side of the gallery
building.

Sidney and Mickey remained pressed against the wall
of the market. Since the building was raised up four feet
from the ground and he stood only five foot eight, the only
way Sidney would be able to get a look inside would be
by stepping away from the market building and toward the
gallery. No inside lights were on except for the nightlight.
A shadow then appeared framed by the light from the window. It went past the window once and then quickly disappeared. Then it returned, only larger in size. It was
closer to the nightlight which meant the intruder was behind the counter near the cash register. What was the person doing? Sidney had to get a look inside.

First he thought about just moving over to the window
and jumping up and down. An athletic move to be sure.
Sidney Lake was no athlete. Walking fast was a challenge
by itself and jumping was not an option. No, he had to
move away from the wall and stand directly in the rectangle made from the light. As he and Mickey were about to
move, the intruder came toward the window and stopped.
The shadow was that of a male. He appeared to look out
the window and then moved on back around the short end
of the 'L' shaped counter.

Sidney waited. Where did the man go? Finally, with
Mickey moving first, Sidney followed the black Lab over
toward the light from the window. He decided to keep
Mickey out of view as she was invisible in the dark. Sidney
felt that he probably couldn't be recognized in the darkness as long as he was alone. Having a black Lab next to
him would be a dead giveaway. Although, in reality, he

also realized that if someone tried to chase him it would be
no contest. He moved into the rectangle. The checkout
counter stood out clearly, but there was no one there. He
moved back into the shadow where he had a view of the
inside of the front door. Still no one. He and Mickey
moved under the beam of light coming from inside and
over next to the rectangle of light on the wall. From this
angle he could see the area in front of and to the right of
the counter. There was someone behind the distant shelf.
His image was blocked by cereal boxes. He seemed to be
looking for something in the shelves. The man moved to
his left and Sidney instinctively moved to his right for a
better view and stepped into the light of the window. He
bumped into the invisible black Lab as he did and dropped
his flashlight. It popped on and flashed at the window of
the market. The man peering between the boxes saw the
flash and pulled back. When Sidney recovered, his first instinct was to check on Mickey. He whispered, "Are you all
right?" A tail wagged. Sidney then looked up and saw that
the man had disappeared from view. "Come on Mickey,
time to leave. Let's go."

Mickey, hearing the tension in Sidney's voice, immediately perked up. They both headed down the walkway to
the street. Not wanting to cross directly in front of the
store, Sidney led the two of them up Cedar Street to cross
away from the streetlight at the corner by the market. Midway up the block it was completely dark.

When they started across the street a car came around
the corner by the market. Its lights were out and headed
straight for them. Sidney quickened his pace and pulled
Mickey with him. There was a car parked at the curb ahead
and Sidney moved to his left to get in front of it for protection. He moved as fast as he could and Mickey—used
to staying directly at his left side when they walked—kept
pace. The car swerved at them. It barely missed Sidney as

he made it to the front bumper of the parked car. He could feel the rush of air as it went by his pants legs. Mickey wasn't as lucky. Although she was alongside Sidney, her body length extended beyond him. She got hit a glancing blow in the right rear. The force spun her around and forward toward the curb. Sidney held tight to the lead which, while preventing Mickey from falling on her head and skidding on the ground, pulled Sidney off his feet down and to his knees, where he fell fully to the ground on his side. Mickey tried to scramble to her feet while heading to Sidney and fell on top of him. The car kept going, picking up speed as it disappeared down the street.

ᏒᎤᏒ

Sidney sat on the curb holding Mickey in his arms. The EMS attendant tried to get him to release his hold on Mickey, but he refused. He kept petting Mickey's head with one hand while the other one held a handkerchief over the cut on Mickey's right rear leg.

The female EMS attendant said, "It's okay Professor Lake. Just stay there, but I want to take a look at your leg." Sidney's right pant leg was torn at the knee and blood could be seen on the fabric all around it. "Just stay put. I want to see how bad it is." She talked quietly and calmly to him and then carefully cut the fabric so she could get a sense of the injury. He didn't answer, just sat holding Mickey, who didn't move, but Mickey's eyes were open and watching the attendant as she worked. Sidney's jacket was torn at the elbow he'd used to break his fall. There was blood on his face from the cut he received on his forehead when he hit the ground.

For all of Sidney Lake's criticisms of cell phones, he would never complain again. His phone, which he usually forgot to take with him, had been in his jacket pocket.

Lying on the ground with Mickey, he had called 911. His second call went to Hattie. When he got to the curb Sidney and Mickey huddled together and waited. Hampton Butler was the first to respond and found Sidney at the curb in front of the parked car that saved his life. On seeing who it was, he immediately called Sam. A second uniformed officer had arrived at the same time as the EMS truck.

Hattie stayed on the phone and talked quietly with Sidney when he called her. He told her he had called 911 and that he and Mickey were at the curb. Hattie could tell from his voice there was more to it than the simple comment he made. Hattie called Tillie and then the emergency number for the Morgan Animal Hospital and Clinic.

Within minutes Sidney's support troops began to arrive. As she lived nearby, Hattie was the first to get there. Five minutes later Sam Cashman arrived followed quickly by Tillie. Dr. Peabody from the animal hospital came a few minutes later.

Hamp stood near the front of the parked car and Sam walked over to him and said, "How's he doin'?"

"Okay, I think. He's pretty shaken up. Dog too. Lots of cuts and bruises for both of them. EMS people seem to be more worried about the bangs on the head than the leg problems."

The EMS attendant said to Sam, "I need to get him to the truck, but I don't want to separate him from the dog. They're both in shock."

Tillie heard the comment and said, "Lemme help. He'll let me take Mickey. We'll all go to the truck together. Don't want to separate em either."

"Agreed," the attendant said. She then waived to another EMS officer to help get Sidney up once Tillie had Mickey.

Sam looked at Sidney for a long moment as Tillie and the EMS driver started to get Sidney up. What he saw came as a shock. The formidable English professor with the inquisitive, probing mind had taken on the simple appearance of an old man and his dog.

Once inside the EMS truck and sitting down, Tillie put Mickey back in Sidney's arms.

Sam said to Hattie, "Any idea what happened?"

"He jabbered a bit on the phone. Said he saw someone in the closed market. A man. Car came after him when Sidney tried to get away. He then just went on about Mickey being hurt. Didn't say any more. Mickey better be all right. You have no idea what that dog means to him. Especially after his wife Cynthia died. Sidney puts up a good front but—."

A man interrupted, "Excuse me. I'm Doctor Peabody from Morgan Animal Hospital."

The female EMS attendant answered, "Good. Glad you're here. Come on up. They're both in shock and I don't want to separate them yet. Professor Lake doesn't have any visible broken bones but we need to get him to Emergency to be properly checked out. I have no idea what condition the dog is in."

Peabody moved up next to Mickey, "Mickey and I are old friends. Been taking care of her since she was a pup."

Mickey's tail wagged upon hearing Peabody's voice and her name. Sidney looked up and asked, "Is she okay?"

"Let's take a look."

Chapter 11

Recovery

t was after midnight Tuesday evening when they all came back to Howard Street. Sidney and Mickey, appropriately bandaged, would spend the night in the library on the sofa bed, so they wouldn't have to climb the stairs. Tillie made up the spare room for herself so she could watch over them. Although Wednesday was not Tillie's usual day to be at Sidney's, she had no trouble changing her schedule to make sure she could play nursemaid. There were no protests from Sidney. Hattie stayed around for a while and helped settle everyone in before leaving. Not a great deal was said. There would be plenty of time for talk on Wednesday morning. Everyone was exhausted.

Sam had stayed around the hospital emergency room until Sidney was released and made attempts at getting as much information from him as he could. Doctor Peabody had checked out Mickey and didn't find anything broken but wanted to see her on Wednesday. An appointment was set up for two-thirty for them to bring her into the animal hospital. He wanted to run some tests and properly treat her scratches and cuts. Sam instructed the market to be secured so Mary Coffey's people could examine it before anyone else came in. No crime scene tape was put up but a sign appeared in the front window that the store would open late. Sam advised Sidney that he would be in to see him on Wednesday morning.

Sidney and Mickey both slept late. Being in the library at the back of the house, which the sun did not reach until late in the afternoon, helped. It was dark in there to begin with, given that four walls were filled with books. The sofa-bed that sat against the wall was one of the few non-bookcase pieces of furniture in the room.

It was Tillie's cooking in the kitchen that aroused Mickey, who woke Sidney. Hearing some movement in the room, Tillie opened the door and peeked in. "You decent?"

"Yes, Tillie, we are."

"I need to let Mickey out to do her business. You can use the bathroom."

"Well, I appreciate that."

Tillie ignored the smart-alecky comment and continued with her instructions. "Put a change of clothes in there for you. Also got one of the canes from the hall so you can get around. Doctor said you need to stay off that leg for a while. Don't put no weight on it. Miss Hattie said she needs to talk with you. Told her I'd give her a call when you ready for breakfast. Come on Mickey."

Getting up and reaching for the cane he said, "Thanks, Tillie. Those crutches they gave me...I just can't get the hang of them."

Gingerly, Mickey got down from the bed and limped over to Tillie. As they left the room Tillie closed the door behind her.

It took Sidney a little over a half hour to get himself together and Hattie had arrived by that time. He greeted them as he came into the kitchen. "Ah, all three of my lady friends in one place."

They turned and watched him come limping into the kitchen struggling somewhat with the cane. It was obvious he didn't have the technique down very well. As he started to take the nearest chair at the breakfast table, Hattie said, "You wish. You may have Mickey wrapped around your finger, but we're not particularly happy with you."

As Sidney began to respond, Tillie held up her hand, palm out. "Hold it right there Professor. I got you set up in the living room. Too many things for you to trip over in here. Doctor said you need to stay off that leg for a while so you go sit in the soft chair inside an' get that leg up. All set up for you." Seeing he was about to protest she stood up straighter and pointed to the exit from the kitchen. "The living room, Professor."

"My goodness, we're bossy today. They being that way with you too, Mickey?" he asked looking for an ally.

"Never you mind about Mickey, she takes instruction well. You could learn from her."

He turned and started for the living room with the parade following him and said over his shoulder as he went, "Does she have an appointment with the vet later?"

Hattie answered, "Two-thirty. Tillie and I will take her over after lunch."

"What did Doctor Peabody actually say about her? Last night's still a little fuzzy."

Hattie answered, "He's pretty sure the leg isn't broken, but he wants to make sure. Positive that muscle is paining her where she was sideswiped. Wants to have a good look at the tendons too. Luckily the cuts are more scrapes than anything else. Can't tell what kind of pain she may be in. He'll give her a good check-up."

"Yes, I know he will. Have to thank him for showing up last night."

"He's a good man," Tillie said.

Sidney sat slowly and carefully and put his leg upon the

upholstered footstool that Tillie moved flush up against the chair so it spanned the whole front of it. With both his legs now up on the stool, he became a virtual prisoner. His bulk made it difficult to get out of chairs to begin with and with the arrangement Tillie set up, he wasn't going anywhere.

Tillie brought him breakfast on a tray and Hattie grabbed herself another cup of coffee and sat down on the sofa beside Sidney's chair.

"So, how're you feeling?" Hattie asked.

"Better. It all seems like a dream, though. I can't believe someone would do that. Whoever was in that car tried to kill us."

Tillie, having finished making sure Sidney was comfortable, positioned herself directly in front of him, folded her arms across her chest and said, "Professor Lake, what did you think you was doin'? You was threatenin' a killer. That man already destroyed the lives of two good people and he ain't gonna worry about messin' with a third. This ain't research on a book that won't try to hurt you. This ain't like writin' a paper or sumpthin' where you can make it come out the way you want it to. You ain't in control. The bad guy is. You didn't tell nobody where you was goin' or what you was doin' except maybe Mickey here an' she just goes along with anythin' you want. Professor Lake, you got to join the real world. They's lots of people around here that really care about you and what happens to you. You ain't alone. I know you usually rely on Mister Morton, but he won't be back till the end of the week. We're a team. If you think we should be doin' sumpthin', let's talk. Miss Hattie an' I be glad to listen an' so will Mister Morton when he gets back. That man, the killer, he thinks you know sumpthin'. If you do, you got to tell us an' you got to tell Mister Sam. The more people know the safer you are. 'Cause, like it or not, you're walkin' in danger right now. When Mister Sam gets here later you tell him everythin' you know an' if there's sumpthin' you can't tell him then, at least tell us. We'll work it out. We always do. Besides, I know plenty of folks who'd love to help get the man that killed Mister Amos and Mister Beasley. That's what I got to say."

Silence. Even Mickey, who took her usual position next to Sidney's chair, lying down very gingerly and in obvious pain but couldn't tell anyone where it hurt, stayed quiet. Her tail never wagged during Tillie's speech. She just stared at Tillie the whole time. Hattie, sitting on the sofa on the other side of Sidney, remained quiet and focused on her as well.

Hattie broke the silence, "I agree. I agree completely. I wish I had said it myself. Tillie's absolutely right."

Mickey's tail finally wagged and slapped against the skirt of Sidney's chair.

Sidney took a deep breath and let it out with a whoosh as he looked from Tillie to Hattie and then Mickey, who he patted on the head. "Thank you, Tillie. You're absolutely right. And I apologize." His eyes filled up as he continued, "I have been careless. You're right, I've been looking at all of this as an intellectual exercise and I unnecessarily put myself and Mickey in danger. I won't do that again. Admittedly, I do use Ray Morton as my sounding board, and he keeps me on the straight and narrow. He's the professional and understands the danger. I'm the amateur. This won't happen again. I'm sorry."

With a nod of acknowledgement Tillie said, "Good. No more to be said. Right now the important thing is to get Mickey to her appointment with Doctor Peabody. That'll be at two-thirty after lunch. Miss Hattie an' I will take care of that. Mister Sam said he'd be here in a little while. Reverend Prentice said he would come over an' stay with you while we take Mickey to the vet. Then we'll work on findin' out who murdered Amos Dunn."

᭒᭒᭒

Sam Cashman and Hampton Butler arrived at ten-thirty and replaced Tillie and Hattie in the living room. Sam took the sofa and Tillie brought a chair from the dining room for Hamp. Mickey stayed put next to Sidney's chair. Coffee was offered and refused politely. With pleasantries out of the way, Tillie and Hattie retired to the kitchen where they could listen to the conversation without being seen. The kitchen had a pass-through window to the dining room outfitted with louvered shutterette doors, one of which Tillie immediately opened a few inches while keeping the louvers in a closed position. They poured themselves some coffee, pulled up a couple of chairs and began to listen.

Sam began, "You're okay, Professor, nothing broken?"

"Thankfully no. It looks as though I may have torn something in my knee. They'll need to take some more pictures but need the swelling to go down somewhat first. Afraid I'll be confined to this chair for a while. Have to keep the whole leg elevated and supported." He motioned to the way Tillie had set the foot stool up against the chair.

"You sure were lucky." Then he pointed to Mickey. "How's she doin'?"

"Mickey?" Sidney's hand reached down to her as she began to wag her tail. "We'll know for sure after she visits the vet this afternoon. Hattie and Tillie will take her. Doctor Peabody didn't think there was anything broken, but she could have the same type of tendon pull or tear as I do. We just don't know for sure. It's obvious something hurts, we just don't know where."

"I take our Brittany to Doctor Adams over at Morgan Animal Hospital, good people. They'll figure it all out." Sam then maneuvered to the matter at hand. "Someone going to be with you when Mickey goes to the vet? I can arrange for Hamp to come by again later."

Hamp said, "It wouldn't be a problem, Professor. Be happy to do it. Wouldn't want anything more to happen to you."

"Well I do appreciate that, but Cal Prentice will be here later while they're gone," Sidney said.

"Good," said Sam, "who reached into the inside pocket of his suit jacket and removed a small notebook. "So, let's see what we have. Picking up from our conversation last night, why don't we go back over what you can remember again just to make sure we have it right. See if anything pops into memory that you didn't recall in the emergency room."

Hampton Butler also had a notebook out and looked at it as Sidney and Sam spoke.

Sam continued, "You said you were certain it was a man you saw in the market last night, is that correct?"

"Yes, it was definitely a man."

"How tall?"

Sidney became animated and enthusiastic, "You know, I've been thinking about that. I never actually got a look at him. All I have is shadows to go by, but I remember at one point seeing him standing behind the far shelf. This view was not a shadow reflection. Although I couldn't see his face or anything, I'm sure his head reached the top of the fifth shelf and that would make him just slightly taller than me."

"Which shelf would that be?" asked Hamp.

"Based on what I've learned of Amos' murder, this would be the one directly across from where Amos Dunn was standing when he was hit from behind. It would have been off of his left shoulder."

"Okay," Sam said. Then thoughtfully, "That was the only actual view you had of the man? Aside from the shadows on the wall of the art gallery?"

"That's correct."

"And you don't remember being able to see the car in the parking lot?"

"No. There's no way I could see it. I couldn't see over the fence and the slats of the fence were tight against one another."

"What made you notice the car that came at you?"

"The sound. It was quiet on the street. I don't think it even slowed down at the stop sign that's at the corner of High and Cedar. Just went right through it. I'm not sure if I heard tires squealing or a loud engine noise. I just looked up and saw the car coming at us. When it turned the corner it immediately stayed on the right side of the street. If that other car had not been parked where it was…well, I don't think Mickey or I would be here right now."

Hamp asked, "And you couldn't see the driver?"

"No. Just knew I had to get out of the way."

"So, you really don't know if the person in the car was the same person that was in the store. You don't know if there was one person involved or two," Hamp said.

Sidney thought for a moment and said, "You may have the answer to that."

A surprised Hamp said, "Excuse me?"

"Was the door to the market locked or unlocked when you found it? If it was unlocked it would be because the intruder didn't have the time to close and lock it and still get to his car to run us down meaning they were one and the same person. If he did take the time to close and lock it, he had time to tell whoever was waiting in the car and that person came after us."

Sam had a smile on his face when he said, "The door was open and unlocked. However, we would still leave the option open that a second person, possibly in a second car, took off after you and the first person panicked and just took off leaving the back door open."

"True. But which option do you believe?" Sidney said.

"One man not two makes the best sense. But let me focus on the car a bit. You said you didn't really see it, so let's work on that. Was it a truck or a car?"

"Not a truck."

"Was it a big car?

"I don't think so. The reason I say that is because of the headlights, which were off. I remember being focused on that left front one as that's the part of the car that was coming straight at me. It appeared to be simply a headlight, not a combination of lights like you often see on SUVs."

Sam said, "The left front?"

"Well my left front, which would be the driver's right."

"Okay, that makes sense." Sam thought for a moment and then said, "So, it wasn't an SUV?"

Sidney paused this time. He closed his eyes and tried to visualize the previous evening. "No, I'm almost positive it was a sedan of some type."

"All right. Not a truck and not an SUV. So were looking for a sedan. Let's work on color. Was the car itself light or dark colored? Don't think about the actual color just the shade."

"I'm sure it wasn't white, if that's what you mean? It was definitely a dark shade. Black, dark blue or green. Definitely a dark shade, yes."

Sam turned to Hamp, "Hamp, what I'd like you to do is tell the guys on the street to keep an eye out for a dark sedan and just make a note of the license. SCDOT can give us a listing of the sedans registered in Coastal Rivers County." Turning back to Sidney he said, "One of the interesting parts about living in the south is that dark sedans are a rarity. Everyone seems to have a pick-up or an SUV and, because of the heat, if they have a sedan it tends to be a light color, usually white."

Sidney said, "Yes, very true."

Sam continued, "Professor, let me shift gears here a bit. Let's talk in some detail about why you were over there in the first place last night."

Sidney shifted slightly in his chair, expecting the question. He explained that his walk with Mickey to the market was not purposeful, but one drawn from necessity. Mickey's necessity. While he told Sam and Hamp about becoming curious about the alleyway between the market and the art gallery, Tillie and Hattie listened from their position in the kitchen. Tillie whispered, "He ain't gonna tell them the whole reason. The professor can be pretty slippery when he needs to be. Oh, he'll tell the truth, but the careful truth."

"I'm familiar with Sidney's word management, as he likes to call it. You have to be very precise when you want to know something he doesn't really want to tell you. He'll never lie, but don't be surprised if the *whole* truth doesn't come out. You got to keep pressing him."

"Can be awful frustratin' sometimes."

"At least he's not like some people who intentionally spread lies and then blame other people for them. Claim they're just repeating what they heard someplace else."

"Can't disagree, but that's not Sidney. When he's wrong, he owns up to it and admits it. That's why he's so good at the research he does. His facts are well documented and supported. He may not always let you know what he's thinking, and he may disguise what he's working on, but he always brings everything out into the open when he's finished."

Tillie held up her hand palm facing Hattie, "Sounds like they're finishin' up in there. Heard Hamp talking on the phone thing he always has with him. Somethin' about a family argument over in The Point they want him to check up on. Yeah, he just got up an' he's going out."

"What about Sam?"

"He's still sittin' down. I think I'll go in and see if they need a coffee refill or somethin'."

Chapter 12

Friends

Hattie Ryan arrived a few minutes early for her scheduled time to be with Sidney, Cal Prentice having cancelled due to an emergency. Mickey had a two-thirty appointment with the vet and their new plan had Tillie taking Mickey while Hattie kept Sidney company. Tillie was insistent that he not be left alone on the assumption that whoever tried to kill him yesterday did so because he thought the professor could identify him. Sidney objected until Sam offered to have an officer stay with him for protection for the same reason. Under no circumstances was he to leave the house. Sidney objected and used the argument that the killer knew by this morning that, as no one tried to arrest him, he had not been identified as a suspect. The compromise finally agreed to involved someone being with Sidney for the next forty-eight hours, as by then the killer would surely believe he was in the clear. Sam knew the possibility existed that Sidney couldn't identify the intruder in the market because he had never seen him before, but in a lineup might be able to pick him out. Sam had every intention of keeping Sidney under surveillance for his own good, he just wouldn't let him know it. So Hattie happily took her shift.

After some logistical discussions about how to get Mickey into a vehicle without hurting her, Tillie came up with a solution. Mickey was curiosity personified and when in a vehicle, always positioned herself so she could see over the driver's shoulder and watch the route being taken. So the plan was for Tillie to sit in the back seat and hold onto Mickey while one of her housekeeper network friends drove. The procedure involved a soft towel being folded lengthwise and inserted under Mickey's midsection to form a sling. Tillie would get in first and then, to avoid Mickey trying to jump up into the back seat, Hattie and Tillie's friend would just lift her by the sling and put her into Tillie's arms. "Well, I think that worked pretty well," Hattie said as she closed the car door and headed back inside to Sidney.

"Do you need anything before I sit down?" Hattie asked Sidney.

"No, I'm fine. So, you got her in okay."

"Yeah, she knew what we were doing."

Some benign chit chat ensued as Hattie became comfortable on the sofa but didn't last long as she had some pent-up questions for Sidney. "So, tell me, what's going on with these murders in the neighborhood."

"Thought you'd never ask. I just wish I had more to tell. We seem to be getting nowhere."

"That's somewhat unusual for you. How about bouncing some ideas off me?" Hattie's question was not unusual for the two of them, as she often served as a sounding board for Sidney.

Sidney looked up at her and said thoughtfully, "To be honest, there's something missing in all of this. Amos' murder makes no sense and everyone seems to agree. Mark Beasley's is even more confusing. The only action that could make sense would be the attempt on me. In that case the motive is relatively clear: I could identify the person in the market that night."

"You can?"

"No, I can't. Never saw him, but the person believed I did. So his action makes sense. At least I can see a motive. I'm still in the dark about Amos and Beasley."

"There has to be a link, of course. I mean, Beasley was killed in Amos' house." Hattie paused and thought for a moment. "I've heard a few rumors that believe it had to do with real estate or some other business activity, but, quite frankly, I think that's a red herring. I didn't know Amos very well but I did know Mark Beasley, as well as the other tenant in Amos' building, the lawyer Marvin Colvin. Their offices are just down the street from Saint Luke's and they've been very helpful to the local community. I can't see them being involved in anything illegal, or for that matter, unethical—even if they are accountants and law-yers." Hattie stopped and smiled.

Sidney had the same look on his face and said, "Can't disagree, but they are in professions that lend themselves to creative reading of the law for their client's sake—and their own."

"Try to twist it to meet their needs."

A wry smile appeared on Sidney's face as he said, "I could comment about how a lot of that goes on around Church Street.?"

"Let's just stick to Amos and your problems."

"My problems?"

"Yes, you're right in the middle of everything now. Even if the police wanted to keep you out they can't. You're a principal, a victim, they have to deal with you. You have a valid, vested interest, as they say."

Sidney smiled, "You know you're right. Even if Chief Hornig would like to keep me on the sidelines, he can't. Very good, Hattie. I feel better already."

"I'm glad. Now tell me what you think is going on."

∽∾∾

Tillie's visit to the vet lasted for more than an hour, but it was worth the wait. No broken bones for Mickey. Her right thigh would be sore for some time. The cuts were mainly superficial except for one that required a few stitches. In all, a clean bill of health. Dr. Peabody wrote a prescription for pain medication as it became obvious she continued to have difficulty getting up and down. He also advised them to tell Sidney to keep an eye on the back hip. Labs always have trouble with their hips and the accident might trigger some other problems. He said he'd like to see her again in two weeks.

After a stop at the front counter of the vet's office to pick up Mickey's prescription, Tillie and Mickey were back at Sidney's by late afternoon. Tillie had called ahead with the good news and both Hattie and Sidney were waiting for them when they arrived.

While Sidney talked at length with Tillie and Mickey, Hattie stepped outside and made a phone call to Ray Morton and explained to him what had been going on. Sidney said he didn't want Ray disturbed on his vacation and she honored the professor's request. However, after spending all that time at the hospital with Sidney last night and worrying about Mickey this afternoon, she felt it was time to get Ray involved.

Ray Morton retired from the Morgan Police Department four years ago. After leaving the Marine Corps. he spent twenty years as a detective with the Coastal Rivers County Sheriff's Office and subsequently with the Morgan Police Department. He and his wife Marie lived just a few doors away from Sidney on Howard Street and had become one of Sidney Lake's closest friends in town and his primary resource on all things police related. Sidney admitted that he didn't really understand how police organizations worked and certainly had no feel for the political infrastructure and jostling that went on between the Sheriff's Office, Morgan Police Department and the mayor. To the public, everything ran smoothly. Ray knew better. He was also a member of St. Luke's and Morgan Rotary and often worked with Amos Dunn in the food truck at art fairs and charity events. Hattie felt that Ray could be a valuable resource on a number of fronts and Sidney's stubbornness, in not wanting to disturb Ray during his vacation, was misplaced.

The plan for the balance of the day revolved around keeping Sidney immobilized but busy. Hattie stayed on for another half hour after Mickey returned and then went on an errand, but promised to come back before dinner so they could all talk before she left for her appointment with the rector of St. Luke's. They expected the meeting to take about an hour and then Hattie would come back and relieve Tillie, who could finally get back to her own family. Hattie would stay the night in the spare room.

After dinner, while Hattie and Tillie cleaned up, Sidney attempted to work on his literary forgery project. Hattie had set up a table next to his that contained his laptop and research folders. He tried to work but his mind kept drifting back to Amos Dunn. He couldn't shake the feeling that he already knew the primary bit of information he needed to make sense of why the two murders occurred. He was staring into space when Hattie came into the room.

"My, aren't we in a deep trance."

"Oh, Hattie, sorry. Just thinking about the links between Amos and Mark Beasley.

"Ah, well, I'd love to hear your thoughts on that," Hattie said as she walked over to the sofa and eased into a comfortable place next to Sidney's chair.

"Has Tillie left?"

"No, she just took Mickey out. I was puttering around the kitchen putting some things away."

"Well, before you meet with the Rector, keep in mind that I don't think either of the murders was intentional. In fact, I'm convinced that neither of them knew why they were killed."

"That's a bit of departure from conventional wisdom."

"Be that as it may, I'm convinced of it. The killer was intentionally looking for something of value to him that Amos Dunn didn't know he had. Beasley, he merely burst in on the killer looking for what he didn't find at the market. The killer and Beasley knew one another so Beasley had to be silenced...permanently."

"But what in the world was he looking for?"

Sidney continued, "The book. Whatever is in that stupid little spiral notebook of Amos' is the key to everything."

"Possibly," Hattie said. She thought for a second and then continued, "In reality, you may not need the book itself, you may just need to know what's in it."

"I'm not so sure we can do without the book itself." Sidney shifted his bulk in the chair to get comfortable and replied, "We might figure out a motive but without the book I'm sure the police would never be able to put a case together."

"Well, you can work on that for a while. I've got an appointment with Shirley Walker over at Saint Luke's in a few minutes. Any new lines of questioning you'd like me to pursue?"

"Mention the book. See if she was aware of why he kept notes in it. Why he carried it around with him. Did she ever see him take it out at a meeting and make a note? Did he ever mention it? Does she know what's in it?"

కు

The rector's office, waiting area and library at St. Luke's took up a third of the space in the basement of the education building. The Reverend Doctor Shirley Walker had been rector for more than five years and she and Hattie had become good friends. Each had made their way through typically male dominated professional structures, religion and academia, and had many experiences to share. It was this issue of a woman's role in the world where Amos Dunn entered the conversation.

"Was he really that much of a chauvinist?" Hattie said.

"Oh, I wouldn't use chauvinist when it came to Amos. No, his view of women related to his biblical education. The bible is a book written by men for men, as they dominated a 'might makes right' male controlled society. It was only logical to do so. Of course, in today's world of the twenty-first century, if Jesus, Mohammad, the Buddha, etc. were to give it another shot, women would get the nod, as they now dominate the populations of law schools, medical schools and just about all other professions. Again, it would only be logical to do so."

"So Amos was stuck in the sixteenth century?"

"Yes, but only from a religious perspective. As a businessman, women were his customer base. He talked with them all day long. He listened to their family problems. Knew of the economic difficulties they were facing. Commiserated with them when a family member was ill. Heard about their problems paying medical bills. He would become particularly irate when he heard of spousal abuse or when a woman was being taken advantage of financially. Whether you agree or disagree with his view, he saw women as the weaker sex. He saw it as his duty to defend them and to be on their side."

"Interesting. Let me bring you up to date about what

has been going on." Hattie then went on to give the Rector a brief overview of what Sidney and Mickey went through the evening before. She also mentioned Amos' now famous 'walk' and that she, the Rector, had said she saw him the night he was killed. Hattie brought up the man who called to Amos that night on Church Street, but the Rector said she was just too far away for her to recognize him.

Hattie then brought up the 'book.' "Do you know anything about the book he carried with him? It's one of those small spiral bound pocketbooks. About the size of an index card, three by five."

"Why…yes. If it's the same one I've seen him with. He said it was his Alzheimer's book."

"His Alzheimer's book. Amos had Alzheimer's?"

The Rector paused, then said, "I…really don't know. I don't know if he really suffered from memory loss or that it was just a joking reference for a 'to do' list he carried. I mean, I pretty much do the same with my schedule. I write down a bunch of things I need to do and people to see. I have an electronic calendar on my phone, but that's more of a backup. It's a lot faster just to pull a piece of paper out of my pocket than to rummage through a purse, find my phone, turn it on, navigate a menu and hope the sun isn't around so I can read it—if the type isn't too small. I know that's some form of heresy in the 'electronic' age, but I prefer convenience and a hundred percent availability."

Hattie laughed, "Bravo! A woman after my own heart."

"Thank you."

"So, you think it might have to do with helping him remember things? I wonder what he was trying to remember." Hattie asked. "Something he saw on his walk?"

"I really don't know, but you might ask William, his grandnephew. Amos said he explained everything to him, everything he was doing and why he wanted to retire. I think if Amos had been diagnosed with Alzheimer's,

William will probably know. Although he and William weren't getting on as far as I can tell. Amos told me William wanted to sell off everything and get out, but Amos said he could talk him out of it."

"Oh, I'll definitely tell Sidney and have Tillie to speak with William Dunn again."

Hattie didn't make it back to Sidney's until after eight o'clock. As planned, she would spend the night in the guest room and give Tillie a break. This allowed Tillie to get back to her family and reschedule her customers.

Hattie, on arrival, noticed how quiet everything was. Even Mickey didn't make a sound or move. She peeked into the living room and saw Sidney sound asleep in his chair. Mickey was out cold as well in her usual spot next to him. Tillie, who'd promised to stay until she returned, was not in the room.

Chapter 13

The book-of-numbers

illie set up Sidney's bed in the library and got the professor's comfortable overstuffed chair arranged nearby. She decided to stay in the room and took the opportunity to browse the bookcases while Sidney and Mickey napped in the living room.

After only a few minutes, she heard a key in the front door lock. Suspicious and cautious, she came out and stood in the library doorway with her cell phone at the ready until she could see who it was. When Hattie came into view she stepped into the clear and waved to her to be quiet. Tillie whispered as Hattie tip-toed over to her, "Didn't want to disturb them. The pain medication they're taking knocked them both out." She put her phone away.

"I don't think that was unexpected. When is he due to take it again?"

"Ten o'clock."

Hattie looked at her watch. "Good. I'll leave them alone for a while. Could you do me a favor and take Mickey for a short walk before you leave."

"Sure," Tillie said.

"How did it go?" Sidney said, sneaking up behind Hattie, who still stood in the doorway. Mickey also peeked around the corner.

"I thought you were asleep?"

"Just dozing. Mickey, on the other hand, did a passable imitation of a snoring uncle of mine. I'm afraid I woke her up when I got out of the chair. I think her medication is stronger than mine."

"How's the knee? You certainly made it out here pretty well."

Tillie answered for Sidney, "Oh, I think he's doin' pretty good with that cane."

"Actually, it is comfortable using it. As awful as those crutches were, I could get used to this." He lifted it up and gave it the once over. "Got out of that chair pretty easily this time." Looking at the brown stick again, "Might invest in one a bit stronger and with a bit of style."

Hattie said, "That's all you need. You'd end up using it as an extension of your arm and index finger when having an argument over a literary interpretation."

Laughter from Tillie. "Come on Mickey, let's you and I take a short walk. I'm not going to get into the middle of this."

As soon as Tillie and Mickey left, Hattie and Sidney secured the door and made their way back into the library. Sidney sat down at the table he used for research, a duplicate of the one in his office.

"Can I get you a cup of tea and maybe some toast or something? You're not due for your medication until ten." Hattie said.

"That sounds good, but hold on a moment. I want to hear about what the rector had to say. Take a seat," he said pointing to the other chair at the table.

Hattie sat down. "She said some interesting things for us to consider. But I have to tell you, I called Ray Morton before I saw the rector." She held up the palm of her right hand to him. "And yes, I know. You said you didn't want to disturb Ray while he was on vacation, but after what happened last night, when you became a target instead of an observer, well…I think we need all the help we can get."

Sidney did not comment for a moment. Finally, "You're right. I came to the same conclusion this afternoon. Being confined to a chair for extended periods of time gives one a great deal of time to think. Not just to think, I suppose, but also to analyze…in depth. I planned to call him tomorrow. I figured I was safe here till then. As tomorrow is Thursday and Ray's due back late Saturday, I'm only interrupting a few days of his time away."

"From my conversation with him, I had the feeling he'd had enough of sitting around on the front porch of the place they rented just watching the tide come in and out. He seemed anxious to get back here. Remember, police work has been his life. His current hobby is sitting around the City Hall Café and the county council meetings and commenting on the goings on—whether anyone is interested in his opinion or not."

Sidney laughed, "You're right. So what did he have to say?"

"Basically, he said you should not hold anything back from Sam Cashman. Sam has a great future in police work. He has the right temperament for it. He listens. He doesn't jump to conclusions and he likes what he's doing. Ray seemed delighted that Chief Hornig has given Sam the opportunity to move to the detective side and he would appreciate it if you didn't screw things up for him."

Sidney acted offended. "What did he mean by that?"

"*What did he mean by that?* Are you serious, Sidney? There are times you appear to be a bull that maintains your own portable china shop just so you can carry it around with you when you get a destructive urge. Instead of demanding that people agree with your evaluations you might want to practice something called diplomacy. Bring them along. Coach them into seeing your point of view. You're not in the classroom anymore, where you were the expert with thirty years of research and experience behind you." She stopped. "Sorry. Didn't mean to get on a soap box. You gave us all a big fright last night and it's not fair to beat up on you like this, especially after what you've been through."

"It's all right, Hattie. Believe me, I've been doing it to myself all day."

Hattie gave a sigh and sat back in her chair. "I'm sure you have. If anything serious had happened to Mickey you would never have been able to forgive yourself. Look, Ray said he would call you tomorrow and you can tell him yourself how you feel, but right now I have to tell you about my conversation with the rector."

Hattie reached down and took a piece of paper from her purse which she had placed next to the chair when she sat down. Her report to Sidney followed the same sequence in which she heard it. The rector knew Amos well and elaborated on each of his usual concerns: the excessive cost of medical care, spousal abuse and the ineffective way the court and police protected abused women, and his concern about the elderly being taken advantage of by the medical profession and insurance companies by threatening non-payment of claims. None of these issues were a surprise to Sidney. Rarely did a Morgan Rotary meeting go by without Amos bringing up one of his constant complaints to someone. But now Hattie got around to the book, the book with all the numbers in it.

Sidney said, "So there is a book. And he calls it his Alzheimer's book?"

"Well, Rector Walker said she didn't know if he was serious or not. I mean, she didn't know if Amos had actually been diagnosed with Alzheimer's or he was just joking about it. All I know is that he called the book his 'book-of-numbers.' She said she didn't know what numbers he was referring to and he didn't elaborate."

Sidney looked surprised. "And that was it?"

"Not entirely. She had the impression that Amos' grandnephew, William, knew something about it. Amos had been having discussions with him about taking over the business. He introduced him all around. Brought him to church. My understanding is that William really doesn't want to move to South Carolina. He likes the Philadelphia area. The idea of him being stuck in what she heard him refer to as the rural south didn't appeal to him. Amos kept pushing the profitable side of the business: The income from three commercial spaces in two buildings and the apartment over the market. He admitted that the market was no barn burner, but it was necessary to the community. Even so, he made sure it was profitable. Amos even took William into the bank to see the manager, Randolph Byron, and introduced him to the director who oversaw Coastal Rivers Community Bank's lending policies. Rector Walker said Amos let it all out to William. Told him everything and if there was anything medically significant in that numbers book, Amos would have let William know."

Sidney sat back in his chair. He shifted his leg a bit. Fiddled with his cane. The knee felt a bit different since he had both feet on the floor rather than up on a stool. He folded his arms across his chest and then reached up and stroked his chin with his right hand. "Make a note to remind me to ask Mary Coffey about that tumor that she found when she examined Amos. We need to know if it could have been impairing his memory. We also need to know how much William Dunn knew about the numbers book and how much Amos revealed to him about his health. I would really like to talk with him. Think we might be able to get him to stop in?"

"Tillie and I will work on that."

Sidney shifted his leg again and Hattie saw him wince.

"Are you okay?" Hattie said.

"Yes, yes, I'm fine."

"No you're not. You need to get that leg up again." She got up from her chair. "I think I hear Tillie and Mickey. Look, your pajamas and bathrobe are there on the bed. I'll go and talk to Tillie for a bit while you get yourself ready. You and Mickey have some medication to take as well. We'll talk again in the morning."

"Before you step out, do you know who Amos Dunn's doctor is?"

"I'm sure Tillie can find out. I asked Reverend Walker that when the Alzheimer's was mentioned. She remembered that it used to be Doctor Cooper but around the time Cooper ran for coroner they had a falling out. It had something to do with Obamacare. She didn't know exactly what and she never heard who he switched to."

"Interesting."

Chapter 14

The morning after

The following morning Tillie opened the front door with her key so she wouldn't disturb anyone, including Mickey, although she knew the Lab would know it was her and wouldn't make a fuss. She usually arrived between seven and seven-thirty, but she'd had some extra things to do this morning so she made sure to arrive before six-thirty. It was easy for her to spot the unmarked police car sitting on the corner of Howard and King Streets. Sam Cashman kept his promise to watch over Sidney and she made a mental note to thank him. As she came in, Tillie listened for some sounds from Hattie upstairs and didn't hear anything. Breakfast would be her first chore. She usually didn't make breakfast for Sidney. He was on his own for that.

Tillie had another reason for being at Sidney's early and it had to do with the phone call she received last night from Grace Carter who sometimes opened up for Amos. Grace finally figured out what didn't look right in the market the morning after Amos Dunn was killed and she wanted to tell Tillie right away. Grace also promised to call Sam Cashman once she got to the market. She said she would wait until about nine when the morning early-bird customers had left.

Hattie came down at seven. She knew Tillie had come in earlier as she could smell the fresh coffee brewing.

Not hearing anything from the library, Hattie assumed Sidney wasn't up yet. As she entered the kitchen, she noticed the oven was on and she whispered, "What are you making?"

"Mornin' Miss Hattie. Fresh biscuits. Haven't heard him yet but I've got to wake him soon. Mickey'll have to go out an' they both got medicine to take."

Hattie took a look around the kitchen. "You're doing eggs and bacon as well?"

"Yeah. Thought I'd spoil him a bit. Also saw Officer Green out there in the police car. Tryin' to hide down the street. Gonna ask him to join us if he'd like. At least give him some coffee and a biscuit or two. Show 'im we appreciate their watchin' over us."

Hattie walked over and gave Tillie a hug. "You are an amazing person, Tillie. We are so lucky to have you as a friend."

"Or a boss," Sidney said, suddenly appearing in the doorway duly bath-robed and leaning on his cane. "But a benevolent one. Mickey needs to go out."

Hattie said, "I'll take her. Come on Mickey, out you go." The two of them headed for the back door off the kitchen.

"How you feelin' this mornin', Professor? Where would you like breakfast?"

"Actually, I'd prefer right here in the kitchen. But only if you're agreeable."

Tillie smiled. "Long as I feed you, you'll do what I say, huh?"

"Absolutely. And yes, I'm feeling much better. A bit stiff, but I'm sure that will work itself out." Sidney limped over to the kitchen table that already had two place settings on it.

"Good to hear. Now you just got to do what the doctor ordered to get well."

"I promise. By the way, are the police hiding out there someplace?"

"Yeah, spotted Officer Green down the street. Not exactly hiding though. Gotta remember to thank Mr. Sam." She brought the coffee pot over and filled his cup. "Oh, I got somethin' important for you. Grace Carter. She said she remembered what she forgot."

Sidney, surprised, looked up from the coffee cup in his hand. "I didn't know she forgot something."

"Well, she didn't really know she forgot it."

"What does that mean?"

"It means that in all the excitement she saw something that didn't look right in the store when she finally got to see it. She's the one that opened it up when the police and Mr. William agreed it would be okay. The police said that nothing had been changed. The check-out counter was set up wrong."

Sidney interrupted her and said, "Wait. Grace originally said that Amos set the counter up for her with the calculator, pads, pencils and other stuff positioned to the right as she was right-handed and would be opening up the next morning. He always did that for her on Wednesday nights. When I first saw it set up that way I thought it was a mistake because Amos was left handed and he always opened up."

"Not on Thursday. Amos liked to do some stuff on his computer at home on Thursday mornings so Grace would always open up that day. Grace said that would normally be the case but that Wednesday afternoon she called to say she would be about an hour late."

Sidney understood the implications and said slowly, "So...he   never...changed...the   check-out   counter settings. It should have been arranged for a left-handed person. Just as I thought. The killer did search the area and he knew Grace would be the first one in on Thursday morning, not Amos. He spotted the Ambers coming back from dinner and in his rush he put the setting back as he knew they should be for the following Thursday morning."

"You got it."

Sidney, now getting excited, made a motion to get out of his chair.

"Hold it right there Professor. You sit, I get."

He stopped and looked at Tillie. "But I've got to call Sam. This confirms that the killer not only knew Amos, but also knew the routine at the store. Knew it well enough to know the Wednesday-Thursday routine and how to set up the counter. He planned it all. He planned for it to look like a random act of violence."

"Yeah, that's what I think too. But it's not your story to tell. Let Grace do it. She's due to call Mr. Sam in about an hour. Let her do it. She told me she'd give us a call after she talks to the police."

Sidney sat back down. Hattie came back with Mickey and saw the movement by Sidney and the looks on both their faces. "What's going on?" Hattie said.

Sidney answered. "I was right about the set up at the market being wrong." He paused and looked at Tillie. "Right for the wrong reason, but right none the less."

Hattie hung the leash up by the door. "What does that mean?"

"Let me explain."

Sidney went over what Tillie had revealed while Hattie got herself a cup of coffee and sat down with Sidney at the table. During breakfast, while waiting for Grace Carter to call, they reviewed the difference in how the checkout counter would be set up for a left-handed person versus a right-handed one, but still couldn't come up with a motive for Amos Dunn's murder.

The motive for Mark Beasley's murder seemed easier: the murderer, while searching and ransacking Amos Dunn's office, was surprised by Beasley, who recognized and challenged him.

Sidney said, "I still have to believe Amos' book-of-numbers is the key to everything. If we could just find it."

Tillie, who had been busy serving breakfast and had just finished putting together a cup of coffee and some biscuits for Officer Green out in the police car, said, "It's in the market. Gotta be." She put the food with some jam on a plate and poured a large mug of coffee. "Be back in a minute."

As Tillie left, Hattie said, "The market. Where in the world could it be hidden?"

"That's just the point. It's not hidden," Sidney said. "That's why it's so hard to find. I know the police and Mary Coffey have gone over everything not just at the market but also at Amos' house."

"What do you mean by 'not hidden'?"

"Amos had no idea that the person he let into the market that night was there to do him harm. Also, since he just finished his walk, he should have had the book with him. It should have been on him."

"That's why the body was moved. The killer was looking for the book. And he was looking in the right-side pants pocket where Tillie said he always kept it, but it wasn't there."

Sidney continued Hattie's line of reasoning, "And Amos didn't have an opportunity to hide it since he was always in the killer's company, assuming that they met up on Church Street and probably walked to the market together."

"Right. So where is it? It's certainly not hiding in plain sight. If the killer had it he wouldn't have been searching

Amos' home."

"Hmmmm..." Sidney sat forward in his chair and started rubbing his chin. "That may not be true. What if he did find it, but it led to something that would be in Amos' office at home?"

A frustrated Hattie said, "But *what* is this all about?"

The front door opened and Tillie rushed in. The door slammed behind her. Mickey jumped up, ignoring her injured hip, and, uncharacteristically, barked. Sidney and Hattie were startled as Tillie yelled out. "They found the book. They found the book."

Hattie got up from her chair and Sidney twisted in his. The only one who could actually see Tillie come in the door was Mickey who moved toward her with a tail wagging furiously in excitement.

Sidney said, "They found the book? Amos' book-of-numbers? Where? Who?"

Tillie was out of breath. She had taken the four steps to the front porch in two leaps. "At the...market. Grace has it."

"Sit." Ordered Sidney. "Tell us. How do you know? Was it Officer Green?"

"No. He don't know yet."

"Then who?"

"Grace found it." Tillie pulled out the chair.

Hattie said, "Let me get you some water. Relax a bit."

Tillie sat down and took a deep breath, "Wow...these seventy-year-old bones ain't used to runnin' like that. Must be getting' old. Didn't think I was gonna make it up the front steps. I was trying to hurry, walk an run all at the same time. Didn't want Officer Green to see me excited so I came down the street on the other side an then ran across in front of a car an then up the steps. Wow."

Hattie put a glass of water in front of her. "Take a sip and tell us what happened."

"Well, I delivered the coffee and biscuits and we did a little chattin' an my phone rang. Saw it was Grace an told Officer Green I had to go. Told him to stop in before he left an I'd have some more for him."

Sidney said anxiously, "And?"

"I'm gettin' there. Anyway, Grace said they had the electrician in this morning to fix one of the fans up toward the front of the store. The one that sits over the front shelf before you get to the check-out counter. He was fiddling with the electric box tryin' to get it to work, but it looked like there was sumpthin wrong with the fan itself but he couldn't get to it because there was too many people around the check-out line. When things eased up he went an' got a ladder from the back and set it up right by the counter. He worked on the fan all the while Grace was on the phone with Sam Cashman tellin' Sam about how the counter set up was wrong the day Amos was killed. Grace moved away from the counter while the fan man worked. She told Mr. Sam everything she told me and I told you, but she didn't tell him she told me. Anyway, the electric man took the fan all apart, found a loose wire, fixed it, put the ladder away all the time she was talkin' on the phone. She'd paid no attention to him. Then when he was all done and brought the bill up front for her to sign for it he said, 'Oh, by the way I found this up on the fan.' He had the little notebook. 'It was sittin on one of the blades. Can't imagine how it got there. Never saw it 'till I got up on the ladder. Darnedest thing I ever saw.' Grace knew exactly what it was. She knew it was Amos's book from his walks."

Hattie said, "Oh my goodness."

"That's just what I said, sorta."

Sidney, all serious, said, "Where is it now?"

"She still got it. Told her to bag it with one of those plastic baggie things an' put it in her purse."

"Excellent. Of course the electrician's fingerprints and hers will be on it, but that's okay. If the killer was looking for it, it probably means he never had it in his possession. Did she tell Sam about it?"

"No, not yet. She found out only after she hung up with him."

"Okay, good. Now this is what I want you to do. Call her back. Tell her to put it in the storeroom where those oatmeal containers are. Leave the door to the storeroom open. Tell her not to call Sam Cashman again until we call back."

"Okay, but why?"

"Because we're going to borrow it. Hattie, I want you to go over to the market, sneak in the back door, get into the storeroom, take the book and bring it back here. We'll make copies of everything in it and then get it back to the storeroom. Then Grace can call Sam and tell him she found the book and it's in a safe place waiting for him."

Hattie looked at Sidney questioningly, "Why are we doing this?"

"Because that's the only way we'll ever get to see what's in it."

"But why so sneaky?"

"I want Grace to be able to say, honestly, that as far as she knows no one else has seen it. She bagged it, put it in the storeroom and that's where it was when Sam took possession of it."

Tillie had a smile on her face and shook her head from side to side.

Chapter 15

A book-of-numbers found

illie did her best to walk at a normal pace, but it wasn't easy. Amos' book-of-numbers, carefully placed in a plastic sandwich bag and then wrapped in a second one, laid securely in her purse. The transfer from Hattie to Tillie had come at the rear kitchen door. Tillie had Mickey with her and they traded a dog's leash for a plastic wrapped book. Hattie and Mickey headed down the driveway to the front of Sidney's place, while Tillie went in the other direction toward the Presbyterian Church and its large commercial grade copier with a magnifier capability.

Tillie knew who would be working at the secretary's desk in the office, so she just called out as she opened the door, "Mornin' Miss Alice."

A cheerful response came back to her, "Tillie, how nice to see you." Alice Ringfoot had been the secretary to the pastor since the 1960's and knew not only everyone in the Presbyterian Church but also just about everyone who ever attended a church in Morgan. "Don't tell me Professor Lake has more copying to do. I swear he uses the magnifying thing on that machine more than I do. I wouldn't be surprised if Reverend Prentice bought that machine just so

Professor Lake could use it."

"Wouldn't be surprised either with all that forgery work he's investigatin'." Tillie chuckled, "You got him figured out too. Funny how they all thinkin' they got one up on us an we always know what they's doin'."

A smile from Alice in return, "Sure is the truth. You go right ahead. You know how to use the copier as well as I do. It's been a slow day. I haven't even taken the cover off it yet."

Tillie walked over to the machine and before she removed the dust cover asked, "Miss Alice, that box of gloves still in the closet?"

"Actually, ah have some in the drawer right here." She reached over and pulled out the bottom left hand drawer of her desk and removed a small box of food service gloves. "Somethin' old and sensitive again?" Alice was used to Tillie showing up with something old and delicate to be copied.

"Yeah, Professor Lake said to be real careful with it. Doesn't want any finger smudges on it. Writin's real tiny." Tillie took the box, removed two gloves and put them on. Alice watched her. She didn't miss much. It was just her way. She, instinctively, mentally recorded everything. Fifty years of watching and recording, a difficult habit to change.

Alice said, "Doesn't look too fragile."

"It's not the outside that's the concern, but the inside."

Tillie now picked up the little book and then removed the copier's dust cover. Alice reached over and took it from her and started to fold it while carefully looking at the little notebook in Tillies hand. "Looks like one of those little books you see in the stationery section of the Food Lion."

"Could be."

"Amos Dunn used to carry one like that. Kept numbers

in it to help his memory."

⌘

Sidney Lake looked exasperated, "You're not serious? Alice said that? She knew about the book and what he was using it for?"

"I didn't say that. Alice said he was concerned about getting' old an losing his memory, like they keep sayin' all the time on TV. So he figured the best defense is good offense. Lose it or use it is what Amos always said."

"You mean 'defense is the best offense.' "

"No I don't. I'm just tellin' it the way she said Amos said it."

Sidney gave a sigh, "Okay, but either way I can't argue with the approach."

"Me too. Yeah, well, Miss Alice said it didn't make a lot of sense to her anyway. Said Amos had a mind like a steel trap. Kept everything in his head. Knew how much of everything he had in that store. Knew who owed him money. Who paid on time an' who didn't. Oh, that Amos, he never forgot nuthin'."

Sidney sat back in his chair and looked up at the living room ceiling. He placed his elbows on his mid-section, brought his hands together on his chest and made a church steeple out of his index fingertips. "Interesting. Amos was always a cagy, clever fellow. I wonder what's really in that book."

"You mean there's more than numbers? All I saw was numbers. All I copied was numbers. Although I did see a few letters now and then." Tillie sat down on the sofa across from Sidney and picked up one of the copier sheets that sat on the tray table alongside Sidney. "What you're sayin' is that these numbers may not be rememberin' numbers but somethin' else. He didn't want someone else to know what he was doin' so he made up a story? Hmm, sounds like Amos all right."

"You think so?" Sidney said while collapsing his church steeple and shifting in his chair so he could look directly at Tillie.

"You know when he bought that building where Mr. Beasley and those lawyers have their offices, he gave everyone the idea he was lookin' way on the other side of town. Yeah, I think it's possible, but what were the numbers for?"

Sidney looked directly at Tillie and said, "Think we could arrange a meeting here with William Dunn? Could really use one. Convince him to stop by to see me and have a chat. Tell him Amos' book-of-numbers has been found and the police have it. They do don't they?"

"Oh, yeah. I got it back to the place where Hattie took it from. Grace didn't see me put it back. Then I went up front and bought some stuff. Didn't say anything about the book, but she knew. Yeah, she knew. Expect she called Mister Sam after I left."

"Good. He'll turn it over to Mary Coffey right away. Now let's figure how to get Sam and William together with us being present."

享⁊ᕦ

William Dunn wondered what he had gotten himself into when he told his Uncle Amos he would consider moving to Morgan, South Carolina. The plan had been that Amos would fully retire and William would take over everything and have complete control. It was pretty evident that he and Amos had different ideas about what 'full control' meant. They agreed there would be a transition period of about six months at the end of which Amos would step out of the picture. William told this to Sam Cashman and

Tillie when they met with him in the breakfast area at the Holiday Inn Express. Sidney's plan to get everyone together at 111 Howard Street wasn't feasible.

"I hope you don't mind me asking Tillie here to be present? It's nothing personal. I just feel more comfortable with an independent third party in the room."

Sam said, "No, no. Not at all. I think it's a good idea for all of us. Besides, you are a lawyer and I sort of expected it."

"Yeah, but I also think you know what I mean: you're black but you're also a cop."

"I know, which is why Tillie being here helps me as well. I don't think any of us has any illusions about the real world. All I do know is that the murder of your uncle and then Mister Beasley is more than it seems, and I really want to get to the bottom of it. I don't see any of this being a racial issue, but I'm enough of a realist to know that when push comes to shove it's always a fallback position for a lot of people. I wanted this meeting, on a strictly informal basis, to do some exploring on a number of levels. I need your trust and I know I have to earn it. I need you to be relaxed, as I believe you know some things that will help us find not just the killer but the reason behind all of what's been going on. Little things that Amos may have mentioned that have no meaning to you, but mean a lot to us in the context of Amos' history here in the town."

Tillie sat quiet at the table, but it wasn't her intention to stay that way. Not making a comment would be way out of character for her so neither William or Sam were surprised when she said, "I want to know about that book. What it means? Why he kept it? That's what I want to know."

Sam smiled and said, "Okay, good place to start. Let's talk about Amos' book-of-numbers. I'm assuming you both know it's been found?"

"Tillie just told me before you got here."

Sam looked at Tillie, shook his head and said, "I'm not going to ask how you found out. Given the way this town works, I'm guessing I was last on the list to be notified. Well, maybe not me, but the police, which isn't really the same thing...although it is. Anyway, Mary Coffey of the coroner's office has it at the moment." Then looking directly at Tillie, "I do appreciate someone telling Grace to bag it." Tillie didn't respond and Sam posed his question to William. "Just how much do you know about it? Did you ever question Amos about it? Did he ever talk about it?"

"The answer is yes and no. Yes, I knew about it."

Tillie said, "Everybody seems to have *known* about it."

"I'm finding that out," Sam said. "However, I can't get a good feel for what it contained."

William sat forward and leaned on his elbows, "I did ask him about it and he flippantly just said it was his Alzheimer's book."

"Do you know what he meant by it?"

"Not really. I do know he had a fear of losing his memory."

"Did he ever show the book to you?"

William Dunn thought for a moment before answering. "I've seen the book. I remember coming into the store one time when there were no customers present and found Amos standing by the cash register with his eyes closed and the book in his hand." William paused and looked into the distance trying to visualize his uncle in the store. "It was in his right hand and he seemed to be drawing something in the air with his left. It reminded me of someone trying to memorize something. You know, you read something, look away and then try to repeat it verbatim."

"Could you see what was on the page?"

Tillie kept quiet. She knew what was in the book, she

saw it, she copied it, it was all numbers. This was not the time to say anything. Besides, Mary Coffey would eventually tell him as she now had the original book.

William continued. "No, he closed the book while he was writing in the air. Sorry, I just can't help you with it."

"Too bad," Sam said, obviously disappointed, but very curious as to why he would want to commit the entries to memory. *Maybe this is all about memory loss and we're overthinking everything,* he hesitated and then said, "Moving on for now, there's been some speculation that Amos was about to make another real estate purchase. Did he ever say anything about that?"

"No. I asked him about that too. He said that would be up to me. He just wanted to retire. Needed a break."

"So…there's a possibility he could have been looking into something. He just didn't want to make the decision if you were taking over."

William thought for a moment. Then, shaking his head, "No…no. I don't think so. He was pretty straight with me about the store and everything. I don't think that book and what's in it had anything to do with the store. There's got to be something else. Something he didn't tell anyone about."

The questions and answers went back and forth for a half hour. Tillie could see a comfort factor building between the two men. William Dunn also spent some time asking about Sam's background and his family. Asked him about the local police and what Sam thought about Chief Hornig and the other people in the department. Tillie also added some background information on the region, the town and the Gullah community. Topics, William said Amos didn't spend too much time on, since he didn't live on Deer Island and didn't have a Gullah connection. Everyone relaxed and smiled good-naturedly when the interview concluded.

Chapter 16

Crisis at City Hall

Sam left the meeting first. He thought it went well and felt William Dunn had acquired a degree of comfort with him. Tillie helped with her endorsement of him and the outline she presented of how the families in the Gullah community were tied together. She and Sam acknowledged the good and the bad elements that existed on the islands, which were not that much different from any hard-working, low to middle income community regardless of race. Racism, especially the subliminal kind, filled with code words and the mismatch of words versus deeds, was another matter. There also seemed to be a problem with regard to the perception of a black man in a blue uniform on a mostly white police force. His motivations seemed to be suspect by everyone, which in itself was another form of racism. However, the real objective of the meeting, the development of a comfortable and trusting rapport, seemed to have been met. Sam was convinced that William Dunn knew something important that related to Amos Dunn's murder. The problem would be to draw it out of William, especially as William didn't know he possessed it and Sam had no idea what it was.

As soon as Sam got into his car, he called Mary Coffey. He needed to know what was in that book.

"City Hall Coroner's Office, Mary Coffey."

"Mary, Sam."

"Oh, hi Sam. That's an interesting little puzzle book you gave me."

"Puzzle book?"

"Yeah. There's no writing in it."

"Wait, I took a quick look at it before I sent it over to you and I saw writing in it."

"You saw numbers, not one word is spelled out any-where. It's all numbers with a few letters interspaced."

"Is Amos' name even in it?"

"No. Nowhere."

Mary stood in a small conference room in the basement of the City Hall building as she talked with Sam. The main location of the coroner was in the annex of the county hos-pital but, as coroner inquests were held in the City Hall building, a temporary Coroner's Office was kept in the basement of the building for convenience purposes. Sam had just started to pull out of the Holiday Inn Express park-ing lot to drive the two and a half blocks to City Hall. He stopped the car.

"Sam, it's the strangest jumble of numbers I've ever seen. If it's code of some type, it's a really good one."

"It has to mean something."

"I'll be right with you." Mary said addressing noise she heard coming from the Coroner's office next door. "Hold on just a minute, Sam. Someone just went into the office." She put the phone down and walked toward the conference room door that led directly to the small office used by the coroner when he was at City Hall.

The lights in both rooms went out. Even though it was mid-day, it became dark. There were few windows in the basement and none in the coroner's office or the conference room.

"Hey!" Mary yelled

"Mary, what's going on?" Sam yelled into the phone.

"Who's in there?" Mary demanded.

Sam heard a loud crashing noise as he listened to his phone and immediately put his car in gear and headed for City Hall. The line to Mary was still open, but quiet.

It took Sam less than two minutes to reach City Hall. He made it downstairs in another half minute followed shortly afterwards by Officer Shawn Green, who he yelled to as he came in from the parking lot. Green was working backup at the rear door security checkpoint. The Coroner's office and attached small conference room at City Hall served as a convenient location for the coroner when holding an inquest in one of the hearing rooms upstairs. When Sam reached the bottom of the stairs, seeing the long, dark hallway with no light coming from the rooms at the back where Mary should be, he quietly waved to Green to call for backup. Cautiously making his way to the office doorway, he spotted Mary lying in a heap on the floor. The office and attached conference rooms were small and even in the dim light he could tell the office area was clear. He bent over and checked Mary, but still kept watching the doorway to the conference room. She was alive, breathing, but with a nasty wound to the head. He immediately called EMS for medical assistance and stepped back cautiously to the light switch, a grouping of four that controlled the lights for both rooms. He turned on the light to the office and then the light in the small conference room. He could hear someone running down the hallway toward him as he stepped toward the conference room and peered in at the small table and its chairs. It was empty. The telephone Mary had used was on a small table in the corner. The receiver in the same place Mary put it when she spoke with Sam. He touched nothing. Went back to Mary. Shawn

Green appeared at the door.

"Holy shit!"

Sam looked up and said, "I've called EMS."

A moment later Detectives Kent and Patton were at the door.

"I was on the phone with her when it happened. Whoever did it could still be in the building."

With his phone to his ear, Kent took off down the hallway back the way he came. Detective Patton came over and joined Green and Sam. "She gonna be okay?"

Chief Hornig appeared in the doorway.

Sam said, "Still out. Took a nasty hit from behind. Someone must have been in the corner over there." He pointed to a dark space between the door frame to the conference room and the wall that ran next to it, where the copier, with its control panel blinking, stood against the back wall. "I was on the phone with her in the conference room when she heard someone in the office. She went to see who it was and the line went dead."

Patton had a puzzled look on his face. "Why? Why attack the coroner? Who attacks coroners?"

Mary moved slightly, moaned and mumbled something.

Sam dropped to his knees next to her and said, "Stay still. EMS coming."

"What did she say?" Chief Hornig asked.

"Sounded like 'Take pictures. Book.'" Sam replied as Mary passed out just as two EMS officers came in from their station upstairs near the back of the building.

Sam looked up at the copier as he got up. "The book. Shawn, check the conference room. The papers by the phone."

"What book?" Hornig demanded.

"Amos Dunn's book." Sam stepped over to the copier and checked the flashing light. The enlarging feature had been turned on. He carefully opened the cover. No book. He looked around the copier and on the desk next to it and then called out, "Shawn, anything?"

Hornig stepped carefully into the room, but did not interfere, letting his people do their jobs.

Shawn called back. "All I see is a notebook and some papers."

"Amos Dunn's?"

"Don't think so. It's an eight and a half by eleven binder with the coroner's name on it. Couple of loose sheets. One with some numbers on it."

Sam moved quickly into the conference room, carefully moving around the EMS people. Another EMS technician now stood in the doorway next to the chief. Sam looked at the material on the table: Mary's loose-leaf notebook opened to a report page she had been filling out, a ballpoint pen and a single page of copier paper with the image of what had been copied: a page from a small notebook with strange numbers on it.

"Okay, anybody want to tell me what's going on?" Chief Hornig said to the assembly of police officers in front of him. They were all in his office with the door closed. No-one sat. Shawn Green instinctively took a step back. Since there were detectives all around him, he intended to do his best to stay in the background.

"We found Amos Dunn's notebook," Sam said. "Mary was copying it when she was attacked. I was on the phone with her at the time."

"Tell me about this book. Why is it important?"

"We really don't know, but we believe it has some damaging information in it that someone is very uncomfortable about. Could be the motive for two murders."

Chief Hornig didn't immediately reply. He then said, "Know what's bothering me?"

Silence.

"The fact that Mary Coffey was attacked in this building. This should be the safest place in town to get in or out of."

Detective Patton spoke up. "You think we should be looking for someone who works in this building. We shut everything down. Identified everyone. Still doing it. Have video cameras all over the place…" Patton got the point. "Except the basement. It's not public space."

"Right." Hornig said. "Where's the book now?"

Sam said, "Don't know. Mary had it. I gave it to her earlier today and she was looking it over when I called her. I believe she was making a copy of the pages to work on when she was attacked. Shawn found one of the pages in her notebook by the phone in the conference room. We haven't found the original yet, but if it's anywhere in the building we'll find it."

Hornig again, "Think Mary saw who hit her?"

"No way to tell yet. Hopefully she suspected something. If her attacker is still in the building he's probably hid the book someplace by now. Given that he knew he didn't have much time." Sam paused and looked at Shawn Green. "You were at the back door that goes to the parking lot when I came in, did anyone go out past you immediately before I came in?"

"No. The security people were checking handbags and briefcases. Except for you, no-one came in or out for at least five minutes before or after you."

Hornig said, "Okay, I want every nook and cranny from the Coroner's office—and that means the whole basement—and everyplace nearby checked." Speaking to Detective Kent, "Coordinate this. Every available body you can find I want in here. Nobody leaves before they are identified, searched and interviewed. You know how to do it. Sam you stay here. We need to talk."

csɔcɔ

Although Sidney felt secure in believing the danger to him was over, Reverend Prentice still insisted in coming over and relieving Hattie while she did some chores. No one told Cal what those chores were, since they involved Hattie meeting with Tillie and driving over Amos Dunn's evening walk route with the copy of the numbers book in hand. Cal wouldn't normally have asked anyway as it wasn't his practice to pry into the lives of others. As a pastor, he got enough information voluntarily passed his way that he didn't need to go looking for more. Sidney also knew Cal would never divulge something said to him in confidence. Everyone acquainted with Cal knew that, but Sidney thought it best to keep him out of the loop just the same. The less he knew the less information he could provide to a third party. Information that Sidney would prefer the party not have.

Hattie left on her errand within two minutes of Cal's arrival and, while Cal expected Sidney to object to having a keeper, he was surprised at not only being welcomed but also being bombarded with a whole series of questions about Alzheimer's.

"Do you know many people in town with the disease?"

"It's not uncommon these days. People are living longer so it's not unreasonable to assume that dementia in a variety of forms will appear."

"I understand that. My interest is in your experience with it…as a counselor. I mean, you talk to medical people as well as patients, are there techniques recommended to ward off the disease? Are there memory games and exercises that are recommended? I know I've seen advertisements for an on-line program for people to use to keep their minds active. Sort of promoting the concept of 'use it or lose it.'"

Cal thought for a moment and said, "I think it would be safe to say there aren't many retirees that don't have it as a concern. But more to your specific question, yes, I see a lot of people doing lots of different things. Crossword puzzles are a good example. Also, old fashioned picture puzzles are another. You see card tables set up in a good many places with 1,000 piece puzzles spread out on them. Then there's reading mysteries and trying to work out the solution to the crime. There are all sorts of memory exercises and techniques being used and, to some degree, they all seem to be helpful."

"How about made up games?' Sidney suggested. "You know, just trying to remember everything about a room you just left or the color of houses in their proper order on a street."

"Yes, yes. I come across that. What's this all about, Sidney?"

"I'm wondering about Amos Dunn. You know that in famous little notebook he was always writing in, Tillie spoke with Alice earlier…"

"At the office?"

"Yes, she was there on an errand for me and in conversation Alice said Amos referred to the book as his Alzheimer's book."

Cal surprised said, "Oh, that's right. Yes. I'd forgotten about that. Yes, his Alzheimer's book. He did say that. Said it once when I saw him jotting something down."

"Did he ever show you what he put in it and what it meant? You know the coroner found a tumor in his head around where he was hit. Admittedly a tumor is not a sign of Alzheimer's, but apparently he didn't know he had it and it could have been affecting him."

"I see what you mean. He could have thought he was losing his memory, but it would have been for a different reason and not connected to Alzheimer's at all. Amos was notorious for bad-mouthing doctors. He didn't seem to like most of them and never went for check-ups. Had a partic-ular dislike for Doctor Cooper, the coroner. Something to do with a diagnosis of one of his elderly customers. Don't know the full story behind it."

"No, no. That's all right. You've been most helpful. Most helpful."

Chapter 17

Deciphering numbers

Tillie sat with the copied pages from Amos' book of numbers on her lap as Hattie, driving, turned onto Marianne Street. "Why don't you just pull over anyplace along here an' let's take a look at what I got here."

Hattie eased the car over to the curb and found a spot under a live oak tree with lots of shade and Spanish moss. "How's this?"

"Good."

The two women leaned close to one another as they looked at the papers in Tillie's hand.

"This the first page?" Hattie asked.

"Yes. I've been lookin' at this since I copied it an' I think this page and the couple following it is a little different than the one's later on."

"In what way?"

"Look here." Tillie held up the first page. "See how there ain't nothing but numbers. No letters at all. So I got a feelin' these is house numbers. When Amos walked, he was on the other side of the street and headed toward George Street, where he made a left. Now Marianne Street is kinda like no-man's land in that it ain't part of *The*

Ridge, where the rich folks live, an it ain't part of down-town, where the streets is laid out logical, like in squares an rectangles. The numberin' is also different. It starts at 100 on the left and jumps to 113 on the other side of the street." Tillie pointed past Hattie to a black mailbox with white numbers on it and then to one not far from where they were parked.

Hattie turned to look and then refocused on the sheet of paper. "This first line of numbers starts with 100 then goes to 116 120 128. That matches up with the sequence of numbers on the mailboxes on the left side of the street. What's the next line of numbers?"

"113 115 121. He skipped a couple of lines when he wrote these."

"Those numbers are on this side of the street."

"Eggsactly! He's writing down the house numbers on Marianne Street." Tillie then pointed to the third line, which was another couple of lines down the page.

"The next line is the same numbers as the first but in a different order. 120 100 128 116. And there ain't any marks between the numbers so if you ain't careful it would look like 120100128116."

Tillie, now excited continued, "Amos is testin' his memory. He jumbles the numbers again on the next line an' then adds to them as he went down the street."

Hattie had a big smile as she said, "That's why he re-ferred to it as his Alzheimer's book."

The two women did a high five.

"Well I'll be," said Hattie.

"Me too."

"But wait, you said it changes."

"It does. Take us over to George Street. Make the left as Amos woudda done. That's a short street. Only one an' a half blocks long an' the numbers are pretty simple."

Hattie put the car in gear and they headed down the

street.

Tillie continued, "They's like one, two, three, four. It looks like Amos wrote the Marianne numbers on the first page and then on the second and third pages he put the numbers down as he remembered them. You can see where he used his eraser on a couple of them. He then went on to a different set of numbers." She shuffled the pages as Hattie started her left turn onto George Street and the sound of police and emergency vehicles caught their attention. "Boy, there's an awful lot of police sirens goin' off around City Hall."

Hattie completed the turn onto George Street. At the end of the shortened second block the street backed up to the City Hall's parking lot and flashing blue and red lights could be seen through the border foliage.

"Something serious must have happened," Hattie said.

"Bet it's a bad axident. They got five streets comin' together on King Street near City Hall. It's always a problem."

Hattie maneuvered the car into another shady parking spot. "Now what were you saying about four, or was it five?"

Tillie refocused on the sheets in front of her. "Eh yeah…let's see. He kept playin' with the Marianne Street numbers. Mixing them up. Then he added some single numbers like three and five. They'd be George Street numbers." She pointed to the mailboxes with single digits on them. "Now we go on to three-digit numbers again. They must be Pond Lane numbers. That'd be the next street he'd turn on to. The next page looks like he'd be tryin to remember again. Now this is the change part. On the next page we get some regular numbers with letters mixed in. See here." Tillie pointed to specific lines for Hattie to take a look at.

"I see what you mean. It's all very curious isn't it?

Sometimes they're all numbers and sometimes it's a mixture of letters and numbers. The letters seem to be random. 357121WZX825359C0C75 and don't seem to make any sense."

Tillie blurted out, "Oh yes they do! Oh yes they surely do! An look at the next two pages. He ain't trying to remember any more. He's just writin down more letters and numbers."

"What does it mean?"

"Look at this one here: O...2...N...O...H...M. Know what that is?"

Hattie shook her head. "I have no idea."

"That's Miss Geraldine Young's license plate number. I'd know it anywhere. 'Oh to know Him' that's what it says. Oh, yeah. That's Geraldine. An' look. They's all license plate numbers. Old Amos, he's been keepin' track of cars that been parked in front of certain houses."

ᥫᩚᥫᩚ

Chief Hornig spoke in a low-level voice that came out almost as a growl, "You mean to tell me that with all the technology we have in this building we don't have any pictures of what happened downstairs?"

"I'm afraid that's true, Chief," Detective Patton said somewhat meekly. "All the cameras are in the public spaces upstairs: the council chamber, the entrance and exit screening areas, the hallways, the stairways, the information desk, all those areas are covered. The insides of the offices are not. The Mayor's the Solicitor's, your office, the EMS Director, the Coroner, there are no cameras in them. Since the downstairs hallway is supposed to be restricted access, no cameras were put in, but then they never funded the secure access gate at the top of the stairs. There's a camera in the main hallway upstairs. It's a ways off, but it does get a limited picture of the top of the stair-way."

"So, we have nothing?"

"Not necessarily, Chief. We have pictures of everyone that came into the building and pictures of everyone who entered or exited a public space, which is everyone in the building. We definitely have a picture of Mary Coffey's attacker. We just don't know what we're looking for."

"And the missing book?"

"Everyone's on it. If it's in the building we'll find it."

Officer Green came to the door of the Chief's office and looked in as he said, "May have a lead chief. Downstairs there's two guest offices, one that's right at the bottom of the stairs and the other to the right. The opposite way from the coroner's office. There's a shredder in there with fresh cuttings in the basket. It could be the notebook. Nobody's used that space all week."

"What condition is the paper?"

"All cut up."

The Chief looked exasperated. "Of course it's all cut up. It's a shredder. Is there anything recognizable?"

"Oh, yeah. Eddie, the custodian, said it was an old shredder. Recycled from the old City Hall building. It's not a cross-cutter like the new ones. Just cuts in a straight line. Sam said one of Cooper's people could probably re-construct it especially if it's the only document in the can. Figured it would take some time though."

With enthusiasm now the Chief barked, "Patton, get on it. Get it done. Now. I'll call Cooper and tell him I'll give him all the help he needs." Green started to turn around, but Hornig continued, "If Kent's out there send him in. Where's Sam?"

"Lookin' at pictures."

"Okay, don't bother him, but get me Kent."

⟨⟩

By the time Hattie and Tillie were over on Pond Lane writing down the numbers of the houses, Tillie had also decided to use her phone to take pictures of the driveways and the way the cars would be parked in them. This was a 'halfway there' neighborhood where the local business people lived. People like Randall Byron of Coastal Rivers Community Bank, Dr. Cooper, the coroner, Ted McGraw of The City Hall Café and a couple of professors at Morgan College. It was called 'halfway there' because, while well off, they couldn't afford the million-dollar price tags of *The Ridge* neighborhood, which began on the other side of Marianne Street.

Hattie said, "How are we doing on time?"

"No problem. Professor said not to rush it. Think it through. Said we should try and put ourselves in Amos' place. I think he's wrong there. Professor Lake is figuring Amos is trying to remember stuff, but I don't think so anymore. Maybe in the beginning. Not later. He'd come across somethin else. A whole new puzzle."

"I agree," Hattie said. "We've got to know who lives along this part of George Street and the part of Pond Lane between George Street and King Street. Once we have that and the license plate numbers that relate to them.... Wow, listen to that racket over at City Hall. There's more than an accident going on."

"Think you're right. Sounds like they called in every police car in the county. You think it could be terrorists?"

Hattie looked surprised. "Terrorists in Morgan, South Carolina? Really?"

"You don't know no more. You can't. Can't take a chance. Everybody's got guns. Good people, bad people, sick people. When I was young if you got real mad at someone you punched them in the nose, now you pull out a gun an' shoot 'im an' everyone with 'im. Police say the most dangerous thing they do now is stop a car for runnin a red light or try to stop a family from fightin' with one another. Betcha that's what it is. Somebody got mad at someone at City Hall and started shootin'."

"I sure hope you're wrong, but I know you could be right."

"Yeah, don't understand it. They say folks like Wyatt Earp tamed the West by forcing everyone that come to town to turn in their guns to the sheriff. Give 'im back when they left. Keep the peace. Now days they tellin' everybody to get a gun an' shoot everybody back. That's just nuts. You know the other day I saw a picture of Jesus carryin' a holster an' a gun. What kind of Christian is that? Don't remember Jesus sayin' 'Turn the other cheek, but make sure your six shooter is loaded.' "

Hattie smiled, "Tillie for Mayor. You've got my vote. I'm just glad Sidney and Cal are safely at home and not headed for City Hall trying to be of help."

When all the noise started, Sidney Lake and Cal Prentice decided to move out to the front porch where they might find someone who knew what was happening. It wasn't long before the rumors began coming down the street.

"Somebody held up the bank over by City Hall. Think there's hostages," said the old man wearing a baseball cap.

"Found a bomb at City Hall," said a man walking slowly with a cane.

"Someone shot the mayor," said an old, angry looking man with a scowl on his face.

Once the speculation spreaders had passed them by a convenient distance, Sidney whispered to Cal, "I have a feeling that last comment was more wishful thinking than accurate information."

"You think any of it was accurate?"

"Probably not. Otherwise we would have to conclude that a group of terrorists tried to unsuccessfully explode a bomb at City Hall, tried to kill the mayor and, in making their escape, hid out in the bank across the street, took a hostage and the whole event caused a major accident on King Street."

Cal feigned serious concern, "Ah, I think Chief Hornig is going to need some help."

Sidney said with a smile, "Chief Hornig is always in need of help."

"Seriously, Sidney, there is something going on over there."

"Don't worry, Tillie and Hattie are due back in a little while from their investigation. I have full confidence in Tillie's ability to know more about what happened that anyone else."

"They're over by City hall?"

"Not far from it."

Cal gave Sidney a stern look and said, "What are you up to this time?"

Sidney didn't answer, but appeared to be visualizing something, as he focused on the porch ceiling.

"Sidney? What do you have them doing?"

Again, quiet for a moment, then he finally answered. "Grace over at the market found Amos Dunn's book-of-numbers. Tillie got a look at it and now she and Hattie are going over Amos' walking route to see if they can make sense of it. They're two of the brightest minds around. One comes at a problem with an incredible instinctive approach while the other is pure logical research. Between them they see every side of every issue"

A new round of sirens could be heard in the distance.

Cal held up his hand and halted Sidney's analysis. He then said, "I recognize that sound. It's an ambulance this time, not a police car. You hang around hospital emergency rooms like I do you can tell the difference. I think we can assume that someone is definitely injured. Let's hope it's not a shooting. You sure they're okay?"

Sidney said, "You have your phone with you?"

Cal pulled it from his pocket.

"Call Hattie and let's make sure."

As Cal dialed the number, Hattie and Tillie were standing on the corner of Pond Lane and King Street, one block from the City Hall complex. Tillie continued speaking with Hampton Butler, who just finished setting up a police barrier to keep traffic away from City Hall, while Hattie answered her phone.

"Yes, Cal, we're okay."

"Let me put Sidney on."

He passed the phone over to Sidney who said, "Hattie, where are you?"

Chapter 18

The troubles at City Hall

Hattie gave Sidney a quick rundown of their re-exploration of Amos' nightly walk route and Tillie's discovery of the license plate numbers in his book-of-numbers. She then said, "Tillie's been talking to officer Hampton Butler about what's been going on at City Hall. Let me put her on."

Tillie took the phone. "Professor Lake, looks like there's a big mess downtown an' we're right in the middle of it."

"What! Hattie just said you were north of there on Pond and King."

"We are. That's not what I mean. It's Miss Coffey, the coroner lady. Somebody knocked her on the head and stole Amos' book. Just found out from Mr. Hamp. Looks like we have the only copy. An' we ain't supposed to have it."

Silence from Sidney.

Tillie continued, "City Hall is all locked down. Nobody allowed in or out. They think whoever hit Miss Coffey is still in the building, but they ain't got a clue who it is."

"Any idea how Miss Coffey is?"

"Said there's an ambulance over there now. Nobody's said nothin else. He's settin' up barriers to get traffic out of the area."

"Can you get back here?"

"Yeah, we're okay. Can just scoot back up to Marianne and come down Market, the way we came."

"Good. Do that."

When Hattie and Tillie got into the car Tillie said, "Professor Lake said you always carry a big note pad with you in the car."

"Yes, I do. There's a briefcase on the back seat that has a yellow pad in it. What's he up to now?"

The question didn't surprise Tillie. "He wants me to take the copies of Amos' book I made and write it all out by hand. Said we need to have a back-up copy an' then we can make a photocopy of the back-up."

Hattie thought for a moment while Tillie reached into the back seat and grabbed the briefcase. Hattie said, "You know, I think he has another reason." She started up the car and turned back down Pond Lane. "He wants to be able to say we were working from a hand-written copy. He's trying to avoid revealing that we removed the book from the market where it was found."

"Yeah, I thought about that right away. That way we can still give Mister Sam a copy without gettin' into real trouble. That's Professor Lake all right."

While Tillie and Hattie made their way back to Sidney's, Chief Hornig assembled detectives Kent, Patton and Cashman in his office.

He paced behind his desk as he spoke, "Okay, I'm betting the person who did this is still in the building. The security people have confirmed that from the time Mary Coffey was attacked—and we have the exact time from the phone call Sam made to her—until Kent issued the order to lock-down the building, no one went past security on the way in or out. Sam, I want you in that office in the basement. Nobody goes near it. And I mean nobody. I want Cooper's people in there by themselves when they get here. Did he say how many are coming?"

"Chief, with Mary Coffey out of action, he's only got two people."

"He can always ask for more—and he better. If Shawn's right and that book full of numbers is in the shredder, it's all we have."

"Let's hope it's all we need." Sam said, "We haven't really ruled out anything yet. Whoever did this had to have been in a hurry. That works in our favor. You're in a rush, you make mistakes."

"Do we know when the room was last used?"

"I'll check. If we're lucky, no one will have been in there for a while."

"By the way, you been talking with Sidney Lake lately?"

"Indirectly. Kept a watch on his place after someone tried to run him down. Also, Tillie James, his housekeeper, attended my meeting with William Dunn. She took the pressure off with William. Was very helpful. Plan to get back with Lake when things quiet down around here. Tillie said some interesting things at that meeting that I want to follow up on."

"Okay, you guys all know I hate amateurs, but this Sidney Lake guy's different and don't you dare let him know I said that. I got two dead people and an officer of the law in the hospital. You see a lead, you follow it. And Sam, don't be bashful about asking for help. Patton and Kent here are ready to step in and help in any way. Right now I need that room protected for Cooper."

Before Sam could comment, Hornig's phone rang. It was Mayor Wilcox. Hornig and the mayor were not fond of one another, but they worked side by side when they had to.

Hornig said, "Hold on Steele. Sam, everybody, that's

all for now. We'll talk again later."

As they left the office, Sam gave the chief a quiet wave and indicated he would go straight down to the guest office in the basement.

Chief Hornig had no interest in talking with Mayor Wilcox. Unfortunately, unlike the Sheriff who owed his job to the whims of the voters of Coastal Rivers County, the chief of police of Morgan ran a police department and had to deal with a mayor who could demand his resignation at any time. Hornig liked his job, but he didn't like politics. The mayor, Steele Wilcox, lived and breathed politics and saw everything through the ever-changing kaleidoscope of the next election. Two people dead and one in the hospital made the people of Morgan uncomfortable and nervous citizens are unreliable voters. Wilcox wanted the Amos Dunn murder out of the headlines. He wanted it solved and quickly.

Much of the problem between Hornig and Wilcox re volved around their perceived self-images in the community. The chief of police considered himself a professional with an extensive background in both military and civilian policing. He looked on Wilcox as a jerk and an opportunist whose background revolved around the funeral parlor he inherited from his father. After obtaining all the certifications needed to run a funeral parlor in the state and taking a variety of courses designed to lead to a forensic science certification, Wilcox sold off his interest in the business to one of the national chains—for a substantial sum—and decided to run for coroner, as his entry vehicle into the world of public service. Although meeting the minimum requirements for coroner under South Carolina law, including being an official advisor to the county sheriff's office and the then county coroner—who decided to retire—it became clear to Chief Hornig that Steele Wilcox had no real interest in being a coroner. The chief predicted that Steele wanted something else but needed the coroner slot as a stepping stone. Steele Wilcox became the mayor of Morgan, SC last November.

Wilcox growled over the phone to Hornig, "Pete, what the hell is going on around here?"

With traffic detours in place around City Hall, it took Tillie and Hattie an additional ten minutes to make the drive back to Sidney's. The intense sun and rising temperatures of the approaching noon hour had driven Cal, Sidney and Mickey off the front porch and back to the comfort of the living room and air-conditioning.

"My goodness, it's getting hot out there," Tillie said as she came in the back entrance and into the kitchen. "It is that," Cal said. "We just came in. Mickey's the smart one. Just got up and stood in front of the door until we were forced to let her in and we followed her."

"Always figured she was the smart one in the group."

"Hah," laughed Cal. "I didn't know it showed."

Mickey struggled a bit as she got up to greet them. There was nothing wrong with her tail though, as it wagged enthusiastically and seemed to help propel her across the room to Tillie and Hattie.

"Ah," Sidney said as he twisted in his chair to see them. "I'll bet traffic is a real mess out there. Come on in, I'm dying to find out what you've learned."

Hattie spoke as they took up positions around Sidney. With the professor being somewhat immobilized, Tillie had rearranged the furniture so his visitors could surround him as he held court in his oversized chair. "We have a lot to tell."

Sidney asked, "Do you know what's going on over at City hall?"

"Pretty much," Tillie said. "Had a long chat with Hamp Butler. It's the coroner lady, Miss Coffey, she was attacked in that basement office they use in City Hall. Mister

Sam was on the phone with her when it happened."

Cal exclaimed, "So it *was* an ambulance I heard."

"Yeah, don't know how bad it is. Somebody gave her a pretty good bump on the head."

Cal got up. "I'll call the admitting desk in emergency. I'm sure I can get some information from them." He pulled his phone from his pocket and stepped to the other side of the room.

Sidney then took over. "How much was Hampton Butler able to tell you?"

"Well, some I got direct from him and some other I got from that radio thing he has on his uniform. Mister Hamp said they locked down alla City Hall. Nobody allowed in or out. I guess they think whoever did it is still in the building. Said Mister Sam heard her call out to someone in the office. She musta been in that little conference room next to the room the coroner uses. Probably workin' on somethin' in there. Wouldn't use the desk in the office. Doctor Cooper's kinda funny about anybody touchin' stuff in there. Even has a code for the copier behind the desk."

With a look of surprise Sidney said, "Hamp told you that?"

"No, he don't know anythin' about that. Eddie told me."

"Eddie?"

"He's the custodian for the building. All the cleaning supplies an' stuff is in a room across from Doctor Cooper's office. Office ain't used much. Only when there's somethin' goin' on upstairs where the coroner has to be at a meetin'. Although Eddie said he does find somebody uses the place off hours sometimes."

Sidney thought for a moment and then said, "So Mary Coffey wasn't expected to be there today?"

"Don't know. Didn't hear that either way. Have to wait for Miss Coffey to wake up to find out."

"Maybe not. Didn't you say that Sam was on the phone with her when she was attacked?"

"That's what Mister Hamp said."

"So, he knew where she was."

Hattie said, "Not if he called her on her cell phone."

"But he gave her the book. Where did they meet for him to do that? Did she come to the store and receive it directly from Grace? Did Sam and Mary go off in different directions—Sam to the meeting with you and Mary to City hall?"

"Mister Sam would know."

The conversation continued among the three of them: Sidney, Hattie and Tillie. They explored the events of the morning while Cal continued speaking first to the emergency admissions desk and then a good friend at the emergency room nurses station. Cal learned that Mary woke up in the ambulance, but only briefly. After being rolled into a treatment room she awoke again and spoke to the physician attending her. After some tests were completed, she slept.

Sidney sat quietly with his hands in the church steeple position on his chest. Putting pieces together he began to get a sense of a larger problem, one that involved those who worked at the City Hall building itself. Small towns were notorious for having somewhat porous systems that local officials could manipulate to their advantage. Two murders and an attack on a county official, could it all be a cover up of wrongdoing of some type? He wondered if what Amos discovered could lead to something rotten in City Hall. The book of numbers turned out to be a book of house and license plate numbers and Tillie had now discovered something else, something that could tie everything together—a date code. It seemed Amos had an unusual way of writing the date. He used all numbers and no spacing, putting the year first—all four digits—and then the month and day using two numbers each, ending up with 20141015. She learned this in the meeting with William Dunn and Sam Cashman. Mark Beasley, the accountant murdered in Amos' house, suggested it as a good way to be able to list items by date so they could be sorted chronologically across multiple years. Amos liked the idea and used it on everything. Including his now famous book-of-numbers.

Tillie's phone rang and she checked the caller I.D. before she said, "Sorry, Professor Lake. It's William Dunn. I think I better take it." She got up from her chair and moved across the room toward the windows that looked toward the front porch and Howard Street. She could see the heat rising from the street and, as she answered, a woman on the sidewalk stopped and opened the umbrella she carried for protection from the pop-up thunder storms that had been forecast. She would use it to create her own island of shade.

"Mister William, what's up?"

As Tillie spoke with William Dunn, Sidney inquired about Cal's call to the emergency room. "So they think she'll be all right?"

"I would say yes, based on the way my contact framed his answer to my question. There are certain nuances you pick up. They're not supposed to give information to non-relatives, but there's a number of ways to answer other than yes or no. The clergy in town have discussed this and each of us have our own contacts in the emergency room. It's almost a code we've worked out. In this case, so far, things look pretty good."

Cal's phone rang. The pastor peeked at his phone and, seeing the I.D. for his church, Cal held up his hand to indicate he had to take the call. "Hello, Alice…Yes, I'm still at Sidney's…Oh, I'm sorry to hear that…Yes, I'll be leaving right away…I'll come back to the office first anyway.

I walked over. My car's in the parking lot…Thanks Alice."

"Problem?" Sidney said.

"Yes. Mrs. Woodwright is on her way to Doctor Cooper's Medic-aide place. Looks like she may have broken her leg in a fall. She's in her eighties so anything like this is serious. I'm going over there right away."

"You go right ahead, Cal. I'll keep you up to date on everything that goes on here. Why is she going to Cooper's instead of the Emergency Room at the hospital?"

"It's a long story. She was Old Doctor Cooper's patient and she won't see anyone but his son. I'll tell you the story when I get back. As long as I'm heading in the direction, I'll stop in and check on Mary Coffey at the hospital."

As Cal headed out the front door, Tillie finished her conversation with William Dunn and came over to rejoin Sidney and Hattie. She had a serious look on her face as though she was trying to piece together the information she just learned. Something seemed to be really bothering her.

Chapter 19

Thinking about numbers

Tillie's relationship with William Dunn began as one of suspicion on William's part. Not because of anything Tillie said or did, but because William, born and raised in Philadelphia, had a natural suspicion about people he didn't know. Anyone he met that was from outside of his natural comfort zone would be kept at arm's length until his gut made a decision about them. Big city people were like that and Tillie knew it, so her approach followed a time-tested pattern of actions speak louder than words. She demonstrated real caring about William's great uncle Amos and adopted the same manner with William. She wanted to help. She wanted to protect. Having people you don't know do something nice for you just because it's the right thing to do, well, such occurrences were uncommon in the world William Dunn knew best. The meeting earlier with Sam Cashman proved to be a change maker. Tillie stood with him against the badge in the suit across the table. Not that he didn't trust Sam Cashman. No, Sam came across as straight forward and honest. It was the badge he carried that made him cautious, regardless of Sam's skin color.

Tillie realized something had changed when she took

the call from William—his voice changed. No longer the halting suspicion, he spoke openly and freely.

"Tillie, I did what you suggested and called Uncle Amos' doctor and you were right. He had no idea about the tumor. Uncle Amos wasn't too high on doctors to begin with and the last time he saw one was about a year and a half ago. Doctor Clark, that's who he goes to over on Deer Island, said he only found out about the tumor because Mary Coffey called him to get Amos Dunn's medical records. She told him what she found and promised to send him a copy of her report. The main thing is I don't think Uncle Amos knew."

"I think you're right."

"Another point, I don't think Uncle Amos thought he had Alzheimer's."

"But what about the book?" Tillie asked.

"We're over thinking it. Tell Professor Lake that Uncle Amos liked to play mind games just for fun. Although I have a feeling he already knows that. Amos told me a number of times that he loved going to Rotary meetings because he liked to needle the members who were ninety percent white and eighty percent Republican. He often made challenging remarks with a smile, but with a stinger hidden inside. Oh, how he did enjoy needling them."

"But what does the book have to do with it all?"

"I'm convinced it all started out as one of his mind games, but then he saw something and everything changed. The Alzheimer's explanation was just a ruse, a cover-up for what he was doing. For something he discovered."

"But what was it?"

"I don't know, but the key has to be in his office. That's why Mark Beasley was killed. That's why Amos' office was ransacked."

Tillie finally asked, "Is there any other place where

Amos might be keeping somethin' other than his office?"

"He had a safe-deposit box, but I haven't seen what's in it yet. I'm not a signatory so I can't get into it."

"Mister William, I appreciate all this and I'll tell Professor Lake, if it's okay?"

"Tillie, please do. Use your judgement. I trust you. And if I can help in any way, I will. Uncle Amos stumbled onto something. Something that got him killed."

As Tillie ended the call, Sidney watched her. "Everything okay, Tillie?"

"Yes." She reworked the conversation with William Dunn as she came back to her seat near Hattie and Sidney.

Sidney said, "William figured something out didn't he?"

"Yes, he did," Tillie then went on to recount the conversation. "He said he wanted to help."

"Good. He's right about Amos liking to tweak the Rotary people—me included—but I figured out what he was doing and he knew it. He liked to challenge me on knowing living black writers instead of only dead white ones. We used to have some interesting conversations. There was always a bite to what he did."

Hattie couldn't resist, "I guess you two had a lot more in common than either one of you would like to admit."

"Oh, we knew it. Tillie, tell William to keep pushing with regard to the safe-deposit box. He may have a case for getting a look at what's in there if his father is the executor. The police, of course can get a court order and have it opened, but they have to have a reason and if they do they don't have to tell us what's in it. Also tell him to go over whatever business documents he received from Amos just to see if anything pops out that looks strange or doesn't make sense.

"Hattie do you have that pad you usually carry around with you?"

"Tillie has it. That's what she made the handwritten copy of the book pages on."

"Good. Tillie, quickly make two copies of what you wrote out. Use the printer in my office, it has a built-in copy feature. Just tear off the pages you need and give the pad to Hattie."

Tillie got up and walked across the entry hall to Sidney's office. "Keep talkin', I can hear you."

"Okay, the first thing I want to know is who lives on Pond Lane and who lives on George Street. Let's do George Street first since that location comes up on Amos' walk first. How many houses…. Let me change that. How many addresses are there on the left side of George Street as you walk south as Amos did?"

Hattie said, "I think there are only three."

Tillie called out from the other room, "That's right. Only three. The lots is bigger on that side of the street. They get smaller after you pass Pond Lane."

"Who lives there?" Sidney asked.

Silence.

"Tillie, any help?"

"Not really, Professor." The copier could be heard churning out page after page and Tillie raised her voice to be heard above the noise. "Don't think I've ever been in any of those places. There was a family by the name of Alston, in the middle house. Florence Mikel did housekeepin' for them, but they moved away 'bout five years ago. Sold to some folks from Charlotte and they redid the whole house last year—inside and out. Use it for a summer place. Don't know much about them."

"Find out who's in the other two addresses. How about the other side of the street?"

Tillie hesitated as she gathered up the papers from the copier. "Pretty sure there are four on that side. Good sized places but not like across the street. Doctor Cooper's is the most notable one. Been there forever. It's the third one down. Place next to him is a lawyer fella."

Hattie said, "I know him. He does some work for Morgan College and she volunteers at the Library. I'll think of the name. Go on."

Tillie came back into the room and handed Sidney the copied pages and the originals. "Don't know the other two."

Sidney kept writing on the pad as both Hattie and Tillie identified the property owners. "How about around the corner on Pond Land. I know McGraw of the City Hall Café lives in the one on the end by King Street."

Tillie thought for a moment before saying, "Mister Byron, the banker man, I'm sure he has one of the houses on the North side of the street. Doesn't use a housekeeper from the island. Somebody tole me she was foreign. Polish or somethin' like that. Worked for his wife's family. Came with them when they moved here. Don't really know much about her. Did hear Misses Byron came from oodles of money. Don't live like it though."

Sidney and Hattie just looked at her in amazement. Sidney couldn't resist. "Well, I'm glad to hear there's someone you don't know too much about, I can't imagine what the size of the dossier is that you have on us."

"Yeah, well I know what I know," she laughed. "Could find out more if you need it. Yola Carson works for Mister McGraw down the street."

"No, I think that's enough for now. Let's take another look at the pages from Amos' book and pick out more license plate numbers and addresses. See if we can make a relationship of one with the other."

"Sidney," Hattie said. "Before we do that, have you given any more thought as to why Amos was collecting license plate numbers to begin with? I mean, it's all well and good that we believe the Alzheimer's reason turned out to be a red herring, but what other reason could he have for writing all this stuff down?"

Sidney did not answer immediately, preferring to gather his thoughts first. Sitting around the living room trying to keep his leg out of trouble didn't fit in with his usual analysis technique. He should be cooking something. Messing around with one ingredient after the other clearing his mind for theories to run wild. He'd known from early on that the Alzheimer's excuse was just that, an excuse that allowed Amos to pursue putting pieces of something together. But what?

"All right. Let's go down that avenue. What do we really know about Amos Dunn? I mean what were his likes and dislikes? What upset him? What were his hot button issues?"

Chapter 20

Pond Lane

illie spoke first, "I suppose you could say race, but that's too obvious. It's always race down here. So, no, I think we got to look at somethin' else. If there's one thing I remember really getting' Amos angry is old people bein' cheated. That would get him goin'."

"I didn't have a lot of interaction with Amos Dunn," Hattie said, "but I do remember hearing about one incident that I mentioned to you some time ago, Sidney. Remember the computer?"

"What computer?"

"Oh, it was about a year ago. I was just chatting with one of the women who worked in the cafeteria kitchen at Morgan College and she told me she was having trouble coming up with the money to repair her son's computer. He was in middle school. The school has a program to provide all the students in the school with those inexpensive computers they use. Well, it didn't work. Her son couldn't do his assignments and she didn't have the money to have it repaired."

"Yes, now I think I remember that. But how does Amos fit into it?"

"Well, she told him what happened and he said he'd take care of it. I didn't really think much about it until a few days later when I ran into her again. She said Amos got the computer fixed for her. I was curious how he managed it and she said Amos explained that the Morgan School System had a repair contract with a company over in Beaufort where she took her son's computer to be repaired. The owner of the company lives here in Morgan. Amos called him direct and discovered the owner was taking advantage of the woman by charging her for the repair and then billing the school system as well. The owner claimed it was all just an honest mistake and the computer would be repaired without charge to anyone. Although Amos managed to get everything straightened out, he still gave the owner a piece of his mind. He also reported him to the school system. I'm pretty sure he ended up losing the service contract, as this wasn't the first complaint they had."

"Yes, yes, now I remember it all." Sidney sat up in his chair and moved his knee too quickly. "Ooowh."

"What did you do?" Tillie said,

"Damn knee. Twisted it. Never mind. I remember this. There were some people at Rotary made some comments about the owner losing the contract. Said it was unfair. Defended the owner. Sat at a table with Chief Hornig one Wednesday who said flat out 'Don't bother. He's a crook.' Seems he was preying on poor families. Would try it every time with them and if they didn't know better or were intimidated he'd double charge them. Hornig also said the Beaufort police had him on filing fraudulent warranty claims on items he didn't own. Told the owners there was no warranty. Then he'd file a claim after the customer paid for the repair or he'd get a replacement part free and then charge the customer for it."

Hattie said, "So maybe there is a racial component?"

"Hornig didn't think so. Thought he was an equal opportunity crook. Just took advantage of anyone he thought wouldn't have the gumption to report him. If they objected, he'd apologize for the mistake and refund the money. Wonder if he lives over by George Street some place?"

"Oh, they's a racial part to it. You bet. This is the sneaky stuff."

"You mean 'subliminal' racism?"

"That's the word. Way to make sure black students don't get the same advantages as the white. Like they do with votin'. Claim lots of fraud goin' on when there isn't. Yeah, seems to be a racial piece to everythin' lately." Tillie thought for a minute and then began again. "Well maybe that's not really fair. Mindy Dahut, who works at the City Hall Café, she just went to work there because that Mister McGraw is a good man—honest and fair. She used to work for that fancy fish place down on the Morgan River until the owner started deducting waitress' tips to cover the minimum wage he was payin'. Lot a folks had words with him about it. Wouldn't be surprised if Amos got in on that as well. Wonder where *he* lives. Although I guess all the sneaky people can't live on Pond Lane."

"You just said Ted McGraw is a good person and he lives on Pond Lane."

Tillie said with a smile, "Well, they say the exception proves the rule."

Sidney finally found a comfortable position again. "We really have to get a list of all the people living on Pond Lane and George Street. I have a feeling that Amos was on to something that made one or more people very uncomfortable."

Hattie agreed and said, "Between Tillie's cleaning ladies and my college contacts—I know there are some college people over there—we can probably put a list together in an hour."

"How 'bout lunch?"

Everyone looked at Tillie.

"Everybody's got to eat sometime. It's after one. Let's just ease off. We's just runnin' around like chickens with no heads. Got to do some thinkin'. Let's all move into the kitchen an' eat there. Professor, you always say you think better when they's food around an' we need to think things through. That's probably why the police around here miss so much—work through lunch too often."

Tillie prevailed and the three of them made their way to the kitchen table.

Cal Prentice wasted no time in getting back to the church office and following up on Mrs. Woodwright. His secretary had all the information waiting for him. While everyone else in town may have difficulty in finding out information about patients at the hospital, Alice, like Tillie, had her own network in place—one of the EMS workers sang in the church choir. Although Mrs. Woodwright had given the EMS people instructions to take her to Dr. Cooper's emergency medical clinic, they said they had no choice but to take her to the Emergency Room at Central Memorial Hospital. All the way to the hospital she kept saying she promised Dr. Cooper that she would always go to him for everything as she always did. She trusted him just like she trusted his father, Old Dr. Cooper. EMS prevailed citing regulations that required her to be brought to the emergency room. Once there they would notify Dr. Cooper.

After arriving at the hospital, Cal called Sidney and advised him of all he learned. "It was very interesting, the way she kept talking about Doctor Cooper. I've seen it before, of course. The lifeline syndrome. At least that's what I call it. She believes Cooper keeps her alive. She has complete and total trust in him."

"I know what you mean," Sidney said. "I guess it's not uncommon when you're old and alone. Alone in the sense of living alone, no one else in the house or apartment. You may have someone look in on you from time to time or call you on the phone, but it's not the same. That's why pets become so important. A cat or a dog or a bird is a living thing to converse with, to listen to you, to sit with you, to comfort you. Your pastor and your doctor evolve into authority figures—one to guide your spiritual existence and the other your physical one. They have an enormous influence in the life of the elderly, especially the ones that are alone. Will you stop back when you're finished there?"

"Yes. Her son has been called and he's on his way. Alice said she'll come over and stay with her for a while. They'll keep her here until her son arrives. The wrist is definitely broken, she can't stay alone. Hopefully he'll take her back to Atlanta with him."

The phone conversation continued for a short while longer and then ended.

Hattie said, "I take it from what I overheard she's okay. Or, at least they have everything under control?"

"Yes. It does make me think though. This was one of Amos' hot topics. The vulnerability of the elderly."

"In what way?"

"Trust. The elderly tend to trust authority figures more, simply because they become more dependent on them."

Tillie looked at Sidney. "You got an' idea?"

"I got an idea. Get those pages from the book of numbers and spread them out on the table and bring back the pad and pencil with you. Hattie, you have your laptop in that bag of yours?"

"Yes."

"We'll need it."

The items Sidney asked for were assembled quickly on

the cleared kitchen table. As Tillie and Hattie maneuvered around the kitchen and the living room, Sidney sat—quietly.

"Hattie, bring up Pond Lane and George Street on Google Earth." He finally said as all three were seated again. "Tillie, let's put addresses on each building and start matching them with licenses plates and dates."

They began in earnest to map out the area. Hattie drew lines on her pad indicating George Street and then started adding boxes representing each house on the street. Tillie called one of her housekeeping friends who worked for one of the houses on the east side of George Street. Sidney worked with the copy of the book-of-numbers and identified the house numbers on the east side, which were all odd numbers starting with three. Since the lots were larger, the houses were listed as three, seven, and thirteen. On the other side of the street there were four houses with the largest one being Dr. Cooper's. It had a large Victorian style wrap around porch that covered three sides of the building. Toward the rear, the office addition that Old Dr. Cooper put on stood out into the driveway. No longer used as a medical office, it now served as a private den and library for the current Dr. Cooper. It did, however, keep a door off the den that opened directly to the driveway.

The house next to Cooper's looked like a slightly smaller version of it with the same wrap around porch but built fifty years later than Cooper's. The same was true of the next two although they had attached garages. At one time all of the property belonged to Old Dr. Cooper, but he had to sell off lots to survive during the depression.

With the basics laid out, they now began to match up the house numbers with the license plate numbers and dates.

Sidney started a second sheet of paper on which he started to raise some questions. He wrote down three columns: *What were Amos' hot topics? 1. Taking advantage of the elderly. 2. Taking advantage of the poor. 3. Subliminal racism.* Under the three categories he started to list the ways the heading topic occurred. Under the elderly he listed: *money, health.* Under poor he listed: *money, jobs, scams, lottery, gambling.* Under racism he listed: *housing, education, jobs and vote suppression.*

Tillie observed, "If you're black, elderly and poor, things sure are stacked against you."

"Maybe so, Tillie," Hattie said, "but if you're old and poor the color of your skin isn't going to make a difference. The people preying on the vulnerable are usually equal opportunity low-life's who are more interested in the color of your money than your skin."

"Yeah, I know, but Amos was black. The people who come to his store are black. The store's in a black neighborhood. He was killed in his store. I may be wrong, but I got to believe that blacks got somethin' to do with it."

Sidney looked up and said, "Don't argue with Tillie's logic. I've tried. She usually sees pretty clearly while the rest of us keep looking for things that aren't there or miss what's staring us in the face. Keep it simple. Pay attention to what's going on around us and question everything. Never assume it doesn't matter and never assume someone couldn't be involved."

Hattie gave a reluctant nod of agreement. "Lesson learned. Speaking about the obvious, what about all this forensic data I see on television? Maybe the police have some leads we don't know about."

"Oh, I'm sure they do. The smart thing Mary Coffey did was to bring in the state lab people right away. They went over the store and Amos' home with the usual fine-tooth comb. Given the way the place was covered with the wine from the bottle that killed him, I'm sure they have at least a partial footprint, and the murderer's clothes would be full of wine stains. Maybe blood as well. I'm also sure that the clothes and shoes are long gone given that it's been a week now since the attack. Amos' house would be a different matter. It was being searched by the murderer, but even if he had those plastic gloves on they wouldn't have held up in a fight and there are all sorts of possibilities for forensic evidence.

"However, the approach the police are taking is only one way to get to the desired end. They will come up with the evidence to prosecute someone. My interest is in motivation as the way to find the reason for killing Amos in the first place and to search his home in the second. The killing of Mark Beasley I believe is a case of being in the wrong place at the wrong time, but it may reveal the most useful physical evidence. Which brings us back to Amos' book-of-numbers. I believe it's the one solid lead that will get us to motivation, but it's not the only one. There's something nagging at me. Something that you, Tillie, mentioned. I just can't bring it out. It'll pop out sooner or later, let's just hope it's sooner."

Chapter 21

Analyzing the list

Sidney looked across the kitchen table at Tillie and Hattie. "So who do we know for sure lives on George Street and Pond Lane? And let's put labels on them. What do they do for a living? How would Amos view them based on what they do?"

"Mmm. Mister McGraw lives on the corner of Pond Lane and King Street. Owns the City Hall Café." Tillie paused as she visualized Ted McGraw—tall, kind of slim, grey hair, easy going, smiled and laughed a lot. "Most people like him. Haven't heard anythin' bad about him. People who work for him don't seem to have any complaints. See no reason Amos and him would have a problem."

Sidney said, "Hattie what do you think?"

"Agree with Tillie. Seems fine on the surface. Don't really know anything about his personal life. Don't know if he has any other business interest in town other than the café. Runs a good restaurant. Not a woman's place. You know, it's more like a diner than the sort of place women congregate for lunch. More a man's place."

"In going through the pages of Amos's book, I don't see anything that matches McGraw's address. Who else is on Pond Lane?"

"That Mister Byron from the bank is two doors down. Since time began bankers' been trouble. Betcha not too many of 'em gets through that 'eye of the needle' thing."

Sidney looked at Tillie for a moment and said, "As usual, you've made a rather interesting observation about the human race. Most of the trouble in the world throughout history comes from those that control the wealth and those that don't have any."

"Perhaps," observed Hattie, "but the same analogy could be made about those who have power and those that seek it."

Tillie had the final word. "Yeah, but the way I see it power and money kinda go together. Those politician people may have power, but it's the money part that gets them into trouble. Fact is you could say that about most things."

"True, Tillie," Sidney said with a small grin.

The three friends were silent for a moment as they looked at the sheets of paper in front of them.

Time passed slowly as the pages were marked and turned. No one spoke. It became so quiet that the silence woke Mickey, who had been lulled to sleep by the constant drone of their voices. She raised her head to see what changed, carefully raised herself up, turned around two times and they settled down again beside Sidney's chair.

After a few minutes, Tillie observed, "I'm lookin' at four addresses. Three of 'um I know, but not the other one."

Hattie said, "Same here. Four addresses."

"Agreed. Four. How about license plates?"

More silence as pencils picked out numbers and letters and circled them. Some blank sheets from the yellow pad were removed and passed around. More notations.

Sidney spoke first, "I'm looking at two sets of plates that show up at two of the addresses multiple times."

"Same here."

"Me too."

Hattie said, "Do you think that Hornig's people are do-ing the same thing that we are?"

"Oh, I'm sure of it. Sam received the original from Grace at the market and he passed it on to Mary Coffey. The forensic people are probably going over it from every angle they can think of. What I'm not sure of is the non-technical part. As with everything else these days, there is a belief that science and technology is the primary path to solutions. It's what will convict the guilty. It's what will cut costs. It's what will assure quality. It's logical. It's im-partial. It's flawed.

"We human beings are unique in our consistency in be-ing illogical. Unpredictability is a hallmark trait we all share. When we are expected to act in our own best interest we often do not. When we are expected to act in the inter-est of others and the greater good—we consistently fail. We have irresistible impulses that move us in directions that are diametrically opposed to everything we profess to believe. Random acts of good or evil do not exist, they are deeply imbedded in the soul.

"Amos Dunn was a champion of those he felt were be-ing taken advantage of, but he was not a kind and gentle soul. He was aggressive, confrontational, opinionated and gave no quarter when confronted. When righting a wrong, the concept of collateral damage would be unknown to him. For the most part he was liked and appreciated, but not loved. In his zeal, I believe he confronted someone who sought compromise, someone not unknown to vio-lence, but someone acting in a way inconsistent with his or her image."

Sidney stopped. Quiet enveloped the room.

Tillie finally said, "Well, I think you got a picture of Amos. I can't disagree with it. So what do we do?"

"We need to know who owns those cars that show up on a repetitive basis at the four houses we identified. I only wish we had Ray Morton here to help us."

Hattie gave Sidney a stern look and said, "Well, why don't we just ask him? I know you said you didn't want to disrupt his vacation, but hell, I already did that when I called him and told him what was going on. Look, he used to be Chief Hornig's right-hand man before retiring. He knows everybody in city government and the state as well. If he asked for something, he'd get it. What do we have to lose?"

Sidney sat back. The left arm went across his chest and the right hand started stroking his chin. Should he do this? He knew Ray Morton would jump at the chance to get in the middle of everything, but his wife Marie—Sidney didn't want to make an enemy of her. Although, with only twenty-four hours left in their vacation maybe Marie wouldn't mind too much.

Ray, on the other hand, had no intention of waiting for a specific invitation from Sidney and had been monitoring events on the internet by reading all he could in the local and regional newspapers. In fact, Ray, on his own, checked with detective Patton to get an inside opinion of the investigation's status.

"You're right, Hattie, I'll call him right now."

Sidney and Ray Morton were an interesting pair. The retired professor and the retired policeman. Two busybodies with time on their hands. Both noted for interfering in the affairs of others. Ray Morton couldn't stay away from City Hall and Sidney couldn't stay away from anything else.

Their telephone conversation focused on the business at hand. There were no niceties about how Ray and Marie were enjoying their vacation or how Sidney's knee felt, although Ray did ask about Mickey. Ray had already learned about the attack on Mary Coffee, which did surprise Sidney, but he was more interested in what the police thought of it. Detective Patton, who would be up for retirement soon, had coffee with Ray almost every morning at the City Hall Café, along with the former City Manager. There were no secrets among them when it came to Morgan City politics.

Sidney now found out that he had the only workable copy of Amos' book-of-numbers and confided the fact to Ray, as well as how he obtained it. Ray was sure that the shredded book could be reconstituted based on what he heard from Patton, but he advised Sidney that it would be best for him to get a copy of what he had into police hands. If he didn't he could be facing an obstruction of justice complaint, even though he was working with a copy. Once they had the original reconstituted, the handwritten copy would not be a factor. Ray told him to contact Patton.

Ray also learned a few things from Sidney when he heard what they were doing with the license plate numbers and the addresses. He asked that Hattie fax the numbers to him of all the cars that were listed at the four addresses.

Sidney's being chair bound proved to be an asset, as Ray knew Hattie to be more computer literate than Sidney. At one point he asked that Hattie be put on the phone so he could tell her how to obtain the owner's name for the other addresses on George Street and Pond Lane. It was all public information online obtainable through the assessor's office website. He gave Hattie his access code if she needed it, but explained that she could sign up for her own if she didn't have one by registering with the assessor's office.

Hattie and Tillie immediately started working together on the laptop while Tillie organized the addresses for both streets.

With access to Ray Morton becoming available, Sidney

started asking the questions he had wanted to ask all week.

"What can you tell me about any involvement you may have had with Amos Dunn from a police standpoint? I know you've been away from the department for almost five years, but I also know you discuss just about everything with your old colleagues. What I'm particularly interested in, is situations where he became involved with trying to protect others. We know of a few specific situations and we have a feel for what would be his hot button issues, but we need a motive for what has been going on and we just don't have it yet. I also assume Hornig and his people don't have it yet either?"

After a moment Ray responded. "Well, you're right about the last part. Hornig's been pulling his hair out over this. To be honest, he'd love to have a copy of the book you've been working with."

"I thought he did when Grace gave the original to Sam. What's mystifying is how someone else found out about Mary Coffey having the original."

"Agreed. Hornig had Sam Cashman trace the path of information about finding the book. They knew who handled the book from the time the repairman found it until Coffey brought it downstairs to the coroner's office. They know who touched the book but not who the repairman told about it and where the information went from there."

"But there's part of what you call the touch route they don't know about."

"Whoa...that's right. Tillie got a look at it and made her copy, but Grace said it never left the storeroom." Silence.

"Sidney. What don't I know?"

Silence

Sidney knew he had to tell Ray what he had done. They were always honest with one another. It would have worked out just fine if Mary Coffey hadn't been attacked.

But she had. Sidney hadn't anticipated that. How could he? But he didn't want to get anyone else in trouble. He thought about saying that he made the copies, but he couldn't. He had an injured knee and besides Alice Ringfoot saw Tillie making copies. Presumably Alice didn't know it was Amos' book but...

"Okay, what happened is this." Sidney told Ray the whole story of how the book was copied and put back.

"Wow."

"I know what you're thinking, but there are no prints on the book other than Amos's and the repair man and, possibly, Grace's."

Silence.

"Wow." Ray said again. "Sidney, how do you get yourself into things like this?"

"I have a personal stake in this, Ray."

"Sidney, I know. But jeez, this could be a real problem. There are a lot of people involved at this point."

"Which makes it all the more important that we solve this. Is it at all possible that we can keep this quiet? Let it go as long as Hornig's people can reassemble the original book?"

"Maybe. I have to think about this. No one can swear that the book left the storeroom?"

"No one knows the book left the storeroom except Tillie, Hattie and me."

More silence.

"Look, Sidney, I'll use Patton as my conduit. He won't say anything to anyone. If he confirms that they've been able to put that book back together—and believe me they're working on it right now—we'll hold off until later this evening. What time is it now?"

"Just about two thirty."

"Let me talk to Patton again and I'll get back to you."

"Ray, one more question for you. Why Patton and not

Cashman?"

"Patton's not directly involved. He's just filling in where needed. He's working on something else as his primary. Sam's got his back to the wall and a lot on his shoulders. If he holds anything back for any reason he's gone. He's tracing the touch trail right now. If he comes up with something suspicious, then we'll deal with it."

"But you do trust him?"

"Oh yes. I would hate to see the town lose him, so let's not put him in more jeopardy than we have to."

It was Ray Morton who'd suggested that Sam Cashman think about joining the Morgan Police Department. Sam was only in high school at the time and planning to attend the Technical College of the Lowcountry in Beaufort, but hadn't decided on what he wanted to do with his life. Ray told him about the great courses TCL had if he had an interest in police work.

He did.

It took him four full-time semesters to get his certificate in Criminal Justice Technology and Chief Hornig welcomed him with open arms when he graduated.

"Another thought," Sidney said, "with regard to Amos and the police, have there been any formal complaints against him and if so, do any of those people live up on Pond Lane or George Street?"

"Interesting question. I know a way I can find out. I've still got time. We're not leaving for South Carolina until tomorrow. I take it you spotted something in the book-of-numbers that prompted the question?"

Chapter 22

Who owns what

A mos Dunn had a good many friends who looked favorably on his social advocacy positions but there were some who felt uneasy around him. His habit of painting perceived wrongs with a broad brush often resulted in as much criticism as praise. When complaining about a banker who talked a borrower into a loan they couldn't afford, he put all bankers in the same box. He blamed everyone in the bank for not standing up against corporate policy. He expected them to resign in protest.

The same was true in the way he treated lawyers and doctors when speaking with them. "Got to watch all of you people. If you refuse to stand up and point fingers at the bad ones, then you're lettin' them all get away. You're as bad as they are."

Fortunately, there were a few people in Morgan who saw it as their job to defend Amos Dunn.

Tillie and Hattie fervently searched the Assessor's Office database and printed out details about the four most likely properties. Sam Cashman was at the Cedar Street Market interviewing Grace Carter about not only who'd come in contact with the book-of-numbers from the time the repairman found it, but also who else she told about it. He also called the repairman to find out to whom he had mentioned it.

There had to be a connection somewhere to City Hall.

Six hundred miles away Ray Morton sat in his hotel room working his computer and cell phone in an attempt to obtain the ownership of the cars with the identified license plates.

The forensic team at City Hall continued to put together the pieces of the book from the shredder.

Sidney Lake sat and Mickey dozed. Thinking and planning were Sidney's strong points. Dozing was Mickey's. Everyone doing what they did best.

The chair in the living room did not usually play the role of Sidney's preferred thinking spot. His library housed his real thinking chair. Positioned carefully in a special corner, where he could be surrounded by two sets of encyclopedias and shelf after shelf of reference books. He felt at a disadvantage being stuck in his living room.

He needed to think quietly. Uninterrupted.

Tillie and Hattie worked away noisily at the dining room table. The drone of their comments and chatter occasionally interrupting his thoughts.

Sidney did his best to block out everything around him. Finally, almost trance like, he envisioned what happened at the Cedar Street Market.

The intruder looked out a window from somewhere on Church Street and saw Amos chatting with the pastor of St. Luke's. He followed Amos for a block and then caught up to him. They walked together to the store.

There was Amos Dunn opening the front door. A man stood behind him. They chatted as they came in. "Amos, I appreciate you're doing this for me. I was sure I put coffee and those sweetener packets on the list for the Wednesday night supper. It's my job to make the coffee and I realized we didn't have any decaf. And I wouldn't put coffee full of caffeine into a decaf jug and try to fool everybody."

Amos said, "You know I've seen people do that. Was at that new Jamaican coffee bar on Carteret Street in Beaufort about a week ago and spotted the young kid behind the counter mixing regular and decaf to fill the decaf jug. Boy, I was all over him in a flash. Never knew what hit him. The high school kid didn't see it as a problem. I told him. Told him I would tell his boss too."

Sidney reviewed the scene he just created. What's right and what's wrong with it he questioned? No. There's something wrong. The distance. That's it. Too much distance between St. Luke's and the market. Best place to catch up with him would be at the corner of Queen and Cedar. Amos would be heading to his house on Queen Street and the market is just a block and a half away on Cedar. Makes more sense.

He continued visualizing the meeting.

Okay, so where they initially met probably doesn't matter. Someone could have called him on his cell phone and arranged the meeting at the store. The reason could still be valid.

They meet in front of the store and quickly go inside. Amos turns on the light.

"Have the coffee right over here. Keep the breakfast fixins together. Cereal on one side and coffee on the other."

"Say Amos what's that book you keep writin' in?"

Wait, no need for the light. The Ambers were coming up Cedar Street after leaving the restaurant. They would have seen the light go on. There was a night light over the check-out counter area. Plenty of visibility like it was on the night Sidney and Mickey were attacked. Cancel the light. Besides Amos knew where everything was. He didn't need anything but the night light.

Important question to get answered: Did Amos restock the shelves at the end of the day? Was something out of place that wouldn't be there just because of his being hit and fallen against some shelves? Need to check with Grace on that point.

Sidney kept visualizing everything as he sat in his chair.

"You seem awful quiet in there Professor Lake. Professor Lake?" Tillie leaned over to Hattie and whispered, "He's either asleep or he's figured somethin' out."

"I'll bet on the latter. With all the rest he's had the last few days, I don't think he's sleeping."

"No, I'm not," Sidney said without moving a muscle.

"So whatcha figured out?"

"There was nothing impulsive about the murder of Amos Dunn. I believe this was a well-planned and premeditated act of violence. It was carefully orchestrated to appear that Amos and his killer had an argument and the killer, in a rage, impulsively attacked Amos and killed him. However, the murder of Mark Beasley was definitely impulsive and unintentional."

Sidney turned slightly in his chair and looked at the two women working at the dining room table. "Could you join me here for a few minutes? I have questions and I need to talk some things out."

A knock, both forceful and urgent, sounded at the front door.

All heads in the room turned.

"Wonder who that is?" said Tillie. "We do have a bell."

As she went to get up Sidney took hold of her arm, "Verify who's at the door before you open it."

Tillie looked at him in surprise.

Hattie said, "Really? Is something going on?"

"Just be careful," Sidney said. "Just be careful."

Tillie got up just as the knock came again. This time louder. She made her way to the door, but before putting her hand on the knob she peeked out through the curtain covering the side light.

"It's Mister Sam."

Tillie commented as she opened the door. "You're certainly in a hurry."

"Where's Sidney?" he said as he brushed by her. "Oh, there." Spotting Sidney and Hattie in the living room. "I got a bone to pick with you." And he marched into the room. "What do ya mean withholding evidence from me? You could be locked up fo' this."

Tillie knew they were in trouble the moment he heard Sam's careful and measured way of speaking desert him.

"I know what you're going to say, Sam...."

"You bet you do."

"But wait. We didn't delay anything or interrupt anything."

"You sure did."

"It took no more than fifteen minutes for Tillie to copy what was in that book. She had gloves on the whole time and the book had been bagged so no damage would come to it. Grace didn't see her do it and had no idea a copy was made. We told her to put it in the storeroom where it would be safe. Grace called you the moment she could." Sidney had anticipated Sam finding out about the copy of the book and carefully phrased his answer to make sure Grace would not be implicated.

"Where's the copy now?"

Hattie answered. "It's in the folder on the dining room table. How did you know we had a copy and why does it matter, you have the original."

Tillie went to the table and got the folder with the handwritten copy in it while shifting some papers over the photographed copy.

"The original's been destroyed."

Sidney feigned shock, "What!"

Sam calmed down. "Mary Coffey was attacked at the coroner's office in city hall as she was copying the book. Whoever did it also shredded the book. We're trying to reconstruct it, but in the meantime, you have the only copy."

Tillie said, "So that's what all the ruckus was downtown. Miss Hattie an' me were downtown earlier and saw all the mess. Didn't know what had happened. Figured it was important though."

"Look Sam, I know I probably shouldn't have done what I did, but given the spot you people are in, I'm glad we made that copy. From what I can tell, it sheds some serious light on what and why Amos Dunn was murdered."

Sam took the folder from Tillie. "What have you people been doing? What else in on that table over there?"

He headed for the dining room.

"You've been deciphering the numbers in the book?"

Tillie said, "They's house and license plate numbers. Amos was trackin' people who went to certain houses."

Sam opened the folder in his hand and then started looking at the other material scattered around the table. He looked at the "Google Earth" printouts of George Street and Pond Lane with the names of the owners on them.

Chapter 23

Confrontation

Sam knew of Sidney Lake's reputation for having a bulldog's determination when it came to never giving up on anything once he got his teeth into it. However, he hadn't anticipated that Sidney would be able to get ahead of him in an investigation. After all, Sam had the investigative capabilities of the police department and the coroner's office on his side.

All that technology.

All that manpower.

He was surprised when Sidney and Tillie said they saw Amos Dunn's book-of-numbers as the key to everything that happened and followed its trail all over town. When he realized they were actually ahead of the police and had figured out the book's meaning, Sam was not only embarrassed but also pissed off.

It took him a couple of minutes to cool down.

"Okay. Somehow, I should have known something like this would happen. Chief Hornig kinda warned me it would, but I thought I was close enough to you that I wouldn't be surprised. So much for that." Sam sat down at the dining room table and pushed some of the papers around with his finger. "Can we all just sit down and talk about this? I'll level with you and you do the same."

Sidney made a motion to get up out of the chair. Given the anger that Sam expressed, Sidney had no intention of playing prima donna by forcing everyone to come to him, even though that's exactly what he preferred.

The knee hurt. There had to be something more involved than a simple sprain. Although being as overweight as he was, he knew any twist or unplanned stress would have more severe consequences than it would for someone of a reasonable weight. He needed to have it looked at again, but not now. Sidney knew his restricted mobility would not be an impediment to his gathering information, as long as everyone was willing to come to him.

Seeing the attempted move by Sidney, Tillie made a quick move to help him. It's what she did. She, more and more, saw him as her charge, her responsibility and she stood ready to respond to the challenge.

Once everyone was settled around the dining room table Sam began, "Okay, just what do you have and where do you think you're going with it? And keep in mind that we haven't been sitting around doing nothing. There are a lot of things that you don't know about—technical stuff. Mary Coffey has been very busy and so have the state forensic people. So okay, let's hear it."

The three amateurs around the table looked at one another. Hattie and Tillie deferred to Sidney.

"All right Sam, let me recap a few things. Some of this you already know, but I think it bears repeating. The key to everything that happened revolves around the twilight walks of Amos Dunn. Why did he take it? Why did he begin to take notes in a small spiral notebook? Why did he try to disguise the information in the book?"

At this point, Sam took out his own notebook and opened it to a clean page. "Go on," he said.

Sidney began again. "There are four main events that are tied together, the murder of Amos Dunn, the murder of Mark Beasley, the attack on me and the attack on Mary Coffey in City Hall. I also believe the link is tied to a series of meetings held on George Street."

Sam made as though he wanted to interrupt and Sidney raised his hand to stop him, "Let me finish a couple of points and then you can add your technical information and we'll see how it all fits together."

Sam relaxed in his chair, but it was quite clear he wanted to jump in.

Hattie and Tillie sat quietly, although Hattie glanced at the papers in front of her and moved some of them around so she could peek at them as Sidney talked.

Sidney shifted in his chair slightly and repositioned his knee as he spoke, "So why did Amos Dunn take his twilight walks? Because he felt like it. No real mystery here. He was tired after a long day at the market. He knew he was slowing down—age wise—and although he had some local help, he just decided it was time for him to retire. That's why he wanted someone in the family to take over the business from him. He decided it was time to smell the roses as they say, and one day after he made the nightly deposit at the bank just kept walking. He looked at the trees, smelled the sea air, felt the first cool breezes of early evening and chatted comfortably with tourists and locals alike.

"Now how do I know this?

"He told fellow Rotary members about it. He told William Dunn about it. He told Grace Carter about it and—I'm sure—a lot of other people. The main question is when did the twilight walks change from relaxation to compulsion and why?

"It changed because he had become observant. He no longer rushed from one place to another. He met some of the same people on a regular basis and saw events occur at the same times. Dogs being taken for a walk. The mail being picked up after someone came home from work. A car being pulled into a driveway. He saw and remembered and asked himself questions."

"And the book?" questioned Sam.

"Ah, yes, the book. I believe the nature of his daily walks changed because he observed a strange pattern that intrigued him. Amos became curious about it, so much so that he decided to record what he saw. He also worked out the Alzheimer's excuse to cover what he was doing. He wrote down activity all along his route, but concentrated on a few specific addresses. When asked about the book, he used the memory testing excuse."

Sam was now actively taking notes. "What were the addresses?"

Hattie picked up one of the pieces of paper in front of her and responded. "There are four. Two we've clearly identified and two we haven't. The two we've identified are both doctors. Doctor Cooper's place and Doctor Anderson's." She moved the paper over so Sam could see it.

Sam looked puzzled. "Cooper I obviously know, but I'm not familiar with Anderson."

Tillie noticed Sidney shift his knee again and said, "Moved here about three years ago. Works on feet. Has an office in Beaufort and another one in Bluffton."

"A podiatrist?" Sidney offered.

"Yeah, that's what they call him. Does all kina stuff with people's feet and then sends the bills off to the gov'mnt like they all do."

Sam said, "And you don't have any information on the other two?"

"Haven't looked them up yet," Tillie said. "Got an idea about one of um. They're next on the list."

"Where are you doing the look up?"

"Assessor's office online," said Hattie. "You can keep that paper I gave you. I have the names and addresses on another sheet."

"Humph." Sam stopped writing and sat back in his chair. "You getting some extra help on this?"

Tillie and Hattie looked at Sidney.

Sidney said, "Ray Morton."

"I thought he was on vacation."

"He is. Will be back late Saturday. He's been reading *The Morgan Times* online and has been following Amos Dunn's murder. Sam, you know how Ray Morton is. There's no way he could stay out of this. He also assumed that I would be in the middle of it as well, especially when he read about Mickey and me being knocked down in a traffic accident. He immediately knew there had to be a connection, even though the newspaper didn't mention one. We've had some lengthy conversations and he had some good suggestions." Sidney had no intention of mentioning that Ray had been getting his information from Detective Patton. That would be for Ray to tell Sam.

"So he helped you to get into the Assessor's Office?"

Hattie replied. "Well, we didn't know you could do it online. I always thought you had to go to the office in person and look the information up in those big books they have. Ray said they converted everything over to computers a few years ago. Since none of us knew that we didn't sign up for access codes. He let us use his. I must admit it proved to be very easy once you got the hang of it. Access to lots of information."

Sam asked, "Like what?"

"Oh, they provide links to other areas of the county and the town. Like that house on George Street across from Doctor Cooper's, the one they did all the renovation on, looks like there have been all sorts of lawsuits about the property. The new owners sued the old owners about things they didn't disclose. They fired two contractors who then sued them and put liens on the property. The new owners also refused to pay the real estate agent claiming fraud and deceptive practices. It certainly explains why it took so long to do the renovations."

' "I'm familiar with that. I was called out there myself on a few occasions to calm people down," Sam said. "Yeah, we've been watching that place for a while. I don't think it has anything to do with Amos though."

"I would agree," Sidney said shifting again.

"So what do you think you have?"

Hattie spoke first. "There are definitely three sets of license plates that show up at two of the addresses multiple times."

"Don't tell me, it's the Cooper and Anderson addresses," said Sam.

No one spoke.

"It is isn't it? You're suspecting someone who visits a general practitioner—who just happens to be the county coroner—and a podiatrist of doing something so bad they would kill someone who found out?"

Sidney, now obviously uncomfortable, said, "Not necessarily. But if we believe that Amos' book is the key to everything, we have to assume some type of suspicious behavior. It may not be Cooper and Anderson who peaked Amos' interest but the owners of the three cars that were visiting them. We've already given those plate numbers to Ray. Also, keep in mind, Sam, we're still looking at the book. We haven't finished with it yet."

Sam sat quietly and looked at Sidney, Tillie and Hattie. He began to rock back and forth in his chair. He knew he was in a bind. Throw in with the amateurs and look like a fool if it all turns out to be nonsense or take what they've given him and use it as part of the overall investigation.

He continued to mull over his options. What kept

nagging at him was the attack on Mary Coffey. How did the attacker know she had Amos' book at City Hall? He followed the information trail about who knew the book had been found and couldn't find any connection to anyone at City Hall this morning. The one person he had not been able to speak with undoubtedly held the key and that was Mary Coffey. Who did she tell? Who did she notify that she planned to copy the book before it was turned over for analysis and who would know she would do it at the coroner's City Hall office? The most logical person she would have notified would be her boss. Is it possible that Cooper did have something to do with Amos' death, however remotely? Were the amateurs really on to something?

"I have to make a call," said Sam getting up from the table. "Just everybody hang on where you are."

He walked out of the room, through the living room and out the front door to the porch.

Tillie said, "Are we in trouble?"

Sidney's portable house phone rang. Hattie got up and went into the living room to answer it, as it had been moved to a table next to Sidney's chair to make it easier for him. She spoke quietly and then came back to the dining room.

"It's Ray. He's put some names to those license plates."

Sidney took the phone. "Ray, hold on. We have a very unhappy Sam Cashman here with us. We told him what we've been doing—including your part. He's on the porch at the moment. On the phone. Not sure who with."

"That's okay," said Ray. "Put him on speaker when he comes back in. I need to talk with all of you."

Hattie got up and went to the front door, which Sam had not completely closed. As she opened it Sam looked at her as she said. "Ray Morton's on the phone."

Sam said into his phone, "Okay, thanks for the information. Tell her we're all thinking of her." He ended the call and then said, "Hattie, there's a package here for Sidney. Came while I was on the phone." He reached down and picked it up from the porch chair next to him and handed it to her

Hattie said, "Oh, thanks. I think I know what that is. Ray asked that we put him on speaker so he can talk to all of us."

Chapter 24

The suspects emerge

Thy were all doctors. All those duplicate license plate numbers at both Cooper's and Anderson's," Ray said over the speaker phone. The listeners had a variety of reactions from Tillie's 'I knew it' look to Sidney's merely sitting back in his chair, putting his fingers together on his mid-section and tapping them.

Ray continued. "Now before anyone says anything, I've got to tell you I've made a few phone calls to a good friend who's currently working for the Medicare Fraud Strike Force in Miami. I had a gut reaction to all those doctors getting together in little, out of the way Morgan, South Carolina and I don't think it was a weekly card game. My contact at MFSF doesn't think so either. He didn't say anything specific, but I definitely got the impression there's going to be a sweep in South Carolina very soon. In fact, probably sooner than later now that I've told him what we've discovered. Now, there's something I need to get your agreement to before I say anything else, I want everyone in that room you're in to swear that this information goes no farther."

Silence.

The four people sitting around the table looked at one another.

Sidney shifted in his chair and leaned forward. "I do not have a problem with that." He looked at Tillie and Hattie.

Hattie spoke next, "I agree."

Then Tillie, with a fierce look in her eyes and a knitted brow said, "You sayin' all these doctors got together and planned to kill Amos Dunn?"

"No, I'm not," Ray said. "I have no idea if there is a connection between those get-togethers and the murder of Amos Dunn. Personally, I think there is, but I don't see it yet. What I do know is there is a major investigation into Medicare fraud under way in the state of South Carolina. These meetings on George Street—and other places— could be key to that investigation. I don't want to say anything else at this point. And I certainly don't want any of us to be responsible for messing up a Medicare fraud investigation. Sam what about you?"

Sam sat—thinking. He doodled on the pad in front of him with a pencil

"Ray, you've got me in a tight spot."

"I know that. But keep in mind that you're in charge of the Amos Dunn investigation and you work for the people of South Carolina. You may report to Pete Hornig and feel a loyalty to him, but you also have an obligation to take your investigation wherever it leads you. Right now you don't know who killed Amos Dunn and you don't know what those doctors were doing at those meetings. You don't have anything to report to anyone. If you feel uncomfortable with this, I can arrange for you to meet with my contact in the strike force. He offered to do this. I recommended you to him. They like to work with and need the help of local law enforcement. They don't have an active contact in Coastal Rivers County. Besides, this would give you cover with Hornig when you tell him what's going on. Keep in mind that you're working with Medicare investigators also gives Hornig cover. Sam, what do you say? Can I set up a meeting?"

Sam sat back in his chair and cleared his throat. Well, he wanted to be in police work. He wanted to help the people in his community. He took all those law courses at the Technical College of the Lowcountry and he was set to move on to the University of South Carolina to continue his education. He wanted to make a difference. Well...

"Okay," Sam said. "I'm in."

Sam recognized the problem facing the Medicare fraud investigators because it had been made into such a political issue. Every year at election time candidates claimed Medicare to be a broken system that cost the taxpayers too much, and that it was all because of fraud and waste. They claimed they could fix it. The problem was that Medicare was an overwhelmingly popular government program. Its users loved it and didn't want anyone to change it or even touch it. So, to make sure it stayed in place they bought into the 'fixing the waste' campaign fiction. Medicare had proven itself a form of socialized medicine that actually worked—and did so extremely well. In defending it you just had to just make sure you never referred to it as socialized medicine.

The Medicare Fraud Strike Force had its beginnings in 2007 when the first office was established in Miami. Wherever you had a large population of retirees and an aging population, you had Medicare. Florida always won that contest hands down. It also won the Medicare fraud contest. As a result, it also won the contest as to where to put the first investigative central office. There were now nine geographical locations.

As usual, the problem was funding by Congress and focus by the Justice Department.

Sam knew all of this because it had come up in the

classes he took.

Also, the strike force held workshops for regional and local law enforcement. Ray had attended some of the workshops when he worked for Chief Hornig. The City of Morgan permitted him to take the time off with pay to attend, but, as usual, had no funds to cover his expenses, which Ray paid out of his own pocket.

Ray then said, "Tillie, I don't want you to take this personally, but I really need you to keep this quiet. I know you discuss just about everything that happens in town among your family and friends. The information you share is extremely valuable at times. This one you've got to promise me to keep under your hat."

"Oh, don't worry Mister Ray, I know what I should say and what I shouldn't. Don't worry, my hats on tight with this one."

"Thank you, Tillie, I appreciate it."

Sam, now fully engaged, leaned forward and again picked up the pencil he had been writing with, "About the Dunn and Beasley murders, my reading on Medicare fraud is that it has a white-collar crime reputation. Violence, especially murder, doesn't usually come into it."

The phone went silent for a moment, then Ray said, "You're right. It's a puzzler. But it doesn't mean it couldn't happen, especially if someone found out about it and threatened them with exposure. Frightened people do some very irrational things. Which leads me to a question for you, Sam, what can you tell me about what the forensic people have figured out?"

It was now Sam's turn to be quiet. With all the years he'd spent with the Morgan police department and everything he'd learned in training and on the job, as well as what they taught him at TCL, the correct answer should be 'I can't tell you.' However, being correct at this point didn't seem to matter. With two people dead, one in the hospital and a major federal crime task force about to jump into the middle of things, this didn't seem like a good time to stand on ceremony and just play by the book.

No, this was the time to let everything out there. This was the time to use every tool available to catch a killer, but…

Sam sat in a crouch. He leaned forward, placed his hands down under the table, hooked his thumbs together and started tapping his fingers against one another.

"Ray, you know I really can't say anything."

Ray understood the dilemma Sam faced and said, "Let me give you a hand. Once upon a time there was a break-in at a liquor store over in Beaufort and a man was killed. Everyone said the killing was unintentional and just a run-of-the-mill liquor store robbery gone bad, And it did look that way until the forensic team and the coroner got their heads together. Do you remember that case?"

"Hmmmm. Okay, yes, I think I do," Sam said with a smile, as he moved his hands back up onto the table. "I see the similarities. In that case the coroner came to the conclusion that the murder was, in fact, intentional—premeditated—but made to look like it wasn't."

Sidney decided to play along. "How did they figure it all out?"

"They determined that the victim was hit not once but twice. The first time he was standing looking away from the killer and the second time he was on the ground."

"Let me guess," said Sidney, "the second blow was with a bottle of wine and the positions were determined by the splash patterns."

Sam looked surprised and said, "Yes, exactly. Also, the bottle of liquid came from a lower shelf not a higher one that would match up with someone just reaching out to grab what was conveniently available. The first blow seemed to be consistent with someone using his right hand to hit the victim while the second one was clearly a left-handed hit."

Ray said, "And there was no evidence that there was more than one person doing the hitting."

"Right."

Sidney sat back and folded his hands, "I wonder if there is statistical evidence of how many killers are right-handed versus left-handed. Wouldn't be surprised to learn that the murderer of Amos Dun and Mark Beasley was right-handed rather than left-handed as we all first thought."

The theoretical conversation continued as they explored the physical evidence obtained from the Cedar Street Market and the home of Amos Dunn until Tillie finally said, "Boy you guys is somthin' else. I thought Professor Lake was the only one who talked with double and triple meanins' like this."

ℰↁℰↁ

After Sam left and Ray ended his call, Sidney, Tillie and Hattie continued to sit around the table. They were all relieved that Ray and Sam were on the same page and it looked as though Sidney and his Howard Street irregulars were not going to be pushed out of the picture. Sidney, though, had some doubts.

Hattie said, "Oh, by the way I think your books came in."

"Books?"

"Well, I think that's what the package is that was on the porch. I put them over there." She indicated the living room chair Sidney had been sitting in.

"Ah, the Thomas J. Wise books. I'll bet that's them. Finally. I'm going to solve that Anne Brontë book problem yet. And Hattie, I think I've also uncovered some Shelley authenticity problems for you."

"So that's what you've been working on."

"When I'm not trying to solve this Amos Dunn murder problem. It's not that I don't want it resolved, I do, but I really want to get back to this literary forgery topic. Besides, with this connection I've learned about to Shelly's poetry, I think you might want to work a bit closer with me on it. You may find that you're teaching something that wasn't even written by Shelly."

Hattie looked at Sidney in a clear state of surprise. "Seriously?"

"Yes, seriously. But for now, I don't want you to forget that once you get that e-mail from Ray with the names attached to the license plates, I would still like to go over them and see if there is anything strange with regard to cars not owned by medical people."

Hattie said, "Shouldn't we just stay out of it for now?"

"No. The investigation is shifting over to Medicare fraud and I don't think we should move in that direction. Yes, it's more high profile and I'm sure it will garner a great deal of news media attention, so let Sam and the federal people work on that. It could all be accidental that Amos discovered something devious on the part of those medical people, or maybe it turns out it was all innocent and they were all playing bridge or something. No, there's something else here. As Sam said, this Medicare angle is usually a non-violent crime. The medical people who do the stealing see it as a victimless crime—they're stealing money from the government, not their patients. An awful lot of people seem to think that's acceptable behavior. They see the government as the enemy and turn a blind eye to people that oppose it. Very dicey. Very dicey."

"So what do we do, Professor?"

"Tillie, I would like you to nose around that house that had all those construction problems. Find out what you can from some of the people you know that worked on the renovation. See if anyone remembers Amos showing an interest in it. If the new owners were unhappy with the real estate people and the builder, then the construction workers were probably the people getting blamed for everything. That would be right up Amos' alley."

"Sure would. Okay. That won't be too hard to figure out."

"Hattie, I'm especially interested in the non-doctor cars. I have no idea what to look for. But if there is one car that shows up on a regular basis it may be able to focus my thoughts a bit."

Hattie said, "All right, I'll work on that. But I'm going to hold you to a Shelly conference. In the meantime, what's your focus?"

"I have to rethink the actual murder of Amos Dunn. I was convinced this was all calculated and had no element of randomness to it and it looks as though I was right. I have to go back to that night and strip away the actions of an impulsive man and focus on how and why the killer tried to make a seemingly unplanned action into one that is designed to conceal a calculated one."

While Sidney spoke with Hattie, Tillie was silent, but her mind worked overtime. Her gut feeling told her that the medical stuff had to be at the heart of everything. Yes, there may be some sort of connection to the dispute over that building being renovated, but she really didn't think it would be a big enough reason for Amos to get involved. Sure, he would defend someone who got a bad deal from a contractor or a developer, but that was just Amos. She knew, as everyone seemed to, that contractors and developers always seemed to be in dispute with someone and with a lot of these outside people buying up the old places dirt cheap and taking advantage of every loophole in doing it, Amos would figure they deserved one another.

A contractor having a dispute with a rich outsider from

Atlanta or Charlotte, well that would seem more like entertainment to Amos than a cause to become an advocate about.

Tillie finally said, "Professor, have you given any thought to that 'doc in the box' place of Doctor Cooper's bein' in the middle of all this? Well, I got a funny feelin' about what goes on there."

Sidney perked up. When Tillie had a gut feeling about something he knew she had her finger on an event or action everyone else missed. Somewhere along the way, whatever happened or was said, people either dismissed as irrelevant or gave a benign meaning to it and missed the significance it hid. It would be well after the fact when the incident or comment would pop back into her head. And when it did it looked a lot different from the strict confines of the situation in which the event or comment occurred.

"Tillie, what's bothering you?"

"Professor, a few days ago when there was a fender bender at axident junction between two people that worked at Doctor Cooper's clinic. Mr. Sam came by to help out as he saw one of 'um was Sarah who lives down the street from Mister Sam. He told Deede about it an she told Sarah's mom to let her know Sarah was okay. Marla—that's Sarah's mom—took off for axident junction. When she got there she spent some time talking with Sarah and Kristin—that's the nurse that was in the other car—an they was making jokes about havin' to go to back to Cooper's to have x-rays made of their arms, shoulders and necks because Sarah hurt her index finger on the steering wheel of the car. Kristin just laughed and said something about her probably bein' referred out to a specialist because she stubbed her toe an he'd probably recommend a knee replacement from another specialist."

"Tillie, how do you know all of this?"

"Just talk. We was all sittin around talkin' later that day

an Marla tole us all about what happened."

Hattie just sat and looked at Tillie. Amazed at how information gets around in the lowcountry. Everybody knows everything, but they don't always know that they know something. Don't know that they may have a piece of someone else's puzzle.

Everybody but Tillie, of course. She always seemed to be able to make connections: recalled information that connected to something where it didn't seem to belong. Tillie had a talent for finding a puzzle piece without a home that actually connected two different puzzles.

Hattie, shaking her head, said, "Tillie, I think you just found a can of worms—as some people would say—that Ray Morton and his friend in Miami would love to know more about."

"It would not surprise me," Sidney added, "if that task force in Miami already has something in their sights. They just don't know the full extent of it. The problem, as I see it is there does not appear to be a connection to Amos Dunn. Or, at least, one that we can readily identify yet."

"It's hard for me to believe that Doctor Cooper could be mixed up in some kind of a fraud scheme. I mean hasn't his family been here for generations? He's got that big house over on George Street and a good reputation—as far as I know."

Hattie waited for an answer but none came.

Finally Tillie, who had folded her arms in front of her while Hattie spoke, unfolded them and said, "It's Old Doctor Cooper that people liked. Still made house calls until the day he died. I guess he was the last one to do that. Knew the people he took care of and they knew him. His wife ran the office. They was a team. Young Doctor Cooper never wanted to come back to Morgan. He did his doctor practisin' up in Charlotte. Got married up there too. When Old Doctor Cooper died his mother talked him into comin' back to Morgan and he finally did, but that wife of his wasn't happy. Thought the house was a dump. Old Missus Cooper refused to let it be fixed up. She expected her son and his wife to just move right in and pick up where she and her husband left off.

"No way was that goin' to happen. They got themselves a fancy new condo on the water over in Beaufort. They did set up the office in the old Morgan house at first. Just took over the old space. But no more house calls. Cash, credit cards and insurance customers only. Lost a lotta people from the islands that always went to Old Doctor Cooper. The new Coopers was business people first and doctor people next. Guess that's the way it is all over now. Probably can't blame 'um. A lot of the old folks kept goin' to 'um outta habit. They had Medicare gov'mnt insurance. Old island people change doctors as much as they change churches. It don't happen. The Doc is the boss. Whatever he says they do. He's their lifeline."

Sidney asked, "As long as I've been in Morgan I don't remember Doctor Cooper being married, what happened?"

"Story is when old Missus Cooper fell down the stairs in the house she ended up in a nursin' home in Charleston where she died. The new Missus Cooper wanted to sell the old house and buy and fix up one of the big places on the water in *The Ridge*. One of those million dollar ones. Doctor Cooper said no. Big fights goin' on all the time. Things quieted down a bit once she got that new German car, but it didn't last. She left about six months later. Divorced. Things settled down after that. Doctor Cooper fixed up the old house and moved his office to that medical building on Front Street."

"And here I invest in encyclopedias, dictionaries and the internet and you still have better information."

Tillie smiled.

Hattie leaned back in her chair and said, "With the

divorce, renovating the house and moving into new offices with a staff, I wonder where he found all the money to start up Medic-aide Emergency Medical Service, his, as you call it 'doc in the box' place. That must have cost millions."

"Didn't find it," said Tillie, "borrowed it from the bank an' other people in town. People like Doctor Cooper is always able to find the money. Same people as give him the money to become coroner. If my friends need money they end up at the pay-day loan places. Difference is we always pay it back—somehow. They get into trouble they just go bankrupt and start over. Remember that Mr. Byron from the bank is just down the street. Somethin' about him I don't like, but can't put my finger on it."

Sidney said, "You raise some interesting points, Tillie, but I'm still not seeing an Amos Dunn, Doctor Cooper connection."

"Sidney," Hattie said, "do you remember the incident about Missus Woodwright when Cal Prentice was here? If I remember correctly, she sprained or broke something, but she wanted to go to Cooper's medic place rather than the emergency room at the hospital. She had been—originally—one of Old Doctor Cooper's patients. The idea being that the people at Cooper's would tell her who she had to see. Maybe a referral to an investor in the company? And wouldn't this be right up Amos Dunn's alley about taking advantage of the elderly?"

"Whoa," Sidney said, "let's not get ahead of ourselves. Restricted referrals are perfectly fine. Insurance plans do it all the time. In most cases it's the way to get the best care. Our whole medical system is based upon the concept of the 'specialist.' A patient has the right to reject the 'suggestion' of any medical advisor. So let's be careful here."

Hattie stiffened in her chair, her back clearly up, "Sidney, I know that. But you also know that old people are the most vulnerable. They rely on their doctors. They don't 'shop around' for care. Nobody shops around for care. Most people don't even know how to go about getting a second opinion. If a doctor tells an eighty-year-old woman she needs a hip replacement the woman doesn't get two more opinions to back up the first one. And for certain she doesn't go looking for 'Hips-R-Us' to get the best deal on the new hip and she doesn't interview five doctors and three hospitals—much less the operating room team—to make sure she's getting the best 'deal' she can. No. She relies on her family physician to make the decision for her. If the family physician is falsifying records to feather his own pocket nobody seems to care as long as the patient isn't the worse off for it. It's one thing to bill the insurance company for a hip replacement that didn't take place and another to actually replace the hip when the patient only bruised it in a fall. Any referral made for a second opinion would be to another doctor that was in on the scheme."

"Now you sound like Amos," said Tillie giving a shake to her head.

"And now we see how Amos could have put himself in danger if he did accuse someone of falsifying records or doing unnecessary procedures," said Sidney.

The discussion evolved into one of motive. Why would someone like Cooper get involved with a Medicare fraud scheme?

Chapter 25

A quiet time to think

After the meeting earlier with Sidney, Hattie, Tillie and Ray on the phone, Sam felt uneasy and sat in his car mulling over the information he obtained. He didn't move for a full five minutes before finally driving off. Medical fraud in Morgan, local doctors falsifying records, a government task force about to descend on the town. Who might be involved? Who could he confide in? He knew he had to tell Chief Hornig, but he still didn't know what was going to happen or when.

He pulled away from the curb and drove down Howard Street to Market and stopped. Should he head to City Hall and police headquarters or turn to the right and go the other way? There were now two cars backed up behind him. One of the drivers honked his horn. Sam had to move. He turned right and away from City Hall and toward the hospital. Mary Coffey was awake, and he needed to speak with someone he could trust.

Back at Howard Street, Sidney had returned to his chair in the living room and Hattie now sat across from him on the sofa. A TV table sat between them with a pad and pencil placed within Sidney's reach. Tillie was in the kitchen making a pot of tea.

"I know I said that it's entirely possible the murder of Amos Dunn had nothing to do with the Medicare fraud accusations now being tossed about, but I really don't believe it. I think there's definitely a connection and I'm also convinced we've seen the connection in action, but didn't recognize it," Sidney said.

Hattie spotted Tillie coming in from the kitchen carrying a tray with a pot of tea, cups, sugar bowl and a small milk pitcher. "Tillie, tell me again what Eddie said with regard to that office reserved for the coroner in the basement of City Hall."

"You mean about Doctor Cooper bein' kinda touchy about people goin' in there when he wasn't around?" Hattie reached the coffee table in front of the sofa and put down the tray.

Sidney, turning quickly toward Tillie, twisted his knee and winced in pain, "What was that again?" he said with a grimace.

Tillie, seeing the expression on his face chided him, "Now why'd you do that. You get yourself back comfortable again."

"But what did this Eddie person say?"

"He said Doctor Cooper was real touchy about anybody bein' in that office when he wasn't there. Kept tight control over the keys. Even had a lock on the copier."

Sidney, now comfortable again said, "Who had keys?"

"'Cordin' to Eddie, just Doctor Cooper an him. Building rules say the custodian has to have a key to every lock in the building. Not to personal stuff, but anythin' owned by the city or county got to have a key available."

Sidney leaned back in his chair, "Ah," he said as his hands came together on his midsection and his fingers began to wiggle. "So, if someone wished to use that office and the copier, they would have to get permission from Cooper directly. And he, of course, would want to know why. Which means Mary Coffey would have had to speak with Cooper before going to that office. She would have cleared it with him. She would have told him about having Amos' book."

Hattie said, "You mean Cooper would have followed her there. He's the one who attacked her?"

Tillie began pouring the tea, a bit of milk for the three of them and then two spoons full of sugar for Sidney. She looked at Hattie. "I don't think so. Need a violent person to do that. Doctor Cooper may be sneaky and a crook, but he ain't the violent kind. I know violent kinds."

"I would agree," Sidney said.

Hattie took a cup and saucer, "Then who?"

Sidney also took his tea, "An employee. A confidant. Someone useful to him. As Tillie said someone used to violence. A person he could control. Tillie, does Sam know about the key situation at City Hall?"

Tillie looked up from her tea serving duties as she finished filling a cup for herself. "Doubt it. He works there, but he don't have no office. The chief has the office."

"Did this Eddie person ever say anything about Doctor Cooper? What sort of person he was. How he got along with him? You can tell a lot about a person by the way they treat people they don't have to be nice to."

"Well, I don't know. Eddie did say Doctor Cooper originally complained about having to provide the key to the coroner's office. Made a real stink about givin' up the keys to file cabinets. Said they had stuff the public ain't allowed to see. Eddie said Doctor Cooper won that fight."

Sidney again had a satisfied look on his face. "Hattie, reach that phone for me. Sam and I have to have a conversation."

⌂⌂⌂

By the time Sam arrived at police headquarters, he had gone over his planned talk with Hornig a dozen times. So much so that he almost caused two accidents, one when he missed stopping for a red light and another when he made a wrong turn on a one-way street. He knew his future was on the line and, while he believed Chief Hornig to be a fair and honest man, he couldn't be sure how Hornig would take learning that the Medicare Fraud Strike Force was about to descend on his town and he didn't know anything about it. Not only that, but the main target would be the coroner, a man Hornig had backed in the last election.

Political relationships were always complicated. The current mayor, Steele Wilcox, had been the previous coroner, but did not have a medical degree. He was a local funeral director who had taken the required forensic courses and had paramedic experience. While Hornig and Wilcox got along it seemed a strained relationship, especially when Wilcox had his political hat firmly in place, which lately seemed to be always. Hornig knew Wilcox had planned a statewide political career for himself and had backed the previous mayor in the election and never expected Wilcox to win the race. He was even more surprised when Wilcox asked him to stay on as police chief. Hornig backed Cooper for the coroner position stating that having a medical degree should be a requirement, a clear criticism of Wilcox, the previous coroner.

Sam kept mulling over how Hornig would take the news that his choice for coroner could now be either the target of the Medicare fraud investigation or, at the least, caught up in its web.

Sam's visit with Mary Coffey proved to be an eye-opener. She did speak with Cooper before going to City Hall and she did tell him why—she wanted to get a copy of the book into police hands as soon as possible. Cooper argued with her at first but finally relented. She had the feeling someone was in Cooper's office with him at the time and giving him some advice. She knew the custodian had the key to the office as well as the copier, as she had to go that route for access once before. The building administration office had a key to the custodian's room in the basement just across from the office used by the coroner. No, she had no idea what Cooper kept in the three locked file cabinets that were in the room. All the coroner's official files were kept in the coroner's official office in the old hospital annex building. She also confirmed that the murderer of Amos Dunn had been directly tied into the Beasley murder by some microscopic pieces of material found in both head wounds.

Sam checked the wall clock as he entered police headquarters and noted the time as six twenty-four. City Hall had finally emptied out of non-essential people, but the ongoing building activity made it seem like mid-day. The difference being that the whole building continued as an active crime scene. Local police, county sheriff's people, forensic investigators, the press and other authorized persons were still actively at work. Hornig and the mayor were in a conference upstairs. Sam found Detectives Patton and Kent and the three of them sat and discussed what had been learned thus far.

While Sam Cashman had been at the hospital, Sidney, Hattie and Tillie continued their review of everything they could remember about any interaction with Cooper's medical emergency business.

Sidney now had the TV table placed squarely in front of him with the hassock under it to support his knee. Mickey positioned herself beside his chair as usual and provided retrieving support in picking up papers and pencils that occasionally fell off the wobbly table. Hattie with her laptop, opened and set on the coffee table in front of the sofa, took notes and documented the information as

Tillie and Sidney spoke. Tillie roamed around the room as she talked and also made mental notes of places that needed dusting. Sitting quietly was not her strong point.

"Professor, I've been rackin' my head and I can't come up with any more funny-business with Doctor Cooper."

"You've done a fine job, Tillie. All these people who left his practice because they felt uncomfortable. Excellent. Not everyone who has a bad experience leaves a negative review on-line. And then the people you mentioned who went to his emergency walk-in business and then were referred elsewhere, yes, that will be a big help. All that paperwork they had to fill out. The fact that not only did the forms that were filled out require the Social Security numbers of the patients but family members and next of kin as well." Sidney picked up a piece of paper on which he had written some notes. He looked at it for a moment and then continued. "Sarah definitely said there were two sets of forms?"

"Oh, yeah. They's probably even more. If you was from the islands you got one. If you was Medicare or Medicaid you got another. If you was really old you got another. Sarah said it was usual stuff. Some people had to fill out lots of forms, some not so many."

"And they were all filed together in the office?"

"Yes and no. The people in the office filed everything the way they was supposed to, but Sarah said that sometimes she would recognize someone as a repeat customer—like they came back three or four months later—and they'd have to start a new file."

"And it wasn't every repeat customer that it happened to?"

"Not accordin' to Sarah. So they just started a new file."

Hattie looked up from her laptop. "I have a feeling I know where those other files are. What did Sam say when you told him about the locked files in the City Hall office?'

Sidney leaned back in his chair and a pencil rolled off the table. Mickey grabbed it on the first bounce. "He said they couldn't just break into the file cabinets, as Cooper claimed they were his patients' personal files used for research and not connected to business related to the coroner's office, which is why he didn't have to provide a key. Sam said he'd need a warrant. Which he could get, but he'd have to have a good reason before the judge would allow it."

Sidney's phone rang. It had been moved to the table at the end of the sofa so the TV table no longer had room for it. Hattie answered it as Mickey delivered the errant pencil to Tillie.

"Yes, Ray, he's right here." She passed the phone to Sidney.

Chapter 26

The raid

While the element of surprise is important when executing a white-collar crime raid, the objects of the investigation have almost certainly anticipated the event. After all, they know they've done something wrong and have made every effort to cover it up. The police, of course, know this too, providing for the ultimate cat and mouse game.

The situation with Doctor Cooper was no different. The trick was for the police to move quickly enough so that some evidence would still be in place. Also, in Cooper's case, he was a late addition to the Medicare Fraud Strike Force's agenda.

After Ray had spoken to his friend in the strike force's office in Miami on Thursday, a good deal of scrambling occurred. Cooper was unknown to them, but once the license plate of the primary target of the strike force's investigation—a podiatrist in Aiken, SC—showed up a number of times on the list of people visiting Cooper's residence on George Street, he was added to their list of targets. The problem confronting the Medicare fraud team centered on the planned surprise raid already having its members in place in Aiken, Columbia and Greenville, SC.

The target date was October 15, 2014. Friday. Tomorrow. Adding Morgan, SC to the list required a personnel shift on short notice and getting the local authorities on board immediately.

Chief Hornig received a call from the strike force leader at eleven o'clock Thursday evening asking for his assistance, which he immediately gave. However, he was told not to divulge any information to anyone until six a.m. on Friday morning, except for two of three key personnel who would be charged with operational management. Hornig was surprised, but not completely. Sam Cashman had sat down with him earlier Thursday evening and explained what Sidney Lake and Ray Morton had discovered. Shortly after Sam explained the situation to Hornig, he received a call from Ray who updated him on additional information he had obtained and passed on to the strike force.

Pete Hornig was a practical man. Having just celebrated his tenth anniversary with the Morgan Police Department as its chief, he had participated with a wide variety of police agencies from the FBI to the border patrol, but this would be a first with the Medicare Fraud Strike Force. He knew of it from Ray's experience with the seminars the Medicare fraud people had given Ray—who had been Hornig's chief detective at the time. But, as the survivor of the administrations of three different mayors he saw some political dangers ahead. The local target of the Medicare fraud team was the current coroner, an elected official he had supported. Also, Hornig's boss, the mayor, was the previous coroner. The leader of the strike force wanted complete silence except for the key officers Hornig would use in the initial raid, but should he tell the mayor? Who should he tell? He needed to assemble the team. If Ray had been in town he would have immediately reactivated him, but Ray was in New England. Finally, he decided there would be three people in the know until six in the morning Friday: himself and detectives Cashman and Patton. At six, every available officer would be called in. He would not notify the mayor until just before entering Cooper's home, emergency medical facility and office.

ↈↈↈ

Shortly after eight on Friday morning, Tillie received a call notifying her that Doctor Cooper's medical clinic had been raided by the police. Her local network took no time in spreading the news around town. Tillie called Sidney to notify him that it was underway and Sidney notified Hattie. The local press found out by their usual monitoring of police activity. Jim Cunningham, the editor of *The Morgan Times*, was not happy about being left in the dark.

Hattie made her way to Sidney's as soon as she could. Tillie could not be there until noon, as her regular schedule put her on *The Ridge* with one of her housekeeping customers. This would be Sidney's first day alone since the attack.

Hattie let herself in the rear door Sidney had left it open for her. "Ah, there you are," seeing Sidney sitting at the breakfast table in front of her as she entered. "Wasn't sure you'd be here or in the living room."

"No, here is fine. Tillie set up everything for me last night before she left. Grab yourself some coffee and have a seat."

Heading for the coffee maker she said, "Have you heard anything more?"

"No, not a word. Tillie, as usual, is fully plugged in and promised to keep me informed." Sidney shifted his chair and his injured knee slightly so it would be out of the way. The newspaper was open on the table in front of him. "Oh, bring me a refill while you're at it."

"Sure. I just can't believe Cooper did all this,"

"All what?"

"Well, the Medicare fraud, the murder of Amos Dunn and Mr. Beasley. And then there's the attempt on you and the assistant coroner. It just doesn't make sense." Hattie came over to the table with her coffee and the carafe for Sidney.

Sidney moved the newspaper, revealing a copy of *Brontë Society Transactions*, the quarterly scholarly publication of all things Brontë sisters related. He moved that as well and said, "Great article in here this month on the Robinson's and Branwell Brontë. And no, I don't believe Cooper 'did all this' as you say. The Medicare manipulation is one thing, but not the others. He may not even know there's a connection."

Hattie sat down across from Sidney. "How could he not know? If they're tied together he had to know."

"That's the tricky part. I think there's a definite connection, but not between Cooper and Medicare *and* the murders. There's someone else who has a stake in the Medicare fraud activity who killed Dunn and Beasley. Someone acting on his own preservation instincts and not tied to Cooper's dishonesty."

"A non-medical person?" In asking the question, Hattie suddenly realized that such a possibility opened up a whole new line of thinking about all of the violence that occurred. "You mean the Medicare fraud people won't be going after Cooper with regard to the murders?"

Sidney took a sip of his coffee. "Oh, I don't think they'd be involved with that anyway. The murders are a local problem not a federal one. That's one of my concerns: that the murders will get lost in the shuffle. Chief Hornig and Sam Cashman can't let themselves be distracted from the serious crimes at the expense of the high-profile, news grabbing headlines of a Medicare fraud case."

The conversation was easy and comfortable between them, although that had not always been the case.

Harriet 'Hattie' Ryan joined the English literature department at Morgan College in 2006, transferring from the Washington DC area, and quickly achieved a reputation as a no-nonsense advocate for the position of women in society. Her direct and un-diplomatic response to any perceived slight or alternate view of an issue she championed solidified her reputation as the sort of person one approached warily in an attempt to avoid leaving her presence with splinters.

Interaction between Sidney Lake and Hattie Ryan did not exist outside of department meetings. Sidney, having a reputation for precision in all things, could be acerbic as well, but only in the strategic defense of an issue he decided to champion. He made a point of not becoming involved in other people's agendas.

Their relationship changed when Tillie James became Hattie's housekeeper and Sidney Lake's wife, Cynthia, was diagnosed with terminal lung cancer.

Tillie spoke with Hattie of Sidney's tenderness with his wife's care and Hattie began to see Sidney in a different light. They met and talked in the Morgan College cafeteria from time to time, discussing students they had in common and course interactions. Hattie understood what Sidney was experiencing as her mother had died of lung cancer. It was Tillie who told Sidney about Hattie's background, without revealing anything truly personal and she did the same when speaking with Hattie about Sidney.

Their friendship grew from that point forward. Cynthia Lake died in 2009 and Sidney took a year's sabbatical away from the lowcountry, spending four months of it in England visiting historical literary venues in Yorkshire and the Lake District. He returned to Morgan in 2010 with a Labrador retriever puppy he had christened Mrs.

Micawber—Mickey.

Hattie took another sip of her coffee, "But if there is a non-medical person involved, how does that fit into the Medicare fraud investigation?"

"I'm not entirely sure."

Sidney's kitchen wall phone rang and Hattie answered it. "It's Tillie."

On the other end of the line, Tillie stood next to her car on Pond Lane holding her cell phone and looking toward George Street and Doctor Cooper's house. Pond Lane was blocked off by two police cruisers with lights flashing. Knowing about the impending raid by the Medicare fraud team, she, at first, assumed they were there to collect Cooper's files and maybe even Cooper himself, but then she saw the paramedics and the ambulance. "Lemme talk with the professor. You can listen in."

Hattie brought the phone to Sidney and turned on the speaker as she handed it to him. Seeing the serious look on Hattie's face, he said, "Tillie, what's happening?"

Tillie spoke as she looked down the street, her heart beating rapidly. "Doctor Cooper's dead."

Sidney, shocked, looked at Hattie as he said, "What happened?"

"Don't know for sure. Getting bits and pieces from folks. Someone said he fell down the stairs and broke his neck." She spoke in a rush and Sidney could hear voices in the background from the crowd that had developed around where Tillie stood. "Doan believe for a minute it was an axident. No matter what they say."

Sidney's doorbell rang and then a forceful knock immediately followed.

"I'll get it," said Hattie, there being no one else in the house but Mickey, who headed for the door with a limp.

Hattie didn't make it to the door before it opened and Sam Cashman came in and gave Mickey a scratch on the head. "You know that front door wasn't locked."

Hattie surprised said defensively, "Oh. No, I came in the back and never thought to check."

Sidney looked down the hallway from his seat at the table and saw Sam. "My fault. Sent Mickey out to get the paper this morning and forgot to lock it." Then speaking into the phone, "Sam's here."

"Good. Can't hear myself think with all the people around now. I'll hang up an you can get the information from him."

Sidney ended the call and put the phone down. "I just heard about Doctor Cooper."

"Tillie?" Sam pointed to the phone.

"Yes."

"I'm not surprised. That's why I'm here." He turned to Hattie, now standing next to him. "Make sure that door is closed and locked."

Hattie turned and went to the front door while Sam walked to the kitchen.

Sidney shifted in his chair to provide a more comfortable view of Sam who entered the room. "Doctor Cooper's dead?"

"Before I get into that, I want to know if either of you told anyone about what we discussed here yesterday?"

"No, certainly not." Sidney called to the front door, "Hattie, you haven't spoken to anyone have you?"

Hattie threw the deadbolt on the front door and turned back toward the kitchen. "No."

"So, the only other person could be Tillie."

Sidney, with a serious, concerned look on his face said, "I can't believe she would have said anything. You know her, Sam. She can get just about anything she wants from someone else, but she's a steel trap if she agreed to be quiet about something. If you're looking for a leak, you won't find it here."

Sam was not surprised at the reaction. He expected no other and he knew Sidney was right about Tillie. He didn't have any real personal background with Hattie so that was still a possibility in his mind. As far as Sidney was concerned, he knew from Tillie and Ray that Sidney could be trusted, but the thought occurred to him that he might blurt something out to that pastor, Reverend Prentice. They were pretty close and open with one another—part of Sidney's inner circle—could he have said something to him in confidence? Pastors were honest people, generally, and not known to be good liars. It could be a possibility. "And you, Sidney. You said nothing?"

"Nothing. Not a word. Did not speak with anyone after we were told not to. Except for Mickey and to my knowledge she is not wearing a wire. So, no. You'll have to look somewhere else for your leaker."

Sam stood quiet for a moment as Hattie came back into the room and said, "Sit down, Sam. Tell us what happened. Can I get you some coffee?"

Sam gave a large exhale, looked at Sidney and Hattie. Mickey took up a position next to him. "Okay, I need a break." He sat down in the chair across from Sidney, the one Hattie had previously occupied. "And yeah, coffee sounds good. I've been running around like crazy all night."

Chapter 27

A review of the raid

S ounds like you didn't get any sleep at all last night," Hattie said as she poured Sam a cup of coffee. "Black or white?"

Sidney and Sam looked at her.

"Oh, sorry. I've had my head in too many British novels lately. Black or cream—or rather milk. I don't see any cream."

Sam smiled. "A little milk will do fine."

Sidney shifted his leg as Hattie brought the coffee over to the table. He could only keep the leg in one position for short periods of time. It felt better when he raised it off the ground and rested it on something which gave it some support. It was definitely more than a sprain.

Hattie sat next to Sidney with her back to the kitchen work area. "I'd be happy to make some toast or something," she said to Sam.

"No. No thanks. This will do just fine. Grabbed a donut earlier."

Sidney, now settled in a comfortable position, came to the point, "How did everything go and what's this about Doctor Cooper?"

The relationship between Sidney Lake and Sam

Cashman had evolved dramatically since the murder of Amos Dunn. The defensiveness Sam originally felt came from what he saw as an intrusion by Sidney, but now he had come to view it as an honest desire on the part of the professor to do the right thing. A simple view of the world that said 'something very wrong has happened here and must be made right.' When Sidney and Mickey were almost run down the other night, something clicked in Sam. He cared for this curmudgeonly old man who only wanted to do the right thing. But then Amos Dunn only wanted to do that too. And that's what Tillie was all about. He knew he had to be honest with these people, he knew it because it was the right thing to do.

"What a mess. We hit the three places simultaneously: Cooper's office, the emergency medical clinic and his home. It seemed a bit clumsy at first. Two officers from the Medicare fraud team had arrived at chief Hornig's office around one thirty this morning and the five of us mapped out how everything would be coordinated. They took care of all the paperwork in Columbia and brought everything with them."

Sam provided a clear and concise outline of what happened around the City of Morgan during the morning hours. He never mentioned the names of the two officers from the fraud team and didn't provide any specific information about the Medicare fraud scheme under investigation. It was all about logistics. How many people the chief could make available at six a.m. and where they should be stationed. The number of teams there would be. They needed someone from the Medicare force leadership to be present at each of the three locations, but since one of those locations, the Coroner's office, was on county property, they merely requested the Sheriff's Office to keep it closed. Detective Patton went over to the county sheriff's office to brief them on what was happening. He stayed there until relieved by part of the team from the emergency medical clinic. Sam had been assigned to the emergency medical clinic and Hornig and the Medicare Fraud team leader went to Cooper's home.

"So what happened to Doctor Cooper," asked Hattie.

"Broke his neck in a fall down the main stairway in his house."

"Oh my," Hattie brought up her hand to her mouth and partly covered it. On the basis of what everyone had said about Doctor Cooper over the past few days, she had learned to dislike him, but, having him die in a fall like that—well, one did draw a line no matter how unlikeable they might be.

Sidney looked at Hattie and then Sam, "Suspicious?"

"…Yes. Very. Don't want to say any more than that right now."

"I understand. Who found him?"

Sam looked at Sidney and remained silent for a moment as he filtered the information he had learned over the past few hours. If Ray Morton were here, Sam would tell him everything. Ray was a professional policeman, even if he was a retired one. Ray would know how to handle the information. But Sam also knew that Ray would tell Sidney everything. So why shouldn't he? Ray wouldn't arrive from Boston until mid- to late afternoon, depending on the drive from the Charleston airport. Chief Hornig wouldn't hold anything back from Ray. They were close friends since their military service days together and worked as police chief and detective after that. Hornig trusted and relied on Ray, Sam rationalized, and Ray trusted and relied on Sidney. So, Sidney would end up knowing everything anyway. But what about Hattie? She would get to know what happened as well. Did it matter? Sidney trusted and relied on Hattie. And what about Tillie? "Oh, hell," He muttered.

"Excuse me?" Sidney said, although he had no doubts about the internal struggle Sam was experiencing.

Sam took a deep breath of air and then let it out long and slow. "Okay, it probably doesn't matter at this point. Besides, sitting with your leg up over the past day, with nothing else to do, you've probably already figured out a few things."

A small smile appeared at the corners of Sidney's mouth and there seemed to be one on Hattie's as well.

Sidney had learned to like Sam Cashman. He didn't really know much about him before Amos Dunn was murdered. Tillie had mentioned him a few times, but Tillie always had news about everyone and whatever she may have said about Sam was just lost in the fog of Tillie chatter. But Sidney saw for himself a young black man with a wife and family. A bright articulate man raised in the island Gullah community and seeing a future achievable through education and he'd grabbed for it. Sidney liked that. He could see why Ray Morton had mentored him and guided him. Sam Cashman was the future of South Carolina. Yes, Sidney liked that. He liked it a lot.

Sam continued, "Let's say we're pretty sure Cooper had some help getting down those stairs. If people really knew how many studies have been done about how people fall down stairs, where the bruises are supposed to be if someone falls forward or backward, if they were running or walking, if they tripped over something at the top of the stairs or on the first step. And then how far down they went before trying to stop the fall. Where they first hit the stairway or the railing. If people understood all of this, no one would ever try to push someone down a flight of stairs with the assumption it would be viewed as an accident."

Sidney leaned forward in his chair, "Or if they did know all of this and did it anyway, that might tell us something as well, wouldn't it?"

Sam looked at Sidney questioningly.

"Didn't mean to interrupt, Sam. When did the fall happen?"

"Best first estimate is between midnight and two a.m. They'll probably be able to refine it better. They usually do."

"And when did Chief Hornig get the call from the strike force leader?"

"I think it was around eleven."

Neither Sam nor Sidney made an immediate comment, but they were both thinking "leak." But where and from whom.

Sidney broke the silence, "And when did the fraud team headed by Chief Hornig find Doctor Cooper?"

"Right around seven this morning."

Yes, there had to be a leak somewhere. Was it in Morgan or in Columbia? Each knew what the other was thinking but said nothing.

Sidney reached over the arm of his chair and touched Mickey's head. She now sat up sensing the tension both men felt. "He was alone?"

"He's lived alone since the divorce."

"Housekeeper?"

Sam answered, fascinated at how Sidney kept asking the right questions, "Comes in daily at eight. Six days a week."

As Sidney and Sam talked, Hattie took notes. She looked up at this point, "Tillie mentioned that her name is funny sounding. She's not from the town or the islands. Has a foreign accent. Originally from Eastern Europe. Keeps to herself. Lives on the edge of town someplace. Tillie's friends haven't had much contact with her so she's a bit of a mystery. Said she's probably an over-stayer who works cheap and keeps quiet."

Sidney looked up, "Over-stayer?"

As Hattie spoke it was Sam's turn to take notes. Useful information from any source is good information. He answered while he wrote, "Came in on a visitor's visa from Eastern Europe and never went back. She's not black or Hispanic so nobody's makin' a fuss. Housekeepers, nannies there's lots of them around. Sorry about that. I don't mean for it sound racist but—." Sam looked at Sidney and then Hattie and shook his shoulder, "It's the way it is."

Sidney didn't reply to the comment as something else more important occurred to him. "You mentioned three locations were being investigated. What about City Hall?"

"Why City Hall?"

"The files in the part-time coroner's office. Tillie said there are three tall file cabinets that Doctor Cooper kept locked in there. The custodian told her about them. Doctor Cooper is the only one with the key."

"You're kidding," Sam said, obviously surprised. "I have to make a phone call." He got up and headed for the front hallway.

Hattie looked at Sidney questioningly. "What do you think?"

"A couple of possibilities come to mind. One is that there is a leak somewhere and it's probably in Morgan. Also, the same person that has been spreading murder and mayhem around town is at it again and everything is definitely related to Medicare fraud. However, the possibility does exist that Doctor Cooper's death is completely unrelated to the investigation and he was killed for a completely different reason, which has nothing to Medicare. And then there's always the possibility that they'll determine his fall to be an accident. He tripped over something in the dark."

"And you believe which one?"

Sidney smiled, "Oh, he was pushed, Hattie. He was pushed and Medicare money is behind it."

Chapter 28

The elusive primary suspect

Sam was on the phone in the hallway for no more than a minute. He came back into the kitchen with a faraway look on his face. Sidney and Hattie were quiet as Sam sat down again.

"Sidney, you too Hattie, I have to admit I don't know where in the world we would be if you two—and Tillie of course—weren't butting in all the time. Chief Hornig believes that we'd eventually get to the same place, he's not a fan of amateurs. As head of the department, he can't be. But I have to believe a warm trail is a bit more useful than a cold one. At this point I just want all of this to stop and how we get to do that I don't care, and I'm not going to worry whose toes are stepped on."

The doorknob of the back door to the kitchen turned slowly and squeaked. All heads turned, including Mickey's. Mickey broke the tension by wagging her tail and Tillie came in.

"You know this door ain't locked? They's a crazy man runnin' around out there and you leavin' the door open. What's the matter with you people?"

"Whoops," Hattie said, "I went and locked the front

when Sam came in, got distracted and forgot the back. I don't think I'll ever get used to keeping all the doors locked. That's not something we usually do."

Tillie closed the door behind her, locked it and threw the deadbolt with a flair. "There that'll do it."

Sidney shifted himself so he could face her. "Thought you were supposed to be in *The Ridge* all morning?"

"With all the police runnin' around everywhere and streets blocked and detours, tole Miss Annie I'd make it up to her tomorrow. What happened?"

Sidney motioned her to take the open seat beside him while they brought her up to date on what everyone knew and then he seized the opportunity to move the conversation in the direction he wanted it to go. For days now, Sidney had been having long conversations with Mickey trying to work out relationships and tying events together, but he needed a discussion, he needed someone to challenge his views and offer counterpoints.

Sidney sat up straight in his chair and asked, "Have the Ambers returned?"

He did not address anyone specifically and Hattie grabbed the bait first. "Ambers, who are the Ambers?"

"Upstairs," Tillie said. "The people who discovered Amos' body."

Sam corrected her, "Technically they didn't find it. Their story is that they never actually went into the store. They just found the back door open by the stairs and called the police. Claimed they called into the store and when there was no answer they assumed something was wrong."

Hattie leaned forward with a questioning look, "That doesn't sound right. Why wouldn't they go in and check to see if Amos was in there before calling the police?"

"Because we advise people not to do that," explained Sam. "It's the standard advice law enforcement gives out: 'If you see something, say something.' We don't advise *doing* anything. So no, I think they did the right thing. Call the police, let them check it out. That's what we get paid to do."

Sidney turned to Sam, "Isn't the conventional assumption one that indicated that Amos and his attacker came in the front door not the back?"

"Not anymore. The front door had a deadbolt. The kind without a key. Since Amos set the locks on the front door when he closed up every night, he used the back door to leave and to open up in the morning."

"You are convinced that the Ambers gave a true account of their movements that evening and would not have had any reason to embellish it?"

Sam looked at Sidney and then moved his chair a little closer to the table. "Couldn't find any reason not to believe it. The timeframe they gave checked out. Even their seeing Amos walk by the restaurant, where they had dinner, and the time they saw him pass by the window proved accurate. We checked. It helped Mary Coffey set the time of death more accurately. Why is it important?"

"Since the door was open, is it possible that the killer was still in the store? Also, it would not surprise me to learn that a conclusion has been reached that Amos' murder was a cool and premeditated act and staged to look as being an impulsive one."

"I won't deny that. Mary Coffey confirmed it pretty quickly,"

"The splash pattern of the wine?"

"Yes, and other things, but I prefer not to go any further. You must have been talking to Ray Morton more than you have let on."

Sidney didn't answer.

Tillie shook her head, "I don't know. I think you're goin' in the wrong way. Doan know a lot about the Ambers, but all I do know is good stuff. Never heard any bad.

They're good people."

Sam looked up at her standing next to Hattie's chair. "Maybe so, Tillie, but an awful lot of good people seem to be doing a lot of bad things lately. We have pretty much written the Ambers off as suspects. To your point, Sidney, yes we're pretty sure they came into the store from the rear door. Amos and his killer, that is. Killer definitely left the same way. We just don't know if he left before or after the Ambers arrived. There seems to be a very small window between Amos' death and the Ambers showing up."

Sidney pointed to the empty chair at the table again, "Tillie, sit yourself down. You don't need to think on your feet with us. Sam, the other night when Mickey and I were noseying around the market in the space between it and the art gallery next door, I noticed that the fence that backed up to the market's parking lot seemed to be easily climbable. Not by me, of course."

Hattie smiling couldn't resist, "Won't get any argue from us on that point."

Sidney gave her a look over his ever-present glasses and continued. "The flat side of the vertical boards were facing me, which meant it would be easy to climb over it from the parking lot and there's a door to the gallery right there. Have you given any thought to Bobby Gray, one of the owners, who, I believe, had words with Amos recently about a rent increase?" Sidney looked at Tillie at he spoke the last sentence.

"Yeah, we thought about that too. He was interviewed and had an ironclad alibi. He was at a reception over in Beaufort at the Beaufort Art Association's gallery. They had a new featured artist they were celebrating, who also exhibited at Bobby's gallery next door to the market. He's definitely out of the picture. We did check the fence though. Mary's people found some fresh marks on the fence's cross pieces that someone used to get over it.

Couldn't prove they were made on the same night Amos was killed, but yeah, it's a possibility the killer could have left that way to avoid the police that came up on the street side."

Hattie gave a quick look at both of them, "How could either of these people fit into a Medicare fraud scheme? We're still looking at that as being the prime motivation for all that's happened, aren't we?"

Sidney looked at Sam, who leaned back slightly in his chair. "Aren't we?" Sidney asked.

Sam agreed that was the case.

Tillie finally sat down and their analysis continued the exploration shifting to motivation. They were back to Amos' book again. Sam confirmed that they had managed to reconstruct most of the original book that went through the shredder. He also said that having, as a guide, the copy that Tillie made greatly speeded up the process. No one disputed the point or even made a comment and Tillie sighed in relief.

Rather quickly, they reached the consensus that Amos probably didn't know that he had uncovered a series of meetings by doctors, and possibly others, who were plotting to defraud the Medicare system. What he did have was a record of who was where and when or, certainly that was what someone suspected he had. For his part, they believed Amos probably thought he had uncovered some form of misconduct or plot to disenfranchise the local poor, which was his overriding objective in keeping such records so he could expose the plot—once he was sure what it involved.

Tillie made the point, "If Amos really knew what was goin' on, he wodda said somethin'. Amos wasn't shy."

Everyone agreed.

The problem was that someone viewed Amos' record keeping as a threat. A threat to the killer personally. Sidney said he believed the purpose of the meeting with Amos at the store was a cover for the killer to get his hands on the book, and that he knew Amos always kept it in his right pants pocket during his evening walks. He needed to confirm what was in it, but he also knew that Amos would not give it up voluntarily. Sam admitted that Mary Coffey had the same theory, as she felt the slight lifting of the body after the attack was designed to take something out of the right-hand pants pocket.

Hattie raised the question about premeditation, "Do you feel that our murderer was prepared to kill Amos from the start? That he got Amos to open up the store on a pretext of some sort so he could make it look like robbery was the real motive?"

Sam took the question, "I think it was 'Plan B.' I'm sure he thought he could intimidate Amos somehow into revealing what he was doing jotting down personal information about people. It didn't work. They got into a row. Amos turned to head for the back door to escort the murderer out and got whacked."

Sidney then began to embellish on what happened and brought up Amos having met someone on the way back to his house or received a call from someone wanting to meet him there. Also, when the killer realized that Amos' pocket didn't have the book in it he had no time to search the store for it as the Ambers showed up. "Sam, any idea how the book got into the fan?"

"Mary did some tests on that. She concluded that Amos actually had the book in his hand when he was hit from behind. Instinctively, his arms went into the air and the book flew up and landed on the fan blade. She managed to get the book up there in three out of ten tries."

Sidney said, "Damn, I should have thought of that."

Sam had a very thoughtful look on his face as Sidney spoke. He liked what he had heard from everyone and continued jotting down bullet points. "Makes sense. That would provide the motive for searching Amos' home office as well."

Hattie, who continued to take notes for Sidney looked up quickly, "Yes, and the attack on Mister Beasley in Amos' house was related to the search for the book. As was the attack on you, Sidney, after you spotted him in the store that night. Poor Mister Beasley, he must have just showed up at the wrong place at the wrong time. So his killing would not have been planned."

Sidney had one more person he wanted to get out of the way before he began to hone in on the core theory he had been developing ever since he'd became confined to a chair. "What about William Dunn? Amos' grandnephew. He said he was alone in his hotel room on the night Amos was killed, so he doesn't have an alibi. Although I must admit he doesn't come across as a particularly hostile sort of person. There have been reports of his having arguments with Amos."

"Oh, that was just family stuff," Tillie said. "William felt he was bein' pushed into something he didn't want to do. Family all around tellin' him how to run his life. I been talkin' to some people and it was kinda a front. I mean William actually found that he liked the lowcountry. Saw it as a chance to break out of Philadelphia, which he actually wanted to do, but didn't want to admit it yet. Just had his back up. Had come around to like the idea of takin' over from Amos. Just wasn't ready to let Amos know it yet."

Sam had a smile on his face as he listened to Tillie. She could always see through people. If she liked you it was pretty certain you were a good person, but if she held back then you could be sure there was a good reason, even if she didn't know what it was—yet. "You're right, Tillie. We pretty much found the same thing. He already told the family in Philadelphia that he would take Amos' offer. And Sidney, to your point about William not having an alibi, he actually does. He just doesn't know it."

"Doesn't know it," Sidney's head came up as though pulled by a string. "I don't understand."

"William said he was alone all evening. Never left the hotel after he came back from dinner. He didn't speak with anyone and didn't remember seeing anyone. And that's true—from his viewpoint. However, he did leave his room about eight o'clock. Walked out to the front lobby and picked up two chocolate chip cookies that were in the reception area. He didn't see anyone, but the night manager, sitting in her office saw him on the CCTV screen that monitors the front door. He never saw her but she saw him. Also, on the main level, after you leave the elevator you have to go past the workout room to get to the lobby. There's also a CCTV camera that covers that area and he's clearly seen coming and going. On the way back he had the cookies and a can of soda as he got on the elevator. There was also a young woman in the workout room. She had just finished on the treadmill and she also remembers seeing William Dunn. Women alone in a workout room tend to be very observant about what's going on around them. Makes a good witness. So, yeah, we've written off William Dunn as much as we can."

Tillie gave a nod of her head, "Knew it."

Sidney got himself comfortable and leaned forward, "Okay, as far as I can tell that would pretty much eliminate the non-Medicare type suspects. I know there are a few people in Rotary that had their differences with Amos, as well as some others in the chamber of commerce, but I can't believe any of them would rise to the level of violence we're dealing with."

"I would agree,' Sam added.

"Then let me offer some food for thought," Sidney

looked directly at Sam as he spoke. "I believe our murderer works at the Morgan City Hall and possibly even in the Morgan Police Department."

Chapter 29

Lock down

Wher Sidney suggested that the murderer of Amos Dunn worked at City Hall and could be a police officer, he expected to hear an immediate protest from Sam, but none came. The silence seemed not only defining but also damning. He knew from Ray Morton that the first instinct of one police officer is to defend another. Like members of the military they had each other's back, they trusted one another with their lives. The longer they served together the stronger the bond became. But they also knew the danger a bad apple could cause and while their instincts initially led them in one direction, self-preservation took them in another.

Post-traumatic stress had become rampant in the US Military, but it was a known and well recognized problem. Post-traumatic stress among members of the civilian police forces around the country was not unknown, especially in large cities, but it didn't have the visibility of the military version. The military had tours of duty that eventually came to an end, even if the memories never did. The police officer's tour was of a different character and seemingly never ending with the stress never stopping. The days of the local, friendly, neighborhood residing policeman were long gone. A policeman's most threatening time has always been in trying to settle a family dispute. Disarming a husband wielding a baseball bat or a wife with a kitchen knife or straight razor, with them yelling at one another and then suddenly have everyone turn on the police officer, was a nightmare no police officer ever relished facing. But now everyone had a gun. Argument and reason disappeared with the placing of a little bit of pressure on the trigger. Everyone on 'the job' knew someone that had been shot. Knew a peacekeeper who'd lost his life trying to settle a dispute. The sense of danger was everywhere and it never went away.

Sidney broke the silence, "Sam?"

Sam Cashman sat at the table, leaned forward and placed his chin into the palm of his left hand and arm, which formed a pedestal. He pressed his lips together and rubbed his chin and then leaned back and released a long breath of air. "I know. It's been bothering me."

Hattie and Tillie remained silent and just looked at Sam. Mickey, feeling the tension in the room sat up and put her chin on Sidney's knee. Everyone looked at Sam.

"Bothering me a lot," Sam said, now looking directly at Sidney.

Sidney patted Mickey's head. "I think the question is, who? There were only three of you who knew about the pending raid, with Chief Hornig and Detective Patton being the other two."

"I know."

⚭⚭⚭

Word of the raid by the Medicare Fraud Strike Force became public with a news conference held in Columbia at eleven o'clock Friday morning. The usual array of people were present, with everyone from the governor, to the mayor, to the local congressman having an opportunity to say a few words before the cameras. Every now and then someone who did know what was happening—such as representatives from the Justice Department, the FBI, and local law enforcement officials—stepped before the microphones.

The scene repeated itself in Morgan just after the report from Columbia ended. This time the local officials were left to deal with the TV stations and newspapers from Charleston, Savannah and *The Morgan City Times*. Mayor Wilcox and Chief Hornig appeared together with an FBI representative spokesperson to explain what was happening. The news conference, by design, followed the Columbia one, so that the information trail would be consistent in not really giving out anything too specific. The same basic questions were asked at both locations and Wilcox and Hornig did their best to answer in the same manner they had seen on the Columbia broadcast. The nature of the news conference changed when the *Morgan City Times* reporter raised the name of the coroner, Doctor Cooper. Nothing had been said about Cooper in the Columbia news conference. But now the questions were more intense and pointed. Wilcox and Hornig did not handle the anxious news-people as smoothly as had been done in the state capitol and kept falling back on the statement: "We do not have any additional information to release at this time."

Sam Cashman had received a call from Chief Hornig's office just as Sidney brought up the leak question and mentioned the names of Hornig and Patton. The explorations stopped at that point as Sam rushed out to get to City Hall. He was expected to be standing in the background on the steps of City Hall for the news conference and be in a position to provide assistance with questions the mayor or police chief hadn't anticipated.

Having a good idea of what was about to happen, Sidney, Tillie and Hattie moved to the living room and turned on the local news. They sat and watched in silence and eventually could see Sam standing next to Detective Patton. The two detectives talked quietly as the camera panned in their direction. Sidney had a good idea of what was being said.

Hattie saw the look on Sidney's face and said, "They look rather intense don't they?" referring to Sam and Patton.

"I'm not surprised," Sidney answered, but elaborated no further and Hattie didn't pursue the question.

Tillie, on the other hand had no problem expressing her opinion. "He's givin' that Patton fella a piece of his mind. You watch the eyes. That'll tell you. Yeah."

The camera then panned the people behind Mayor Wilcox as the mayor spoke, but caught another look at the two detectives. Tillie continued. "You look at that." The TV picture showed Sam give a look directly at Patton who then whispered something to him. "Sam just heard somethin' he didn't want to hear." The camera stayed where it was and they could tell Sam knew the lens was right on him.

Sidney squinted at the television picture in front of him, "Did he just say something to the camera?"

Sam had looked right into the camera lens and mouthed what seemed to be three or four words.

Tillie caught it as well and immediately pulled out her cell phone. As the phone dialed the number she said, "Thought it was 'stay in sompthin'. Deede will know. His wife's good at readin' lips. I'll find out."

"I'm sure that was for us. He knows we're watching." Sidney now leaned forward and looked intensely at the picture in front of him as it moved its focus back to the podium and the mayor.

The phone was held close to Tillie's ear as she got up from her position on the sofa and moved away. Her eyes flashed as the person she dialed answered. "Wad he say?"

Tillie listened and then turned to Sidney and Hattie, "Lock down. The last two words was 'lock down.' Stay in lock down."

"I knew it," shouted Sidney. Then to Hattie he said, "Make sure the front and back doors are sealed." He pulled and pushed to get out of his chair. "Turn off whatever lights are on and let's get downstairs."

Tillie and Hattie did as they were instructed. Hattie went to the front door and realized she didn't know what Sidney meant by *downstairs*. As far as she knew, they were downstairs. In the lowcountry houses were built up not down. The water table was too high and the major problems came from storm surges brought by tropical storms and hurricanes.

After Hattie checked the front door she headed toward the back and found Mickey standing in the hallway next to the closet door that was under the stairway to the second floor. She stopped and then saw Tillie check the deadbolt on the kitchen door and then come toward her. Sidney came around the corner by the kitchen and hobbled along behind Tillie. The closet entrance where Mickey now stood was the small storage room under the stairs where Tillie kept all of her cleaning material.

Hattie said, "We can't all fit in there and what are we hiding from?"

"We'll fit," Sidney said leaning heavily on his cane with a pained look on his face.

Tillie now stood directly in front of the door and opened it, "Oh, we'll fit down there. It's gettin' through the door that's the problem."

Hattie continued to look puzzled. She had no idea that a basement of any kind existed under the house. With all the times she had been in every corner of the building, no one ever mentioned it and she had certainly never been down in it.

Tillie turned on the light and then passed a vacuum cleaner out to her. That was followed by some pails, mops and a large plastic container of cleaning supplies.

Sidney, last in line, took the hose of the canister vacuum cleaner from Hattie. "We'll pull all of this back in behind us as we go downstairs."

Hattie slid the plastic container to the side as Mickey sniffed at it. "Still can't believe this house has a basement."

"Lots of these old houses do. This where the Indians used to live. The high point. Howard Street's one of the high points," Tillie said as she opened the previously concealed door. "Indians ain't stupid. Round here they never built villages right on the water. Always back from it on high ground. Bury their dead there too."

The door was directly under the stairway and opened by pushing in rather than pulling on it. Hattie could see why it would be a tight fit as it was a three-quarter height door with a steep first step down into darkness. The clearance of the entry was approximately five foot five. When Tillie turned on the light, which was a single bulb at the bottom of the stairs, Hattie could see that the height stayed at the level of the opening all the way to the bottom step. Once there, the ceiling measured no more than an additional two inches.

Sidney called ahead, "You two keep going. I'll pull everything in behind me and close the door up here."

"What was that?" Tillie said as she reached the basement floor.

Sidney whispered as he pulled in the plastic container from the hallway, "Someone just came up on the front porch." He put his cane up against the inside wall of the closet as Hattie and Mickey followed Tillie down the stairs. Tillie looked at Mickey and signaled her to be quiet. She hoped no one would ring the doorbell. Sidney grabbed the mops and pails and pulled them in as the male figure moved to his right and tried to look into the living room. Next Sidney grabbed the vacuum cleaner and bumped it into the doorway as he pulled it into the closet. He then grabbed the doorknob and pulled the closet door closed. With his last look toward the front door, he saw a male face peek in the sidelight, which was mostly covered by a curtain. He also saw the doorknob turn and pressure applied against the deadbolt.

As the press conference ended, Chief Hornig motioned to Sam to come over to him.

"Sam, I want you to meet Dan Eberle."

Dan extended his hand, "Glad to meet you Sam. Heard good things about you."

"Good to hear that." Then with a glance at Hornig, "Always nice to have someone say something good about you. Are you with the Strike Force or the FBI?"

"Both. FBI on assignment with the Strike Force. Actually one of my functions is to serve as a liaison with local law enforcement. We would have missed this one if you hadn't spotted it."

Sam corrected Eberle's assumption. "Well, to be honest, I thought we had spotted something else until Ray Morton shifted our focus."

Before Eberle could comment, Hornig stepped in with an explanation. "Ray Morton was my chief detective until he retired a couple of years ago."

"Was he with the Sheriff's Department some time ago?"

"Yes, he was. I talked him into coming over to our side. We knew one another a lot of years ago. One of the best moves I've made."

Addressing Sam, Eberle said, "Understand you were after Doctor Cooper in a murder investigation."

"Well that's not—," Sam's phone rang. He pulled it out and saw it was Tillie calling. "Gotta take this." He stepped back from Eberle and Hornig who continued to chat. "Tillie, you got my message?"

"Sure did," said a breathless Tillie from the dark of the basement. "We're all in the cellar."

"I didn't mean for you to do that. Just take precautions. Sidney has a cellar?"

"Yeah, the professor didn't want to take any chances. Somebody's tryin' to break in."

"Stay right there. I'll be there in a couple of minutes."

"We ain't goin' nowhere."

Sam ended the call and interrupted Hornig, "Chief, Sidney Lake and the two women are locked down and hiding in Lake's basement."

"What!"

"Gotta go. Need some backup." Sam turned to head for his car.

"Sam, I'm commin' with you."

"Mind if I tag along," said Eberle.

Sam looked back and said, "Come on then." And continued toward the parking lot.

As the three of them headed for Sam's car, Hornig placed the call for backup.

In the basement the light from Tillie's phone went dark as she said quietly, "He's commin."

Sidney whispered. "Good. Hattie do you have your phone with you?"

"Yes."

"Put its light on and let's make our way over to the wall in back of you. I don't want to use the cellar light as it might be visible from the inside of the dark closet upstairs. We need to get as far away from the stairs as we can. And be careful. We don't come down here very often and I'm not sure what's on the floor that we could trip over."

"Did you see who it was? Tillie asked.

"No. But it was definitely male. Probably about the same size as the person I saw in the market the other night."

Tillie moved to the side a bit. "Mickey you stay here with me."

In the dark, they carefully moved to the rear of the cellar and positioned themselves against the back wall fifteen feet behind the stairway. They listened quietly. If someone did gain access to the house, Mickey would be the first to sense their presence. The good and bad of old houses was that the floors tended to squeak. Tillie positioned herself to keep Mickey quiet just in case she became spooked and wanted to bark.

Sidney'd had the extra locks put on the front and back doors at the insistence of Ray Morton who had no illusions of Morgan being a safe quiet town. "We have more problems around here in one day than Andy Griffith experienced in a whole TV season," Ray warned. So Sidney'd had the super deadbolts put in. He complained but still heeded Ray's warning. Now he was thankful for it.

Hattie heard something and whispered, "Was that a squeak? Where are we positioned down here in relation to upstairs?"

Tillie whispered back, "Under the kitchen. Around where we was all sittin' earlier. Miss Hattie, put your phone in airplane mode. Don't want 'um ringin' now."

Sidney shushed them both as they fiddled with their phones.

No sounds.

Could someone be upstairs? Did Hattie lock the rear door deadbolt properly? Their thoughts bounced against the walls and one another. An experienced burglar could probably get past the deadbolt, but no one believed they were dealing with a burglar. The consensus belief of both Sam Cashman and Ray Morton was that the murderer belonged to the amateur class of killer. A violent person, but calculating and careful. Robbery and violence were always there, but not as a first option. The opinions they had were formed on the basis of their initial belief that the murders were not premeditated. And then, of course, as professionals, they knew they could be dead wrong. Very dead.

The rear door upstairs rattled. The three of them jumped and held their breath. Tillie grabbed Mickey before she could bark. The rattling of the door sounded again. Whoever it was felt safer at the back door, being not as exposed as standing on the front porch of Sidney's house. They could hear the person upstairs mutter something and then the squeak again. Sidney and Tillie, knowing the quirks of the back porch, assumed the intended intruder had begun to move away from the back door and would check the windows. Sidney's library would be to the right of the door when facing it from the outside. Those windows hadn't been opened in ten years and were firmly painted shut. Sidney didn't want any dirt and dust getting into the library and made sure the windows were always sealed. Even the drapes were kept closed so Sidney couldn't be distracted when reading or doing research. Someone trying to break in couldn't see where they were going, see something positioned behind the drapes that would be knocked over when trying to get in the window. On the left side of the back door was the kitchen. When Sidney had it remodeled a few years ago, a new granite countertop was put along the rear and side walls. The windows were left to look unchanged from the outside to accommodate the rules of Morgan's Architectural Review Board. So while they looked like normal windows from the outside, they were actually only half height windows on the inside. Only the upper half of the window could be opened, something Tillie liked to do in the spring and fall, but the shortened size of the opening above the countertop made it impossible to climb through.

They listened as the potential intruder moved away from the back door and headed to his right and then stopped. They could hear one another breathing as another footstep made a squeak. They kept imagining him moving around the porch and stopping to see into the windows of Sidney's library. The sounds stopped.

Suddenly they heard what they believed to be some heavy, quick steps leaving the back porch.

Hattie whispered, "Did he leave?"

Sidney gave her a low hush and placed a finger across his mouth. An instinctive movement no one could see in pitch blackness of the cellar.

They waited silently.

A very long five minutes had passed when they heard a pounding on the front door. They all jumped and this time Mickey managed to get off a bark.

"Sidney, open up. It's Sam."

"Good heavens a mercy," Tillie said letting out a long breath of air.

Mickey barked again and everyone relaxed. Hattie turned her phone's light on.

"Sidney. Open up." Sam gave the door another pound with his fist.

"You and Mickey better get up there in a hurry before Sam breaks the door down," said Sidney.

Tillie moved quickly to the stairs, flipped on the cellar light and went up followed closely by Mickey. She pulled the cellar door open and then pushed open the closet door, letting Mickey by and moving the canister vacuum cleaner out of the way so she could head for the doorway where

Sam could see her.

As soon as Sam spotted Mickey, he called over his shoulder, "The dog's here and okay. Hold on someone's coming. Check the back," he instructed Officer Green. Hornig and Eberle came up onto the porch.

Chapter 30

A camera sees all

Once everyone came up from the cellar and assembled in the front hallway, Sidney gave Sam a quick overview of what happened.

Sam placed his left hand on Sidney's shoulder. "Knew there were a couple of houses around here that had cellars. Just didn't know which ones. Have seen a few. Didn't know you had one. Originally most people thought they were underground railway stops, but the houses were built after the war. How's everybody?"

"I think we're all okay. A little shaken up though," Sidney said looking at Tillie and Hattie. "Except for Mickey, of course. To her everything is a game so she had a fine time."

Mickey responded with an enthusiastic tail wag.

Chief Hornig stepped forward to join the group. "Hello, Sidney, Miss Hattie, Tillie. Everybody's okay?"

"Yes, thank you Chief. Little scary though," Sidney said.

"Didn't see him too clearly?"

"No, pretty much a shadow on the curtain, which blocked my view, and his as well."

"Definitely male?"

"Yes."

Hornig stepped to the side slightly, "Want you to meet Special Agent Eberle. He's with the Strike Force."

Eberle came forward and extended his hand which Sidney took just as Officer Green came back around the side of the house and called to Sam, "No sign of anything."

"Okay, close everything off and we'll start checking the neighbors. See if anyone saw anything."

Hornig called to a police sergeant getting out of his car, "Rope it all off and get forensics over here to check the doors, windows and grounds." Then to Sidney, "I need to speak with you."

The directness with which Chief Hornig spoke came as a welcome surprise to Sidney, for it wasn't a command for a change, but more in the manner of a comment from a colleague. There was no edge to the chief's voice. It came across as a calm statement.

"Certainly, Chief. Let's step in here." Sidney motioned to his office and the three chairs that were set up around a small table near his desk.

As Hornig and Sidney moved to the side, Sam took over introducing Eberle to Tillie and Hattie, who both had similar looks of surprise as they silently watched the Chief of Police of the City of Morgan, South Carolina carefully guide a limping Sidney Lake across the room. Here were two people they would never have thought to see in a quiet, friendly conversation chatting about Sidney's injured knee and Mickey's supportive nature as they made their way into the office.

Once they sat down, Sidney put his cane aside and moved his leg into a comfortable position, Chief Hornig got directly to the point. "Sidney, you have an idea who's behind all of this, don't you? And I don't mean the Medicare fraud, that's a federal problem. I'm talking about Amos Dunn and the rest. You've also figured out the motive too, haven't you?"

"Yes—yes, I think I have." Sidney paused as he looked carefully at the police chief, taking in the man's mood and manner. He recognized that this was a big step for the chief. One that Hornig decided he had to take, but one Sidney had to deal with carefully, as it presented an opportunity for both men to work together toward a common goal. Sidney knew the approach he would need to take. "Chief, bear with me just a bit as I make a suggestion. I'm not looking to achieve any degree of notoriety in this whole business. I just want all of the evil to stop. So I want to suggest something to you. Rather than just have me tell you who I think the prime suspect is that you should be focusing on, I'd like to see you reach that conclusion on your own. So let me point you in the right direction if I may and have you come to the same conclusion I have."

Hornig gave Sidney a steely eyed questioning look and leaned forward and said slowly, "Okay."

"Good. You will recall yesterday when Mary Coffey was so brutally attacked at City Hall it was determined that there was no CCTV cameras that gave a dedicated and clear picture of the stairway to the basement area."

Hornig nodded his head in agreement and shifted slightly in his chair.

Sidney noted the movement as well as the look on Hornig's face and then continued. "However, there are two cameras that peripherally cover the area. They are focused on more heavily trafficked, public locations, but are too far away to give a clearly identifiable view of the persons going up and down the basement stairs. Now, I understand the people are visible, even if not identifiable in a court of law way, but someone with a specific type of walk or manner or uniform that is well known to the usual occupants of the building could be identified with confidence by any number of people and confirm the identity of the person in the picture."

"Okay, I'll buy that."

"Now, the first thing I would suggest is that you go back to those tapes and count the people based on the time of day. By count the people, I suggest that you begin counting well before you see Mary Coffey go down the stairs. And, as far as time of day is concerned, you should have that from Miss Coffey herself based on what she told the doctors in the emergency room. I'm sure she's quite recognizable even with the distance she is from the camera.

"Once you have a time frame, then I want you to count the people as they came up the stairs. You know how many people were down there. List them out. My understanding is that Mary Coffey believed that the entire basement area was empty when she went down the stairs."

Hornig nodded his head in agreement. "Yes, that's what she believed."

"Fine. Now you need to count and identify all the people who came up the stairs. Everyone down there was a person known to your department. Use the process of elimination if you have to. If you can't identify someone, ask the people who were down there to identify their image as they came up the stairs. Stop your counting after Mary Coffey is brought up the stairs by the paramedics. Then, knowing how many people you have left behind, you should have a matching number of ups and downs."

Hornig again nodded his head in agreement, but didn't say anything. He looked questioningly at Sidney as though he wasn't sure where the professor was going with his commentary.

Sidney continued, "However, you will be one shy on the downside."

"How? How is that possible?" Hornig said with an intense look on his face. Thinking that how could one person going down and one coming up, and all parties accounted for, lead to anything but zero.

"Let me explain. The two cameras in question were not focused on the stairway, as we agreed."

Another nod from Hornig.

"They were focused on the more active public areas and had overlapping sweep patterns programmed into them so they would capture one hundred percent of the activity in the area they were designed to monitor. But not on the stairs to the basement. If you carefully monitor the sweep actions you will find a natural gap where neither camera is looking at the stairway. When that occurs, you can slip past them on the way down, but not on the way up as you cannot see the cameras to time them properly. Mary Coffey's attacker was already downstairs when she arrived. The film should show that Sam Cashman was the first one down those stairs after she was attacked and had been on the phone with her when the attack occurred. You know everyone who was downstairs. Up until now you have been looking for someone who shouldn't have been there rather than someone who should have been and came up the stairs without a record of going down."

Hornig interrupted. "You're saying that one of my people or an EMS person attacked Mary Coffey?"

Sidney didn't answer.

Raising his voice Hornig said in a controlled and angry way, "Well?"

"One of your people, yes, I'm afraid so. I have no idea of exactly why he was there, but I have a feeling it had to do with money distribution records with regard to payments related to the Medicare fraud scheme."

Hornig sat back for a moment and then leaped from his chair and said, "Okay, if what you say is true, all we have to do is identify everyone who came up from downstairs and match them against the people that went down. The mismatch is who we want. The person who was downstairs before Mary Coffey arrived." Hornig pulled himself up to his full height and stood over Sidney. "Where did you get all this information about the cameras?"

Sidney smiled. "From Tillie."

"Tillie?" He quickly turned to see Tillie chatting with detective Eberle. "What does she know?"

"Chief, as usual she has a connection. Down the hall from the stairs to the basement where the cameras are positioned is the Treasurer's office. Tillie's cousin, Lolo Simmons—her real name is Lolita but no one would dare call her that—well, she works in the offices as a counter clerk handling real estate payments as well as other over the counter, in person, payments by residents—dog license fees and so on. There are specific CCTV cameras focusing on each of the payment positions inside the treasury area. However, outside in the hallway there are two doorways at each end of the treasury area, one marked as ENTRANCE and the other as EXIT, but there is only one camera covering them both. It is programmed to scan from door to door. It is positioned on the wall opposite the treasury area and on its left it picks up, peripherally, the stairs to the basement. Across from the Treasury Office is the Assessor's Office and it is set up the same way with similar ENTRANCE and EXIT doors and CCTV cameras performing the same functions. Only, in this case, when its hallway camera peripherally picks up the stairs when it scans to its right. The cameras are not synchronized and every five minutes or so the stairs in the distance are not visible on either camera."

"I'll be damned. If you're right, Sidney—" Another long hard look. "Damn. I hope you're wrong, but if this works out—" He turned away and ran his fingers through his hair and uttered under his breath, "Shit." Looking back at Sidney he pointed at the professor and said, "Don't go anywhere."

Sidney looked back, picked up his cane and said, "No fear of that."

Turning toward the hallway Hornig walked toward Sam and called out, "Sam, get over here. We have work to do."

As Hornig and Sam spoke, Eberle, who had been quietly talking with Tillie and Hattie, but also trying to hear what Sidney and Hornig were saying, got up and came over to Sidney. "Mind if I sit down?"

"No, not at all," Sidney put his cane back in the position it was before Hornig left him.

Hornig then seeing Eberle sit down called to him, "Dan, I've got to get back to City Hall, can you catch a ride with one of the cruisers?"

"Sure, Not a problem."

Addressing Sidney, Eberle said, "I've been talking with your housekeeper, Tillie James, and she had some interesting things to say about Doctor Cooper and his medical practice. I wonder if you could tell me a bit about her. In the short time I've been here I've heard some very favorable opinions about both you and Miss James from Sam Cashman and Chief Hornig. What I'm looking for is reliable information with which to secure my case against Doctor Cooper and his associates. The whole possibility of Medicare fraud here in Morgan was not on our radar until a few days ago and without Cooper's help we may have a problem. The whole issue of the book-of-numbers you found, that was compiled by a Mister Amos Dunn, I believe will play a strong part in making my case. I'd be very interested in hearing your thoughts on the matter and, as I said, what you think of the reliability of Miss James and the thoughts and ideas she has come up with."

Sidney listened carefully. Eberle talked quietly and had a friendly demeanor. Sidney pictured him as playing the role of 'good cop' in the usual good, bad routine, but Eberle was an unknown quantity to Sidney. He hadn't had a chance to speak with Sam about him so Sidney decided on taking a cautious approach. "Well, first of all, I would be happy to provide a strong reference for the honesty and integrity of Tillie James. She's a very kind and caring woman with a strong Christian faith. Actually, I think a better word would be a *confident* Christian faith. Once she has come to a conclusion about something she doesn't waiver. This is especially true in her opinions about people. Her initial reactions are instinctive, but in the long run extremely accurate. She's also truthful. Sometimes in the extreme. She will never lie to you. She may avoid giving you an answer or outright decline to give you one, but she's not in the business of deception or leading you down a false path. If you wish to have her confidence you will have to earn it. You can trust her, but more importantly from her perspective, can she trust you?"

Chapter 31

A killer strikes

Chief Hornig and Sam left Sidney's house after instructing detective Patton to meet them at police headquarters. Eberle decided to stay behind as he decided to continue his discussions with Sidney and Hattie while Tillie took Mickey for a walk around the block. The activity around Howard Street began to subside as the neighbors were getting used to disruptions. The police presence also thinned out, although Detective Kent had now shown up. He obtained a briefing from two of the uniformed officers putting up yellow tape to cordon off Sidney's porch area. He stayed outside until he found out where Agent Eberle was and had a frown on his face when he saw the FBI investigator in deep conversation with Sidney and Hattie.

At police headquarters, Hornig assembled the key people he would need to analyze the CCTV tapes and identify the people going up and down the stairs to the basement office area. They used two monitors to view the tapes from the cameras. They realized that the way the cameras were set up was extremely inefficient, but also had to admit in all the years that they had been in use, there was never a time when anyone ever had to look at them.

Ten people crowded themselves around the two monitors and began to identify each person as they appeared. There were initial disputes over the identification of some of the figures in the distance, but they were eventually sorted out.

"That's definitely Shawn. I'd know that walk anywhere," was a typical comment.

Two administrative staff people ran the tapes quickly and noted each person, giving them a name and a time and the direction they were going on the stairway. The EMS people were picked out easily as were the uniformed police officers and the one woman—in addition to Mary Coffey—who appeared on the tapes. The men wearing suits and street clothes were more difficult, but bit by bit they broke everything down and confirmed the identity of everyone. Although some people went up and down multiple times they had everyone identified as well as the total count of everyone that went each way on the stairway.

Hornig declared the exercise over and said, "Sam, Patton, into my office. Grab those sheets from Sally," indicating one of the tape operators. Then calling to his secretary, "Gloria, get me forensics on the line. There's something I need to check."

Patton's cell phone rang as they entered Hornig's office.

Over at Howard Street, Detective Kent nervously wandered around Sidney's house. At one point he left only to come back a half hour later. He finally had a chance to introduce himself to FBI Agent Eberle and they chatted briefly before Eberle received a call and had to move away. Kent wandered around some more, chatting with the remaining police officers and then passing the time with a few of the neighbors. He was a fixture around the old neighborhood having policed the area for almost thirty years before he retired two years ago. The locals seemed happy to see him back. A familiar face. A Morganite they felt comfortable with—not one of the new young police-men who didn't have an understanding of the heritage of the area.

Although moving from place to place, Kent always kept the front door to Sidney's in sight, especially after Tillie and Mickey went for their walk. He tried to strike up another conversation with Eberle but he had gone back to Sidney's office where the FBI agent was now sitting at the table chatting with Sidney and Hattie.

Finally, tired at being ignored Kent entered Sidney's office and said, "Excuse me Dan, but could I have a word in private?"

The FBI agent looked at Kent questioningly. "Eh, sure. Sidney, Hattie excuse me just a minute. But don't go way, I want to hear more about this Brontë book." He then got up from his seated position across from Sidney and the two investigators moved out to the front hallway by the door.

"Kent, sorry if I haven't contributed much, but when I found out both Sidney and Hattie were English professors at Morgan College, I couldn't resist pumping them for in-formation on the Brontë sisters. I got my undergraduate degree in English literature before going to law school. For me the Brontë story is a fascinating one and when I found out about Sidney being involved in finding that missing Anne Brontë book, I just had to find out more."

Kent looked shocked and said, "You mean you weren't talkin' about the case?"

"Actually, no. That's pretty much under control. We picked up everyone around the state we needed to. Cooper was the only one in Morgan and he's dead. His suspected local partners were in Beaufort and Bluffton and we have them in custody. The team grabbed all the records from the medical express place and Cooper's house. Understand from Sidney there may be some more in the basement at

City Hall where there's an office Cooper used. That's being looked into. Your boss, Chief Hornig, seems to have
everything else under control. The book that the man who
was killed had, I think his name was Dunn, will be useful
to us, but not critical. The murders and attempted murders
will, most likely, stay as local issues. I doubt there'll be a
need for us to be involved."

"That may be, but watch that Sidney guy. Don't listen
to him he's a loose cannon," Kent said with a sneer.

Eberle could see Kent's temperature rise when he mentioned Sidney Lake. "You two have a history?"

"Who? Lake and me? No. He's just a nosy amateur.
Hate amateurs. More trouble than help. And Sidney Lake
is one of the more unreliable ones. Don't know why anyone would listen to him." Kent fidgeted as he spoke and
Eberle took note of the detective's nervousness.

"Your boss thinks different."

"That's just a show. Hornig don't like him. They're always arguing. Lake's unreliable. Don't listen to him."

"What about Tillie James, his housekeeper?"

"She's worse. Hates the police. Big mouth. Will say anything to make us look bad. Don't listen to either of them."

At City Hall, detective Patton finally got off the phone.

"Chief, we got to talk."

"Who was that?"

"Ray Morton. They identified all the other cars that
were listed as being at Cooper's multiple times and one of
them is real curious."

"Who?"

"Kent. Turns out he came in third behind two of the
doctors."

"Kent? You sure?"

"Yeah."

Sam interrupted, "That's strike two. He's the one missing from the tape. He came up, but never went down." A

thought occurred to Sam, "Chief, I need to double check something real quick." He held up his hand to Hornig and turned to Gloria, who was standing in the doorway to the office. "Can you get me Randy Byron of the bank? Call him at home. The bank closes at one Saturday."

Gloria headed for her desk.

Hornig moved in front of his desk and said, "What's this all about?"

"Something Tillie said she heard about a few days ago. Didn't see any connection at the time."

Gloria now in front of her desk outside the door, held up her desk phone for Sam. "He's on the line."

Sam took the phone. "Sorry to bother you Mister Byron, but I have a couple of questions I need to get cleared up...Yes, it does have to do with what's going on around town...Thanks, I appreciate that. I heard a few days ago that there was a shouting match going on in your office with a customer and a comment was made about Amos Dunn's murder. Is that true?... (silence) Mr. Byron?... Can you tell me what it was about and who you were speaking with?..." Sam looked at Hornig and Patton as Byron spoke at length over the phone. Sam nodded his head a few times as he listened to Randy Byron's explanation. "I appreciate that Mister Byron. You've been very helpful...Yes, and if anything else comes to mind please give me a call." He gave the phone back to Gloria.

Hornig said, "What the hell was that all about?"

"Could be strike three. A couple of days ago Byron had a heated argument with someone in his office that was overheard by one of the bank's cleaning people. Tillie heard about it third hand from a friend and mentioned it. At the time it didn't seem to fit into anything, but now it does."

"So? Who was it?" Hornig asked knowing all along what the answer would be.

"Kent. He was delivering a message on behalf of Cooper."

Now Hornig looked incredulous. "Are you serious? Delivering something for Cooper?"

"Kent worked for Cooper's medical express clinic on the side. Did security work for them after he retired. When you asked him to come back to us until a replacement could be found, he kept working for Cooper. The argument had to do with the bank holding up the drawdown of funds the med express place needed for expansion. According to Byron, it looked like Kent had invested a lot of his retirement money with Cooper. Byron wasn't positive about it. Although, that's how Cooper financed the med express business to begin with by getting a lot of small investors in town to put up the money—a lot of them. Kent made some sort of veiled threat that if Byron's actions put Cooper's business in jeopardy, the same thing that happened to Dunn could happen to anyone else that got in the way."

Hornig put his hand up and covered his mouth and then rubbed his chin. "Holy shit. Where the hell is Kent now?"

"He should be at Sidney Lake's."

While detective Kent continued to occupy Eberle's attention, Sidney and Hattie chatted at the table in Sidney's office.

"What do you know about the detective speaking with Eberle?" Hattie whispered.

Sidney looked up at the two men standing in the hallway. Kent spotted Sidney look toward him and continued speaking with Eberle.

Sidney whispered to Hattie, "Not a great deal. Has been a fixture in the Morgan Police Department for as long as I've been living in town. I've never had a reason to engage him in conversation. What little I know comes from Ray Morton. He retired about the same time as Ray. Not long

after that officer Millar left, I think that was her name—
you remember her from the George Reed murder—she
was the one who put together the missing books, well she
took a detective position over in Orangeburg that left a real
gap for Chief Hornig. She was originally on the Chief's
list of candidates for Kent's position. Ray mentioned that
Hornig tried to talk him into coming back temporarily, at
least until he could hire a permanent replacement for Millar. Ray's wife, Marie, put a stop to all the conversations.
He had promised Marie that they would finally do some
serious travelling during the summer months and she put
her foot down—hard—about Ray reneging on his promise. So, Hornig asked Kent to come back. That was, I think,
almost a year ago."

"Well, good for Marie." Hattie gave a firm nod of ap-
proval for Marie's stance.

Sidney gave her his usual look over his glasses. "That's
why they're up in Maine. Actually, Ray is due back today.
He flew out of Boston this morning."

Hattie turned and took a look at detective Kent, "How
old do you think he is?"

"Kent? Oh, probably early sixties. Grabbed his Social
Security early I would imagine."

She turned back to Sidney and whispered, "I have a
feeling he knows we're talking about him. We just got a
couple of looks that gave me a chill."

Sidney couldn't resist taking a peek at Kent.

"Don't do that." Hattie admonished.

Looking away Sidney said, "He does seem intense,
doesn't he? Ray mentioned him a couple of times just in
passing, but I never paid much attention. I wish Tillie was
here right now. I'll bet she has a whole dossier on him."

Sidney sneaked another peek in Kent's direction and
saw Kent's eyes narrow as the detective gave them a return
look.

Sidney said, "I think we're making him uncomfortable."

Hattie reached across the table and touched Sidney's arm. "I think you're right. What should we do?"

They both lowered their eyes as Sidney mumbled to himself. "I wonder...?"

"What was that?"

A very low whisper came from Sidney. "I told Chief Hornig that I was convinced that someone who responded to the attack on Mary Coffey at City Hall was actually her attacker. He and Sam are reviewing those CCTV pictures again, right now. All along they've been looking for suspects connected in some personal way with Amos Dunn, but what if the real suspect has been in front of us the whole time and has no real connection to Amos Dunn at all. What if...."

Hattie, instinctively gave a peek in Kent's direction and wished she hadn't, as he gave her a fierce look back. "Whoops, shouldn't have done that."

Hattie decided that it would be a good idea for her to get up and head for the kitchen as a way of breaking the link with Kent. As she pushed her chair back the sound of a police siren could be heard in the distance.

Detective Patton drove with Hornig next to him and Sam Cashman in the back seat on the phone. Hornig said, "Who are you calling now?"

Sam covered the speaker part of his phone, "Kristin McGuire. She's a nurse practitioner at Cooper's medical express place. A week or so ago she and Kent had a rather intense conversation at 'accident junction.' There were a couple of things she said that are starting to make sense." On the other end of the connection, Kristin took the desk phone from the receptionist. Sam switched to his phone. "Oh, yes. Miss McGuire, this is detective Cashman of the Morgan police again, I need to ask you something...No, not about Doctor Cooper this time…Can you tell me what you believe detective Kent's role is at the clinic?…Yes, detective Kent." Sam listened quietly as the nurse spoke at length. Hornig tried to interrupt and Sam held up the palm of his hand to him. "Interesting…No, no. Please go on…Enforcer?…Ah, I see…Okay, that's all I need for now, but we'll need to talk again later…No, no. Thank you."

Sam ended the call as the police cruiser went down Howard Street and stopped in the middle of the street at number 111. Hornig jumped out and yelled, "Where's Kent?"

A police office on the front porch said, "He's inside."

Sam and Patton got out of the car. Inside the front door, everyone inside froze in place. Eberle and Kent turned to see Chief Hornig heading for the front porch steps in a rush.

Hornig called again, "Kent."

Detective Kent, seeing the look on Hornig's face and then seeing Sam instruct Patton to head down Sidney's driveway, pushed Eberle toward the front door, turned and made a move toward the kitchen in the back of the house, but his path was blocked by Hattie on her way to make a pot of tea.

Kent's face was red, twisted and angry. He was in full panic. As Hattie turned to him in response to the yelling, Kent grabbed her arm with his left hand while simultaneously pulling out his Smith and Wesson .38 revolver from under his suit jacket with his right hand.

Eberle, seeing what was happening, recovered from the shove that almost knocked him down and reached for his shoulder holster and his own weapon.

Kent fired, hitting Eberle in the midsection.

Eberle fell back and collapsed in the doorway blocking Hornig, who now had his own weapon drawn.

Reaction outside among the other police was instantaneous. Sam ran to Hornig's side. Patton stopped at the entrance to the driveway and hit the ground. Two officers took cover behind a police car and another went behind a tree. Patton made the call to Police Headquarters for backup. Guns were drawn everywhere, but no more shots fired.

Inside the house, Sidney sat quietly at the table. In shock as Kent tightened his grip on Hattie, now having his left arm around her neck and positioning her in front of him as a shield. Sidney said nothing—just kept looking at the door and a moaning agent Eberle.

Hornig spoke while staying behind the front doorframe on the porch. "Kent this is no good. You've got no place to go."

"Yes I do," said a panicked Kent. "I'm going out the back and I'm taking Miss Ryan with me. Just let me be and nothing else will happen."

Chief Hornig signaled to Patton—who having reached the cover of the three-foot-high porch floor and peeked over its top—to head down the driveway to cover the rear entrance. Sam now hunched down next to the front stairs moved to his left to get out of Kent's line of vision and made it to the front porch on the opposite side of the front door from where Hornig stood. Sam grabbed the railing and pulled himself up. Once over the railing he could see into Sidney's office and saw the professor still sitting, motionless, at the table. He also saw that Sidney now had his cane in his hand and held it out of Kent's sight.

Sam eased himself over the railing while watching Chief Hornig across from him.

Hornig spoke to Kent again, "Come on Kent, you know how this is going to end. Don't make it any worse for anybody. We've got to help Dan here. Don't hurt anyone else."

"If they get hurt it'll be on your head not mine. Just get everybody out of the way."

Unnoticed by everyone was Tillie and Mickey. When the shot was fired, Tillie had just come to the edge of the back porch steps. On leaving she left the rear door open but closed the screen door as she usually did. Now, she huddled next to the door and instructed Mickey to remain quiet by her side.

Tillie peeked through the screen door as Hornig and Kent traded comments. She quietly opened the door hoping it would not squeak. Sending the signal to Mickey to 'stay,' she slipped inside and eased over to the kitchen out of sight of Kent and his planned escape route. She had a plan. Tillie was used to standing up to bullies. She had known a lot of them in her seventy odd years of island life. She knew Kent was a bully. She knew he was scared. She knew he was unpredictable.

Looking around the edge of the kitchen wall, she gauged Kent's position. He stood even with the edge of the doorway to Sidney's office. The stairway to upstairs was to his left. Tillie had the opening to the dining room ahead on her left and Sidney's library on her right. The canister vacuum cleaner, usually in the under-the-stairs closet, stood against the left wall with its hose and wand leaning against the closet door jam, not having been re-placed after the incident earlier in the day.

Tillie eased into the dining room and made it to the doorframe side toward the front of the opening.

As she peeked around to see if Kent had moved, Sam did the same at the front door and spotted Tillie.

Kent yelled, "Don't do it Sam. This lady's gonna get hurt if you do. Stay right there." He took a few steps backward so now he was clear of the entrance to Sidney's office.

Now, out of Kent's view, Sidney got up from the table.

Tillie grabbed hold of the vacuum cleaner wand.

Outside, Patton came around the side of the house. Mickey spotted him and gave out a loud bark.

At the sound behind him, Kent, holding Hattie around the neck by his left arm, turned his head and swung his right arm around giving Tillie a perfect angle at it. If there was one weapon Tillie was an expert at handling it was the long tube and wand business end of a canister vacuum cleaner. In one quick, clean, smooth motion she brought the rug beater end down as hard as she could on Kent's right wrist. The gun went off as it fell from his hand. As he reached for it Hattie broke free and fell to the floor in front of him. A shocked off-balance Kent righted himself and made a grab for the gun now at Tillie's feet. She kicked it toward the back door. Kent scrambled after it. Tillie managed to get the vacuum cleaner wand between his legs so he tripped again and went down on his knees. Looking up Kent saw Patton come through the screen door and pick up the gun lying on the floor in front of him. Tillie came up behind Kent ready to strike again.

Chapter 32

A long stressful day

The clock in Sidney Lake's office announced the time as six o'clock in the afternoon, but 111 Howard Street continued under the control of the Morgan Police Department. In an effort to stay out of the way and for everyone to take a breather from the harrowing events of the day, Sidney suggested they all retire to the back patio of the Morgan River Grill.

The events of the day proved most unsettling for Sidney. It was one thing to intellectualize an occurrence and another to actually experience it. The image of a man being shot in his front hallway, his best friend being strangled and almost killed, were images he would never be able to forget. Hattie had been very quiet ever since—not like her at all. His home had been invaded. Not once but twice on the same day. The cellar would forever be suspect and he would jump every time he heard the porch creak. His practice had always been to push his chair away from his corner desk, turn it so he could face the front windows and hallway, sit back and stare into the distance while visualizing the solution to a problem. What would he see in the future? A body bleeding and moaning in the hallway? Blood spattered walls? Screaming and yelling? Panic everywhere? And what of Hattie and Tillie? How would they feel about 111 Howard Street? He knew it would never be the same. Could never be the same.

Entering the patio, they commandeered an out-of-the-way corner table and had the hostess and a waiter put two tables with market umbrellas together for them. It was only Sidney, Hattie, Tillie and Mickey at this point, but Ray Morton and his wife Marie were expected to join them at any moment. Their plane had been delayed in Atlanta where they made the connection to Charleston. Also, Sam Cashman promised he would come by as soon as he could.

"So you're sure you're okay?" Sidney said to Hattie. He knew her neck ached, she had bruises on her knees and a stiff shoulder where she hit the floor. The usual feistiness and assertiveness seemed to have deserted her. "You're very quiet."

"Yes, well I'm not supposed to talk too much. I seem to recall you not being very vocal after almost being run over by that car."

Sidney thought. *Ah, that's better.* And then said, "Point taken. That was a hard fall you took. And your neck must have taken a beating."

"No, really. I'm fine. Little shaky still. The EMS folks were great and wanted me to go with them to the emergency room, but no, I'm okay. How about you Tillie?"

"Oh, I'm okay. I'm used to the exercise."

"You do swing a mean vacuum cleaner," said Hattie with a laugh followed by a grimace, as she felt a pain in her neck. Sidney saw Hattie move a hand to her throat and just reached over and patted her other hand.

Tillie said, "Mickey, here," who looked up from her position under Tillie's chair when she heard her name, "she sure barked at just the right time."

"Well, you all look a little the worse for wear if you ask me," Ray Morton said as he approached the table.

"Ah, the mysterious vacationer is back." Sidney twisted in his chair as he spoke and carefully moved his knee to a protected position under the table. "Where's Marie?"

"Back at the house. She's worn out from my getting her up so early this morning. She'll try to join us a little later. Tillie, I hear congratulations are in order. You're now an honored member of the Order of the Vacuum Wand. Great job. You're already the talk of the town," he said light heartedly.

Tillie smiled and in a bashful way waved him away with her hand. "You sure you ain't been in I-land instead of Canada? You full of Blarney—or is that baa-lonee?"

"Ha, ha. Tillie you're the best. Hattie, you all right?" Ray reacted to the look of pain on Hattie's face.

"Yes, I'm fine."

Sidney motioned for Ray to take the seat next to him. "So tell me Mister Retired Detective, what's your view of everything from the inside? We figured out a good deal of what was going on, but we've been on the outside all along." Sidney noticed Ray look up for the waiter. "Don't worry, I ordered a scotch and soda for you. The drinks will be here in a minute."

"You're a good man Sidney. Well," Ray sat back in the chair he just occupied, "it boils down to Kent getting himself in way over his head. I understand Sam will join us in a few minutes and he can give you the technical pieces, but I think a problem of this sort with Kent was long overdue."

"Really?" said Hattie, with a slight whisper to her voice.

"Hindsight's always twenty-twenty, I know. That's just the way it is. People are often surprised by someone doing something they think is out of character, but, for Kent, I think he was very much in character. I worked with him for ten years. He had a number of excess force complaints lodged against him." Ray saw Tillie nod her head in agreement. "Hornig thought about getting rid of him a couple of times. City council said to just let him get to retirement. He'd been with the Morgan Police for almost thirty years. Father was a police sergeant up in Orangeburg. That old Smith and Wesson thirty-eight caliber he carries is his fathers. They grandfathered it for him when the town went to the semiautomatic Glock twenty-twos. He comes from an era of chasing down out-of-state license plates along route three-oh-one. After the fact somebody can always find fault with the police or the FBI or the town council or the principal. It's unfortunate, but that's the way it is.

"In Kent's case, a couple of things played into his violent streak. Personal problems at home for one. Married and divorced young. Remarried about fifteen years ago. Has a couple of kids with college on their minds. Pension wasn't going to help. That's why he went to work for Cooper on the side. Now I hear he went and invested just about everything he had in that emergency medical business of Cooper's. Re-mortgaged his house. My bet is that he knew about the over-billing that Cooper was doing with regard to Medicare and was on the profit distribution list."

Sidney said, "Agent Eberle thought that's what the attack on Mary Coffey in the basement was all about. The records that Cooper kept away from home and the medical offices. How is he, by the way?"

"I checked on the way over. He'll make it. Kent's using the S and W thirty-eight may have been in Eberle's favor. It doesn't have the stopping and killing power of the Glock. Did you know he was a big Victorian literature fan?"

"Yes, I found out during our chats before everything fell apart."

Tillie asked, have "So what they gonna do to him now? The Kent fella."

"Depends on the evid…Oh, here's Sam. I bet he's got the answers."

Sam Cashman came over and greeted everyone and then took the open seat next to Tillie. He looked tired. He hit the chair heavy and let out a long exhale. You could see the strain in every motion he made. This was not a day he hoped to ever have again. When the waiter came over Sam looked up and said, "Bud lite. Cold. Very cold."

"Yeah, I sure know how you feel," said Ray. "Everything tied up?"

"Just about. Lot more paperwork to do. But it'll hold. Chief Hornig told me to get home. Called Deede and she's comin' over in a little while and we'll grab a bite and take a walk along the river."

"Marie and I used to do that too."

"Can you tie Kent to everything?"

Sam looked at first Ray and then Sidney, let out a sigh and answered, "It looks like it."

Speaking directly to Sidney, Sam said, "How did you know Kent would be the missing person on those CCTV tapes?"

"In all honesty I wasn't sure who it would be. I thought about Detective Kent but it wasn't based on anything I could put my finger on. I knew Tillie had some issues with him and the Gullah community wasn't too happy with him either, but you can't convict someone just because you don't like him."

"Well, it proved to be Kent, all right. Once we had a person to focus on everything started to come together."

Ray leaned forward in his chair and asked Sam, "Was the murder of Amos Dunn impulsive or pre-meditated?"

"That may be a sticking point."

Sidney said, "I thought they said he tried to cover it up?"

"Yeah, but that looks like it was after the fact. It looks

like Kent and Amos had an argument with Kent accusing Amos of being a snoop. Of invading people's rights to privacy by writing down their license plate numbers and demanded that the book be turned over and confiscated. Knowing Amos, I'm sure he had a few choice words for Kent. Kent blew his stack, pulled the SAP out of his back pocket and just clobbered Amos with it."

"Excuse me," said Hattie in her now whispering voice. "What is a SAP?"

Ray answered. "Ah, another visitor from the past. A SAP is a tool used to disable someone without using a handgun. Back in the twenties and thirties it was a mandatory item in the policeman's personal armory. It's a piece of lead, usually oval in shape, covered with leather and has a long pliable handle. All one piece. It's sometimes referred to as a blackjack. It's a stopping tool like the policeman's nightstick of old. Very effective but can be lethal. Especially if you hit someone with repeated blows to the head."

"So that's what happened to Mr. Beasley," whispered Hattie.

Sidney shifted in his chair and leaned forward. "Wait, didn't one of you say something about there being some strange material in the head wounds for both Amos Dunn and Mark Beasley?"

Sam responded, "That's right. Mary's people discovered that. It's leather. Small bits. They'll match it against Kent's SAP now."

Sidney was now fully engaged, "And Beasley's murder *was* impulsive, wasn't it? Kent was looking for the book."

"That's what we believe," Sam's beer arrived along with two bowls of snacks. He took a long drink and continued, "I needed that. What we're pretty sure happened is that Kent couldn't find the book on Amos. That's why he moved the body. Trying to get into Amos' front pocket where he usually carried it. He then tried to cover up what he did when he realized Amos was dead. That's when he took down the bottle of wine and hit him in the head with his left hand to throw everyone off. He probably would have hung around longer except the Ambers came home and saw the back door open."

Hattie looked long and hard at Sam and then at Ray before she said, "What I don't understand is how he thought he could get away with hitting Amos in the first place. If Amos had lived what would have happened?"

Sam looked at Hattie and then at Ray as though to say *Ray, you've been around here longer than I have, you explain.*

Ray caught the look. "We kinda hinted at this a little earlier. Kent was an old timer. He would plead self-defense and claim that Amos was uncooperative when he was accused of invading the privacy of others and refused to turn over the book to Kent. Sad to say, but Kent being white and Amos black he'd probably get away with it. No matter what, the book would eventually be confiscated and nobody would have paid any attention to it."

"Yeah, you probably got it right there," said Tillie now entering the conversation. "What he didn't count on was Professor Lake's love of puzzles. That's why he got his self and Mickey almost run over. Still think that was a dumb thing to do. Coudda got Mickey killed," she reached down and gave Mickey a pat on the head.

Sam said, "Another interesting bit of news. When I called the hospital to let Mary Coffey know what had happened and that Kent was in custody, she went and called the forensic team leader to get a sample of Mickey's hair from Sidney's place and take it to the lab. On the way over here just now I learned that they impounded Kent's car and found a couple of black hairs imbedded in the bumper of his car. They made a match with Mickey's."

"Well, well," said Tillie, "Looks like Mister Detective Kent's going away for a long time."

Everyone breathed a sigh of relief just as Deede and Marie came up to the table and Deede said, "My you all look like a satisfied bunch. All problems solved and everyone safe."

Sidney couldn't resist, "There is one loose end."

Everyone looked toward the professor.

"Cooper. Who killed Cooper? Or did he just trip and wasn't pushed after all?"

Tillie sat forward in her chair and looked straight at Sidney with her eyes squinted and her mouth firm. "Professor Lake, don't you even think about it for one minute."

END

Deception

The City of Morgan, SC sat in the middle of the lowcountry and, while the location made it a great draw for the summer tourists, the year-round residents just felt the heat and humidity. Being late June, the hurricane season had begun, but no one paid any attention to the calendar or the southeastern sky until August reared its ugly head. Heat, humidity and bugs, mainly the nasty microscopic no-see-ums, were the main concerns.

When the phone rang, it startled Sidney Lake. He had been reading quietly in his library at 111 Howard Street, and dozed off. That was happening more of late. His life had become too predictable. Retirement had finally caught up with him. He was bored.

Sidney Lake, the retired English professor, didn't know what to do with himself. His plan had been to do research and writing, but much of that came to an end when he finished his project: a meticulously researched analysis of the exploits of Thomas J. Wise, one of the great literary forgers of all time. Now what would he do?

Sidney tried to clear his head as he fumbled for the phone that rang annoyingly on the small table next to his chair. Mickey, his Labrador retriever, paid no attention to it and never moved from her preferred position next to him.

"Hello?" he mumbled almost incoherently.

"Did you see it?" a woman's voice said rather excitedly on the other end.

"Did I see what? Who is this?" Sidney struggled to straighten up in his chair as he continued to fumble with his phone, while trying to shake his head and wake up. His right leg, still a problem after having taken a fall when trying to evade an attempt on his life, stayed in place on the hassock in front of his chair and inhibited his movement. The problem with his leg had become his favorite excuse for his immobility, notwithstanding his failure to lose any of the 230 pounds he carried around on his five-foot-eight-inch frame.

"It's Hattie, of course. Did you see it?" Hattie Ryan said again.

"See what? I have no idea what you're talking about."

"The *Antiques Roadshow*. You're watching it aren't you? You always do."

Sidney finally got into a more relaxed position, if you could call it that, as he huffed and puffed his response, "No…unfortunately I'm…not. I'm afraid…I missed it this evening."

"Oh, no. You missed it. The books were on it."

"What books?"

"Well, actually its one book in three volumes. The Brontë book you've been hoping to find."

Sidney sat up straight, now wide awake and ignored his leg, "You're not serious. But of course you are. This is Hattie, isn't it? It's not a joke?"

"No, Sidney, it's not a joke. Someone had the books at the *Roadshow* to find out if they were worth anything." The phone at Sidney's end was silent. "Sidney are you still there?"

"Yes, I'm here." The tone was level now, the initial excitement gone. His mind raced. *This can't be true. The book out in the open. Ridiculous.*

"Good. I thought you fainted, or something."

"I don't faint."

"Well, I almost did. I spilled my drink."

"I hope it wasn't a good one. Wine or sherry?" He felt himself in control. Assertive. Back to his old self.

"Of course it was a good one. I wouldn't drink anything else. Sherry," Hattie said with a huff.

One of the main attributes of Hattie Ryan that Sidney liked was her no-nonsense approach to just about everything. He couldn't bully her, as he used to do with his students and former colleagues—although she had been a member of his English Literature Department at Morgan College—she would not permit herself to be bullied, by anyone. He liked that. It's also why Sidney liked and admired Tillie James, his housekeeper—although she was more friend and confidant than employee. More than once Tillie had chastised him as an older sister would a younger, arrogant brother. They were an interesting threesome and quite formidable when they got together on a project.

Sidney relaxed slightly. At least the initial tension and shock were gone. "You're positive it's the same Anne Brontë volumes?"

"I can't say that. I wasn't there. But the man who looked at them seemed impressed." Hattie also calmed down and now spoke in a normal tone. "What did he say about them?"

"He said they were the real thing. Right look and feel. Right publisher. Only thing he questioned were the notations inside. Seemed to be by Anne Brontë, but he had no way of verifying it."

"Hah! Yes. I thought that too when I first saw them. Best person's handwriting to forge is someone who left few examples with which to make a comparison. Wise was good at that. But unless we can get some experts to look at it we'll never know." Sidney stopped and checked the time on the large bookcase clock across the room. "The show's still on."

"Yes. Only a few minutes to go. Immediately started recording when I saw the books."

"Good. Keep doing it. Record what you can. Especially the credits. We'll get the book dealer's name. I'm sure they'll show the program again at a different time of day and then we'll get everything. I have a program guide in the living room."

"It's probably streamable also."

"Well, I wouldn't know about that technical stuff. That's your department. I want the name of the book dealer who appraised it. Where was the show from this week?"

"Charlotte."

"Ah, let's hope he's local, so we don't have to chase after someone in Salt Lake City or another remote place."

"Oh, it wasn't the bearded fellow. Actually, I think I recognized the name."

The two friends spoke for another five minutes before ending the call. Sidney Lake, wide awake now and bursting with energy, couldn't tone down the excitement he felt. After finishing with Hattie Ryan, he had to speak with someone and decided on Lawrence Brewster, close friend and the last known legitimate owner of the book.

"Hello, Sidney. What's keeping you up this late?"

"What time is it?" Sidney Lake, startled by the unexpected question, reached for the location of his pocket watch, but he wasn't wearing his jacket. He looked at the clock across the room.

"Just past nine," General Brewster said.

"I'm sorry." He was clearly embarrassed. Sidney's eagerness to communicate the news he had just learned caused him to break one of his cardinal rules: never telephone anyone after nine in the evening. "I had no idea. I didn't disturb you did I?"

"No, not at all. I was just reading one of those books you gave me."

"Which one?"

General Lawrence Brewster looked down at the book on his lap and spotted the title in the upper left corner of the page. "*Now, God Be Thanked.* It's the first volume in the trilogy."

"Masters, yes, I thought you'd like that."

"It's got me hooked. I'm not much of a historical fiction guy, the real stuff is more my line." He reached for the recently refilled glass of scotch and soda sitting on the table next to him. The liquid sparkled as it caught the light from the floor lamp, the only illumination in the dark, quiet room.

"He did go to Sandhurst, you know."

"No kidding."

"Very interesting fellow. Believe he was a brigadier in India and Burma. You would probably enjoy reading his autobiography." Sidney realized he'd wandered off the purpose for the call. "Oh, sorry. Didn't mean to wander." It was not uncommon for Professor Sidney Lake to be easily distracted from a train of thought. Although he would not agree with the use of the word distracted. Tangent he believed would be a better choice, since he always came back to his subject no matter what route he might take to get there. Tangents were surely one of his trademarks: start in one direction and then just move with the flow of thoughts. Not only did this trait permeate his old classroom presentation style and create some confusion for his students, who were never quite sure how one point might relate to another, but also his friends and colleagues were mystified as to where his argument would lead them. Once you became acquainted with Sidney, you moved in one of two directions: found him to be exasperating and opinionated and removed yourself from his company or found him entertaining and fascinating and enjoyed his friendship. One thing was certain: there was no middle ground when giving an opinion of Sidney Lake.

"Oh, thought you called to chat about the books?"

"I do, the three volumes," Sidney said.

"Yeah, I have one on my lap and the other two are across the room on the desk. You need them back?" General Lawrence Brewster, US Army, Retired, truly liked Sidney Lake. That is not to imply he wished to be in Lake's company continuously, no one seemed to be able to do that. Continued proximity to Sidney's precise ways and habitual correctness seemed to be somewhat much for most people. Even his closest friend, Hattie Ryan, realized that the best way to have a relationship with Sidney Lake was to get away from him on a regular basis.

"No, no. Not the John Masters books, the ones that were stolen."

"Stolen?"

"The Brontë books. Remember, back when George Reed was murdered."

"Damn right I do. What about them?" The general sat erect in the chair. The three volume set of Anne Brontë's *The Tenant of Wildfell Hall* had been stolen from the back seat of a police car during the Reed murder investigation. The volumes were believed to be Anne Brontë's own author's copies in which she had made personal notations. The loss of them was a continual criticism of the Morgan police department and a bone of contention with Brewster, as they were part of the inheritance he received from a favorite uncle.

"They were on television tonight."

"What!" Brewster now moved to the edge of his chair and almost lost his drink, as the table next to him was jostled with his sudden movement. At six feet four and 250 ponds, most things in the seventy-six-year-old retired general's proximity became disturbed when he moved quickly.

"I just received a call from Doctor Ryan who said that she just saw them on the *Antiques Roadshow*."

"No way!"

"That's what she said."

"And they're definitely my books?"

"That needs to be verified. We can't say for sure. Doctor Ryan has called Ray Morton to see if he can find out something for us."

"Do the cops know?"

"I don't believe so. Someone would have to look at the volumes themselves, which is why I suggested Doctor Ryan speak with Morton. He still knows more about what goes on in town than anyone else. He'll know the approach to take. Sorry I can't be there myself."

"Where are you?"

"At home but I have to be at Clemson tomorrow and Wednesday."

"Clemson? Getting some tips for your roses?"

"No. Elderhostel program. Giving a series of lectures on Victorian gardens in literature. It fits in with the tours of the South Carolina Botanical Garden, which are the main features of the program."

"How long will you be away?"

"Just a few days."

"Well, I hope you can stay involved. I'm not sure I can trust Morgan's finest. If it wasn't for you we wouldn't have known about the books in the first place, and it was the cops that managed to lose them. Should I be doing anything?"

"No, I don't think so. Let Ray find out what he can and then either Ray or Hattie will get back to you."

"Okay." He paused momentarily. "Say Sidney, Hattie Ryan didn't happen to say what those folks on the *Roadshow* thought the books were worth did she? You know we never did get a chance to have them appraised before they were stolen."

"Hattie said that they put a price of thirty-five thousand on the books by themselves as a rare first edition but could probably double that, at least, if the writing inside could be confirmed as Anne Brontë's. However, verification will probably be tough to do given the very few examples of her writing that exist."

"Wadda ya mean?"

"The accompanying annotations would have to be certified as authentic. Also, there was no mention of the note addressed to Ellen Nussey which had been with the original volumes. Everything would have to be confirmed as being in the handwriting of Anne Brontë. Virtually all of Anne Brontë's records were destroyed by her sister Charlotte, as a way of protecting her from any further criticism. *The Tenant of Wildfell Hall* was pretty much vilified by the critics of the time for its subject matter. Imagine someone in the 1840s producing a female character that would stand up to her husband and run away with their son to protect him from the male dominated macho, blood sport culture of the early Victorian age. Don't let your wives and daughters read it, they said. Today, that would make it an immediate best seller, but in the 1840s it was a killer. Charlotte even said she thought Anne was misguided to write it and wanted to protect her reputation. It has often been wondered what else Anne wrote that went up in flames in the Brontë Parsonage's fireplace."

"Now you've even got me interested. I thought she was supposed to be the meek, retiring, unworldly one?"

"Hah, just the opposite, actually. But it's hard to change the image of someone after a hundred and fifty years."

"Damn, that would be something to do though. I can see why someone would want to steal them. Want to read, unfiltered, anything she wrote that expressed an opinion."

"Yes, but keep in mind there are a good many forgeries circulating about. It's always been a curiosity to me as to why the existence of these volumes was unknown. Brontë material is well catalogued and there appears to be no knowledge of this particular original author's edition of *The Tenant of Wildfell Hall*. Of course, collectors are unusual people. Some are buoyed by just having, in their possession, an object once held by a famous person, regardless of value, while others are more interested in what is known as bragging rights, and don't have a true understanding of what they possess."

"Yeah, well somebody knew about it. Hell, my uncle must have known someone who could vouch for them or he wouldn't have bought the books."

"True. Well, I just wanted to let you know what was happening."

"Thanks Sidney. I appreciate it. I'll wait to hear from Ray."

About the Author

Tim Holland is the author of the Sidney Lake Lowcountry Mystery Series as well as the novel *What the Mirror Doesn't See*. He recently received a Keating award for his fiction.

Over the years, he has written for a wide variety of magazines and newspapers, on a contributing basis, and wrote book reviews and literary criticism for *Recorder Publishing* in New Jersey. He also wrote a monthly column for *The Beaufort Gazette,* Beaufort, SC during his time as Chairman of the Learning Exchange of the University of South Carolina Beaufort During his time with a major financial institutional in New York, he specialized in global finance and product management and wrote numerous articles on international trade and product management for financial trade publications.

His writing career began while at St. Bonaventure University where he studied English Literature and was the editor of the literary magazine, *The Laurel*.

He is currently on the Board of Directors of the Chesapeake Bay Writers organization, the Williamsburg Book Festival, is a member of Mystery Writers of America, The Brontë Society of Haworth, Yorkshire, England, and is a frequent speaker at writing events both large and small.